Suspect Santa

Second Edition

Suspect Santa

Second Edition

Mike Faricy

Library of Congress Control Number: 2023918910
paperback ISBN: 978-1-962080-55-2
e-Book ISBN: 978-1-962080-56-9

MJF Publishing books may be purchased for education, Business, or promotional use. For information on bulk purchases, please contact the author directly at mikefaricyauthor@gmail.com

Published by

MJF Publishing
https://www.mikefaricybooks.com

Acknowledgments

I would like to thank the following people for their help and support:

Special thanks to my editors, Kitty, Donna and Rhonda for their hard work, cheerful patience and positive feedback.

I would like to thank Ann and Julie for their creative talent and not slitting their wrists or jumping off the high bridge when dealing with my Neanderthal computer capabilities.

Special thanks to Ann for her patience.

Last, I would like to thank family and friends for their encouragement and unqualified support. Special thanks to Maggie, Jed, Schatz, Pat, Av, Emily and Pat for not rolling their eyes, at least when I was there, and most of all, to my wife Teresa whose belief, support and inspiration has from day one, never waned.

Prologue

After filling her wine glass, I held it out to Layla. It was our fifth date, not counting the night we'd met at a mutual friend's birthday party. Tonight was the first night in her bedroom. She had a two-bedroom condo in the Blair House Condominiums, a five-story Victorian brick building built back in 1887. Layla's unit was all the way up on the fifth floor. The ten-foot ceilings had elegant plaster crown molding. The woodwork throughout the place was oak with beautiful oak floors, all original to the building. Gorgeous stained glass panels were across the tops of double-hung windows. Her living room and the master bedroom both had fireplaces with glazed antique tiles.

She leaned over, kissed me on the cheek, and took the glass. "Thanks, baby. You are so nice. I'm really surprised."

"Surprised? Are you kidding? I'm one of the nicest guys in town. Why are you surprised?"

"Oh, you know, just what I've heard," she said and extended the glass toward me. I clicked it with my beer can. We were leaning on the pillows piled up against the carved headboard of her four-poster Victorian bed. The walnut dresser, with the carved leaf drawers and antique mirror, seemed to fit the room perfectly. Antique wooden chairs were on either side of the dresser.

"Is that some fancy formal jacket hanging on the back of the chair?" I asked and raised my beer can in the direction of the red velvet jacket with the white fur trim and brass buttons.

"Don't be silly. That's my elf coat."

"Your elf coat? Are you into something? Are you married? I thought—"

"No, Dev. I'm not married. Are you?"

"No, of course not. Who'd have me?"

"Yeah, good point. No, that's my Santa's elf coat. This will be my third year playing an elf in Santa's Workshop. I just love doing it. I take time from work, and we have hundreds of children. They're just darling. All on their best behavior, they tell Santa what they want for Christmas, and he says he'll try, but he can't make promises. You know, I really enjoy doing it, and it's an opportunity to give back something to the community."

"Sounds nice."

"You should think about doing it sometime, Dev. The kids are so wonderful. They really believe in Santa, and the older ones, even if they don't really believe, they're still hedging their bets, just in case. I think you'd be good at it. The guy we had the last two years was such a crab. His name is Arthur, and I was sure he was drinking on the job, but we could never prove it. Unfortunately, I think he's going to be back again this year. God, he's had an entire year to get even crabbier, if that's possible," she said and took a large sip of wine.

"Yeah, I would probably like to do that. I wish I wasn't so busy," I lied and gave a quick glance to see if she had picked up on it.

"I'll put your name on the alternative list. You never know. Maybe Arthur will break a leg or fall down the stairs. Or maybe someone's dad will just hit him for being such a jerk. One can only hope."

"He's that bad?"

"Surprisingly, yeah, he is. He's certainly not fun like you. It would be nice if you were there. Besides, I've never made love to Santa before. At least that I can remember." She set her glass on the bedside table and snuggled up to me.

I'd showered, shaved, and had been home for an hour before Morton wandered into the kitchen. I gave him the proverbial head scratch and let him out into the backyard. It was cold, and there was about six inches of fresh snow on the ground. Morton stood on the back porch, looked over his shoulder at me, and gave me a look as if to say, *Really? I'm supposed to go out there with the snow up to my knees and do my duty? You gotta be kidding.*

He was back inside three minutes later. As soon as I closed the door behind him, he shook the snow off and onto the floor, the walls, and the back door, then headed over to his food dish. I attacked the melting snow with a handful of paper towels.

We were down at the office before Louie Laufen, my office mate, arrived. I got the coffee going and was halfway through my first mug when Louie pulled up in his faded Ford Fiesta. He parked behind my car and gingerly crossed the street, trying to avoid the patches of ice. A moment later, I heard the stairs creaking and groaning as Louie made his way up to the office.

He opened the door and stood there red-faced and gasping for breath. He gave me a slight wave that signaled *Don't say anything* as he entered. I filled his mug with coffee, set it in front of him on the picnic table he used as a desk, and went back to looking out the window. The blinds were drawn on the apartment building across the street, so there was no point in taking my binoculars out of the desk drawer.

After a few minutes and a half-dozen slurps of coffee, Louie said, "So, did Layla spend the night at your place again?"

"No, as a matter of fact, I graced her condo with my presence. She made a wonderful dinner, lasagna, garlic bread, and apple pie for dessert. We had wine, chatted, and I was home around 6:00 this morning."

"Was that your first time there?"

"I'd been there before, but it was my first time spending the night. She has a really nice place. Up-to-date kitchen, and it's on the top floor, so you really don't pick up any street noise. How was your night?"

Louie shrugged and said, "Just the usual. Over at The Spot until about 9:00 then home. Watched, I forget what, on TV and went to bed after the news. I'm in court this morning at 11:00. With any luck, I'll be back in the office before 2:00. I—"

My phone ringing cut Louie off. Well, the ringing and me looking at the caller ID, shaking my head, and saying, "Damn it, Tubby Gustafson. This can't be good."

One

Louie looked over after the fourth ring and asked, "You going to answer that?"

"Yeah, I know. I know." I picked up the receiver and said," Good morning, Haskell Investigations."

"Save it for someone who cares, Haskell. I've got a car waiting out front for you. You've got two minutes to get down there."

"Actually, Mr. Gustafson, sir. I'm…umm…I'm still at my house. I've got a doctor's appointment, and I—"

"Don't fool with me, Haskell. I know you're at that dump you refer to as your office. Now, you can either get in the car waiting for you or drive yourself to the emergency room, where they'll place a cast on both your broken legs. Your choice."

"I'm heading out to the car now, sir," I said as I turned off my computer.

"Wise choice, Haskell," Tubby said and hung up.

I grabbed my jacket, gave Louie a wave, and headed for the door. Morton watched me but didn't move from his pillow.

I stepped out of the building, nodded at the thug seated behind the wheel of Tubby's black Cadillac Escalade, and waited for a bus to pass.

"Thanks for joining us, Haskell," a thug I knew as 'Lollipop' greeted me. He was seated in the passenger seat and wasn't smiling. "I was thinkin' we were going to get to go up to your office and remind you how Tubby don't like to be kept waiting."

"Just finishing up a report and wanted to check it for typos."

"What's them?" the driver asked.

"Yeah, sure you were," Lollipop said. "Don't kid a kidder. You were probably scanning that apartment building with your binoculars, hoping to catch some unsuspecting woman who doesn't know she's got a pervert living right across the street."

The thug behind the wheel chuckled, stepped on the gas, and took off down the street before I'd even closed the car door. It slammed shut as he accelerated.

"Better buckle up. We wouldn't want to lose you along the way."

I did just that, clicking the seat belt and then adjusting it from whatever fat guy had been seated here before me. I laughed to myself, thinking it had probably been Tubby Gustafson.

At no surprise, we ran two yellow lights and a red one and made it to Tubby's mansion on the River Boulevard in record time. But then, that was always the case when traveling in Tubby's car. It used to surprise me that his car was never pulled over for speeding, at least as far as I knew. Now, I'm not the least bit surprised. It's the way things work. People with money get whatever they want, and a blind eye is always turned toward them. Guys like me, the working stiffs, or maybe *sometimes* working class, we have to follow the rules or else. We pay the taxes, pay full price, pay, pay, pay. Folks like Tubby Gustafson, wealthy, privileged, and boss of the world, well, at least his world, get to do whatever they want. The rules folks like me have to deal with don't apply to the likes of Tubby Gustafson.

The Escalade pulled into the circular drive and stopped opposite the front door to Tubby's mansion. A couple of armed guys were on either side of the front door, leaning against the wall. They watched as I climbed out of the car.

"Good luck, Haskell," Lollipop said, sounding like he meant anything but as the car pulled away and headed back out of the massive front yard.

"Assume the position," a guy said and rose out of the lawn chair parked in front of a space heater. He smelled like cigar smoke as he patted me down, then finally said, "He's good. Let him in."

One of the guys leaning against the wall reached over and opened the door.

"Thanks," I said and stepped into the foyer.

A muscular guy was seated just inside. He looked up from the comic book he was reading, carefully set it on the oak bench, and stood. He patted me down again, and just as he finished, Fat Freddy Zimmerman, Tubby's second in command, appeared.

"It's about time, Haskell. Follow me."

I followed him past the staircase with the gilt-framed painting of Tubby holding what looked like important documents. An unsuccessful attempt to make Tubby appear honest and upstanding. We walked down the hallway to Tubby's office door. Fat Freddy knocked on the door as he opened it. I followed him into Tubby's office.

A massage table was positioned in front of the fireplace with the landscape painting above it. Naked Tubby was stretched out on the table. Fortunately, a white terry cloth towel covered most of his large rear. The fat from his massive figure hung over the sides of the massage table. Two attractive women, dressed in black thongs and smiling, were currently massaging Tubby's hairy, dimpled shoulders. Unfortunately for the two of them, they weren't wearing latex gloves. They ignored Fat Freddy and me and continued kneading Tubby's fat figure with their bare hands.

I was thinking Tubby might be asleep. His eyes remained closed, but he suddenly said, "Thank you for interrupting your otherwise busy day, Haskell. I want you to check someone out for me. Frederick, if you would present the file, please."

Fat Freddy seemed to come to attention and said, "Happy to do so, sir." He stepped over to Tubby's enormous antique desk. At the moment, the desk was devoid of everything but a phone, a crystal pen holder, and a thin manila file folder. Fat Freddy picked up the file, took two steps, and handed it to me.

Still keeping his eyes closed, Tubby said, "I'll expect you to provide me with a full report on this individual no later than one week from today."

"Anything you can tell me in advance, sir?" I said and opened the file. There were two pieces of paper. One was a copy of a photograph of a man, I guessed maybe mid-forties. The second page had what appeared to be a very short bio on the guy. His name was Alex Chillcot and, apparently, he lived on the East Coast, Newark, New Jersey, to be exact.

"Everything you need will be in that file."

"Is this Chillcot guy in town? Would you happen to have an address, a phone number, an email, or maybe a place of employment?"

Tubby gave a sigh. "Once again, Haskell, you never fail to disappoint. That is for you to determine. No questions? Good. Send him on his way, Frederick."

"But sir, how am I supposed to—"

"Come on, Haskell, let's go," Fat Freddy urged me toward the door.

"I'm just trying to figure out what you need here, sir."

Another sigh from Tubby. He raised his head so that his triple chin oozed into one, opened his eyes, and shook his head. He stared at my faded Bob Seger t-shirt.

"Haskell, just get me anything and everything you can on this character. Is that too hard to understand?"

"No, sir. It's just that I—"

"Stop. It's just that you never, ever get the damn message, Haskell. Seek and ye shall find. Do I make myself clear?"

"Yes, sir, perfectly," I said and followed Fat Freddy out of the office. Once back in the hallway, I said, "Freddy, what does he want to know about this Chillcot guy?"

"Were you listening to what he just said? Anything and everything, Haskell. Is that so hard to understand? Address, phone numbers. Where he's working. Does he have a wife? A woman? Is he in a relationship? Why the hell is this so difficult for you to figure out? Just do what you're supposed to do. Find out everything you can on this guy."

Two

I asked Louie, "So you've never heard of this Chill-cot guy? You're not aware of a pending case where he might be a witness or a defendant?"

Louie shook his head. He finished chewing the meatball in his mouth and took another bite of his sandwich. "Mmm-mmm, it's not ringing a bell with me. Haven't seen anything in the paper or on the news. Did you Google him?"

"Yeah, I did, but there are a couple dozen guys out there with the same name. No image of what they look like. They're scattered all over the country, so it really wasn't much help."

Louie swallowed and took another bite. "Mmm, I would think, since Tubby wants this information, that might mean the guy is living or maybe moving into this area. Could he be a potential competitor? Maybe he's someone who worked for or with Tubby, and he's disappeared."

"I checked online, and there's no report of a death or accidental injury by anyone with that name."

"What about this?" Louie said and then licked meatball sauce from his fingers. "What if he was some sort of business associate of Tubby's, and he's suddenly turned to witness protection? Maybe that's why Tubby wants to find him."

"I didn't think of that, but it certainly could be the case. The only thing is, if someone did something like that, it would be a name I think I would recognize. This guy's name doesn't ring a bell at all."

"All I can say is good luck," Louie said. He picked up the Styrofoam tray and began to lick off the tomato sauce. Suddenly, a big glob dropped out of the tray and onto his shirt and tie.

"You might want to deal with that sauce on your shirt, Louie."

"What? Oh, for the love of—" He attempted to remove the sauce using his finger, which only served to smear a larger stain on his shirt.

I watched him make a mess of the process for another minute, then picked up the phone and called Aaron LaZelle, my pal in homicide. I was ready to leave a message when he picked up.

"Yeah, Dev, how can I be of assistance? Oh, and by the way, if you've been arrested again, you're on your own."

"Not even funny, Aaron. Thanks for answering. Just wondered if the name Alex Chillcot rings a bell with you?"

"How are you involved with him?"

"Actually, I'm not. I got strong-armed into checking the guy out for Tubby Gustafson. He gave me a file with the guy's picture and a very brief description. Lives in Newark, New Jersey, age forty-six. Nothing mentioned about employment or family. As far as I know, the guy could be a schoolteacher or a minister."

"I think you can assume if Gustafson is interested, the guy isn't involved in either one of those occupations. The name rings a bell. I believe he's involved in gambling, obviously not the legal form. You should talk to Tommy Bishop. You know him?"

"That name sounds familiar, but I can't picture him."

"He's a detective in Special Investigations. Give him a call. In fact, let me send your call to the main desk, and they'll transfer you. Oh, and by the way, it's your turn to buy lunch."

"Thanks, Aaron. I—" but he'd already forwarded my call to the main desk.

"St. Paul Police Department," a male voice said a moment later.

"Hi, I just got transferred to this number. I'm trying to reach Detective Tom Bishop in Special Investigations."

"One moment, please, and I'll connect you."

A few seconds later, the phone was ringing. After a half-dozen rings, I listened to the message, "This is Detective Tom Bishop. I'm unavailable to take your call at the moment. If you would please leave a message, I'll get back to you just as soon as possible. Thank you."

A moment later, I heard the beep. "Hi, Detective Bishop. My name is Dev Haskell. I got your name from a long-time friend, Lieutenant Aaron LaZelle, in homicide. If you would give me a call back, I'd appreciate it." I left my number.

"LaZelle didn't know anything?" Louie called. At the moment, he was standing next to the sink. He had the left side of his shirt untucked and was scrubbing the sauce stain with the rag in the sink. The rag hadn't been washed for a month, maybe two. His effort just seemed to make the stain that much worse.

"He gave me the name of a guy who might know something. I'll see if he calls back." I went on the computer and started going through the list of guys named Alex Chillcot. There were a number of individuals in the UK, a handful scattered around the US, none of whom even remotely resembled the image in the file Tubby had prepared. It was getting close to 4:00, and I was thinking of taking Morton for a walk when my phone rang.

"Haskell Investigations."

"I'm calling for Dev Haskell."

"Speaking."

"Hi, Dev. My name is Tom Bishop in Special Investigations. I'm returning your call."

"Oh, yeah, I got your name from—"

"Aaron LaZelle, yeah, I know, you mentioned it, and actually, I just got off the line with him. He said you were okay."

"He probably said that because it's my turn to buy lunch, and he didn't want to screw that up."

Bishop chuckled at that. "You're the P.I. that works for Gustafson, aren't you?"

"Yes and no. I've done some things for him in the past, never been paid, by the way, but on occasion, he throws me a bone. He asked me, actually, asked is his term. My version of things is he told me to find out everything I could on a guy named Alex Chillcot. If I didn't do that, I'd have plenty of time recovering in the hospital to consider my mistake. He told me Chillcot was from out on the East Coast, Newark, New Jersey, actually. He gave me a file with a picture of the guy and three sentences describing him. Nothing earthshaking and absolutely nothing that would help in any investigation. I've been searching online and came across a bunch of guys over in the UK, a couple of obituaries, and nothing on anyone from Newark, New Jersey."

"Yeah, Chillcot keeps a pretty low profile. I'd be interested in seeing the file Gustafson gave you. Would you be willing to let me go through it?"

"Not a problem. Any information you could pass on to me would be a big help. I literally have found nothing. I should warn you. I was serious when I said all I have is a picture of the guy, actually a copy of the picture, and just that he lived in Newark."

"You have time to meet in about an hour?"

"Today? Yeah, sure, Tom. You name the place."

"There's a bar not far from the station called Alary's on East Seventh."

"Yeah, I know the place. I'll see you there in an hour."

"Okay, thanks,"

"Oh, I'm wearing a Bob Seger t-shirt if that helps."

"I already checked out the department's Dev Haskell file. I saw a couple of pictures of you." Bishop laughed at that. "As a matter of fact, Aaron mentioned you and Detective Manning used to be at each other."

"You name the crime committed, and Manning had me first on his list," I acknowledged.

"I'll see you in an hour, Haskell, and don't forget the file," Bishop said and hung up.

I closed things down, clipped the leash on Morton, and locked the door as we headed out. We walked for three blocks and then climbed into the car and went home. I let Morton into the backyard and debated changing my Bob Seger t-shirt, then remembered I told Bishop that's what I was wearing. I coaxed Morton back in the house with a biscuit and headed out the door.

Three

There was a parking place just around the corner from Alary's Bar. A patio is in back, but since it was winter, that wasn't going to work. I walked into the place and was in the process of unzipping my jacket when a voice called from across the bar, "Haskell, over here."

A guy smiled and waved me over. It was close to 5:00, and you'd think the place would be filling up with folks stopping in after work for a drink, but Bishop was one of only two guys seated on that side of the square bar. The last time I had been in the place, all the bartenders had been scantily clad, attractive young women. Today there was only one bartender. He was an older guy with a beer belly and crew cut. Thankfully, he was wearing jeans and a St. Paul Saints sweatshirt instead of being scantily clad.

I headed over to Bishop. As I came around the corner, I extended my hand. "Tom Bishop?" I said.

"Nice to meet you, Dev. Please, call me Tommy."

"Okay, hey, thanks for making the time to meet me."

"Yeah, I have to warn you. I can't stay for long. We've got a foster child for a couple of days, and the wife is going to need a hand in about thirty minutes."

"What'll it be?" the bartender asked.

"I'll have a Summit IPA. You want another?" I asked Bishop.

He shook his head. "Thanks, but it's strong coffee, and one is my limit at this time of day. I'm on the short leash tonight. You said you had a file from Gustafson?" he said, looking at my empty hands.

I reached inside my jacket and pulled out the two pages of the so-called file from Tubby Gustafson. "Here's what I got from him. An image of Chillcot and three sentences on the guy."

He unfolded the two pages, smiled when he saw the copy of the photo, and shook his head as he read the three sentences. "Man, no wonder they want you to investigate. First of all, this photo is out of date by probably ten years. The description they gave you is obviously worthless. Any idea why Gustafson is interested in him?"

"I have no idea. If I had to guess, I'd think maybe he was involved with some mob out east, turned state's evidence, and is hiding somewhere in a witness protection program."

Bishop nodded and said, "Maybe half-right. Basically, what happened is he ripped off someone or some mob family back in New Jersey. He is, or rather was, connected. So instead of getting his brains blown out, he was able to return the funds. He paid a fee and got the boot out of town. Not sure of the exact numbers, but we're talking a seven-figure payment."

"So a million bucks?"

"At least, but his choice was pay or be killed, so he paid and headed west. That was back in late July or early August. At the time, the word was he was headed to Kansas City. Not exactly clear on what changed that, but the bottom line is he's coming here. That suggests Gustafson either owed someone a favor or he's doing a favor for someone back east and will be compensated."

"Is there a file on Chillcot? I mean, has he done time? I couldn't find anything on the guy," I said just as the bartender set a beer mug in front of me. I tossed a ten-dollar bill on the bar and nodded at the bartender. He tapped the ten on the bar and left.

"Not surprising you didn't find anything. Chillcot was, or maybe still is, connected. It's the main reason he was allowed to leave, as opposed to taking a bullet between the eyes. He has always been a behind the scenes operator. He's got dirt on just about everyone, and the rumor is, should anything happen to him, that information will automatically be sent to the powers that be."

"Meaning the DEA?"

"Yeah, among others," Bishop said.

"What sort of information?"

"Everything from tax evasion to details on a number of illegal operations and even affairs with women. Some of the wives of the higher-ups could make life very difficult. From what I've heard, it's not just the info, but in the case of the sexual dalliances, there are actual pictures."

"So all that information serves as the guy's safety net?"

"Exactly. It's actually pretty clever. I don't know this, but I'm guessing the information is stored up in the cloud somewhere. Something happens to Chillcot, and that info floods out. You can just imagine. On the one hand, the information on you gets out, and you're screwed, charged, and arrested. On the other hand, maybe you're not charged, but the information is out there, and there will be people so pissed off that the safest place for you may be behind bars. It's really pretty ingenious."

"So, Tubby Gustafson is concerned because Chillcot is coming here. Does that mean that Chillcot has something on Tubby?"

"It could be, but my sense is he doesn't have anything on Gustafson for two reasons. First, Gustafson is out here in Minnesota. Secondly, Gustafson is a big player here in town. But he's never made a move or even expressed an interest in doing something that would put him on center stage. He's clearly content in the business as it is, right here in the world's biggest small town, St. Paul."

"I can't argue with your theory, but then why does Tubby want the information on Chillcot? It sounds like he's not going to have any trash on Tubby."

"Because the problem with Chillcot is that Gustafson is suddenly going to have a competitor on the scene. A competitor who is backed up by some very strong individuals. A competitor who knows the business, whatever the business is, gambling, women, drugs, you name it. And, over time, Tubby Gustafson will either be pushed to the side, if he's lucky, or simply eliminated."

"Why wouldn't Tubby just take him out?"

Bishop shook his head. "That would be the logical reaction, except if he takes Chillcot out, suddenly all the bad information, the double-crosses, the stealing, the dalliances see the light of day, not to mention all the prosecutable information. No, if Gustafson took him out, he'd be dead within twenty-four hours, and he knows it."

"You're making this Chillcot character sound untouchable."

"Exactly."

"Do you know when and where Chillcot is going to land?"

Bishop smiled. "I have some ideas, but with all due respect, I'm not at liberty to pass them on. I can tell you this. Word is he's purchased some Victorian mansion down on Summit Ave. Somewhere in the four hundred block."

"I'm just a few blocks from there. I'm not aware of any place with a for sale sign on it."

"Could be it will be more of a private transaction if that translates. I've got a place in mind, a corner lot, double lot, as a matter of fact."

"The homes are so big they're all double lots along there. A corner lot? That wouldn't happen to belong to a state senator? Delvin Durkin, a member of our illustrious state legislature?"

"Former member of the legislature. If you'll recall, Durkin didn't file for another term. I've never heard this, so it's just a guess on my part, but like all the connected people out east, your man Chillcot found out something and made Senator Durkin an offer he couldn't refuse. Namely, sell Chillcot the house or else."

"Oh, man, no wonder Tubby wants any and all information on this guy. Does he have a family?"

"He has a former wife. They divorced almost thirty years ago. She has custody of their two children, or I should say, had custody. A boy and girl. I believe the son is thirty-four or five. He's a practicing dentist down in Orlando, Florida. The thirty-two-year-old daughter lives out in Denver. Last I heard, she was an RN in a neonatal facility. Both children took their mother's surname when they turned twenty-one."

"What's the mother's name?"

"Diane Olsen. That surname ends with the letters 'en.'"

"No ties to the old man's business?"

"To my knowledge, they haven't seen him since the divorce thirty years ago. The former wife filed a restraining order against him prior to their divorce, and as far as I know, he's respected it. Hey, nice meeting you, Dev, but I should probably take off. If I know what's good for me, I better get my butt home. My wife will be trying to make dinner, and I'm on kid duty."

"How many do you have?"

"Just one at the moment, a ten-year-old boy. We do foster care."

"You're lucky," I said.

"Don't we know it. If I can be of any help, feel free to give me a call, or you can send me a private message to this email address. Always interested in what you learn," he said and extended his hand with a business card.

"Thanks, much appreciated, Tommy. Anything I can help you with, just let me know. Well, except for babysitting. I would probably be a bad influence on kids."

He laughed at that and headed out the door.

I finished my beer and headed home. I drove through downtown, up Ramsey Hill, and past State Senator Durkin's house on Summit Avenue. Sure enough, there was a moving van parked in front, actually a large semi-truck. At the moment, two guys were carrying a brown leather couch out the front door and down the half-dozen granite steps to the semitrailer. Not a fun job in the best of weather, let alone a Minnesota winter evening.

I pulled into my garage and entered the house through the back door. Morton trotted down the hallway and into the kitchen. I gave him a head scratch and said, "Outside, Morton. Outside?" as I opened the back door.

He looked at me like I was nuts.

"Outside?" I repeated.

He actually took two steps backward.

"Okay, I get it," I said and reached into the cookie jar where I kept his biscuits and tossed one to him. He caught it in midair and hurried out of the kitchen so he wouldn't have to share it with me.

Four

The following morning Morton and I were in the office well before Louie. I had the coffee on and was in the process of emailing Bishop at his private site, telling him about the moving van last night at Senator Durkin's house. I heard a grinding noise out on the street and turned to look out the window just in time to see Louie pull his faded Ford Fiesta in behind my car. When he turned his car off, a large cloud of black exhaust exploded out the back and then just sort of hung in the air for a long moment. Louie made his way through the slush on the street and into the building. The formerly white snow on the boulevard next to his car was now covered with black debris.

The staircase leading up to the second floor began to creak and groan, and a moment later, red-faced Louie entered the office. He gave me his usual wave, set his briefcase on his picnic table, and draped his black wool coat over the back of his office chair. I stepped out from my desk, grabbed Louie's coffee mug, filled it, and set it in front of him. He replied with a polite nod.

I went back to my desk and began typing notes from my conversation with Tommy Bishop the night before. At least I had the beginnings of information on Alex Chillcot for Tubby Gustafson.

"I thought you were going to come over to The Spot last night," Louie said a few minutes later. "Were you working or playing?"

"I met up with a cop. Turns out he had some information on Alex Chillcot. Nothing specific, just general stuff, a lot of hearsay, but it was more than I got from Tubby."

"Anything interesting?"

"Yeah," I said and began to fill Louie in on what Bishop had told me.

When I'd finished, Louie thought for a long moment and then said, "My sense is that, far from wanting to help someone out, Tubby Gustafson is probably worried about this Chillcot character coming to town and cutting into his business. You said he wants any and all information. Sounds like he's already in the planning stages."

"Yeah, okay, but the way Bishop described it to me, this Chillcot is basically untouchable."

Louie shook his head. "Possibly, or does Tubby just have to come up with a plan that's untraceable? What if Chillcot's in a plane crash? A car accident with a teenage driver? Or what if he simply disappears without a trace? Is Tubby Gustafson supposed to protect this guy? Or is he just being a nice guy and going to welcome him to the city?"

"I get what you're saying. So Tubby is worried about the guy moving in on his business, and he wants as much information as possible on the guy so he can get rid of him and not face any problems."

"There's one more part to this, Dev."

"What's that?"

"You don't want to be fingered as the person who gave Tubby Gustafson the information on Alex Chillcot. In some people's minds, that could make you just as guilty as whoever pulls the trigger, plants the bomb, or does whatever it is that removes Chillcot from the picture. I'd say it seems a pretty safe guess they're going to eliminate this guy. It's just a matter of how. Be careful who you deal with. Be careful what and who you ask about this guy, Dev. Even talking to this Bishop, nice guy and all, but if something should happen and word got out you were checking on Chillcot, you could end up with an awfully big target on your back."

A little later, I took Morton for a walk up to Roosters BBQ and got two Memphis-style pulled pork sandwiches to go. I couldn't get Louie's comments regarding my research of Alex Chillcot off my mind. Thus far, I'd only spoken to two people, Aaron LaZelle, and Tommy Bishop. I felt safe on both counts, but Louie's thoughts served as a note to the wise, or in this case, me.

I was back in the office with the sandwiches fifteen minutes later. Neither Louie nor I said much during lunch, but that wasn't unusual. Amazingly, Louie only had one small drop of BBQ sauce on his white shirt, and that was on the left sleeve. When he finished, he pulled on his suit coat, which covered the stain, not that he even noticed. He placed two files in his briefcase, wrapped a scarf around his neck, pulled on his black wool overcoat, and headed over to the courthouse for his 2:00 appearance.

As soon as his car started and he drove away, I called Sarah Debbens, a real estate agent I dated briefly last year. She answered on the second ring.

"Hi, this is Sarah."

"Hey, Sarah, a voice from the past. This is Dev Haskell."

I could almost hear the air being drawn out of the room. After a long pause, she said, "Hello, Dev. If you're looking to have me represent you in the sale of your home, I'm afraid at the moment, and for the foreseeable future, I'm simply too busy to take on another client."

"That's great news, Sarah. I'm glad the business is working well for you. Listen, I don't want to take up too much of your time. I just wondered if you know who had purchased the home at four-forty-one Summit Avenue? I drove past last night, and there was a large moving van out front. I just live a couple of blocks from there, and I wondered—"

"If you'll recall, I'm perfectly aware of where you live."

"Oh, yeah, I didn't mean to suggest anything. I just wondered if you—"

"Is that all you want? Or is this some lamebrain attempt at apologizing for the damage you did driving my car through the garage door?"

"Actually, I was driving because you had been over-served, and I was just trying to help. The last thing you needed was to be arrested for driving while intoxicated and—"

"And you took advantage of me in my car and turned out to be just as over-served as I was."

"Well, yeah, that part was unfortunate, but I—"

"I'm checking the records now. If I give you the information, will you promise to get off the line and never, ever call me again?"

"Yeah, sure. If that's what you want."

"That's exactly what I want," she said. I could hear her fingers on the keyboard. "Okay, here we are, four-forty-one Summit, the home went for, wait a minute, this can't be right. It says that home went for six-hundred-and-fifty thousand. That house, in that location, should go for at least three times that."

"Does it list the name of the buyer?"

"It should. Let me check. The buyer is, wait a minute. What? A company named Alpha Publishing? That doesn't make any sense. Something's not right here. Are you still doing that detective thingy?"

"Yeah, my company is called Dev Haskell Private Investigations."

"So, are you investigating this sale? Something definitely doesn't seem right here. This is way off."

"No, I'm not investigating that sale. I was just driving past, and there was a moving truck, actually a big semi-trailer out front. Two guys were carrying a couch out of the house and into the truck."

"Something's not right here. Well, unless maybe it's some sort of family deal, a property trade or something. I mean, this can't be the sale price. There has to be more involved here."

"And you said the company listed is Alpha Publishing?"

"Yeah, have you ever heard of them?"

"No, they're not ringing a bell with me."

"And you just drove past and wondered? You're not investigating?"

"No, honest, Sarah, I just wondered if it had sold."

"Strange, very strange. Well, listen, Haskell. I'd normally say it's been a pleasure to talk with you, but in your case, I think I'll just hang up." Click.

Five

Louie returned to the office a little after 4:00. I watched as he parked across the street. This time, he pulled in front of my car. I crossed my fingers, hoping the soot, or whatever the explosion earlier in the day was, wouldn't go all over my car. That didn't work. A large black cloud erupted from the tailpipe of the Ford Fiesta, hung in the air for a moment or two, and then gradually settled onto the hood and windshield of my car. Louie waited in his car until the air was clear and then hurried across the street and into the building.

He entered the office a minute later, red-faced and breathing heavily. I watched as he settled into his desk chair, still wearing the black wool overcoat and scarf. After a couple of minutes, he pulled the scarf off and tossed it on his picnic table.

"Are you cold or just deep in thought?" I asked.

"What?"

"You're still wearing your overcoat. Are you cold? Did everything go okay in court?"

"Yeah, given the circumstances. My client has a suspended sentence, provided he attends an AA meeting weekly for the next six months and doesn't touch any alcohol."

"Can he do that?"

"Let's hope so. Otherwise, he'll have six months locked up to think about it."

"So the overcoat?"

"Oh, no. I'm not cold. I was just debating whether to write up a summary or go over to The Spot for a private celebration. By all rights, my client should be contemplating his behavior in a cell. We just lucked out. My summation can wait until tomorrow. I'm going to head over to The Spot and enjoy the warm glow of a legal victory. Care to join me?"

"I've got to make a phone call first, and then I'll be over."

"All right," Louie said as he stood. He wrapped the knitted scarf around his neck, gave a quick wave, and headed out the door. I watched him as he cut across the intersection, waving 'thanks' to the car heading east that was forced to stop and then to the bus driver heading west. Fortunately, he made it across the street and disappeared into The Spot.

I picked up my phone, called Tom Bishop, and ended up leaving a message.

"Hi, Tom. Dev Haskell here. When you have a moment, please give me a call on my cell. I believe I have some information on your friend, Mr. Chillcot."

I pulled on my jacket, clipped the leash to Morton's collar, and we headed out for a brief walk. Fifteen

minutes later, we entered The Spot. Morton was straining on his leash as we headed along the bar to where
Louie was seated on his permanent stool at the far end.
As we came around the corner of the bar, Louie greeted
Morton with a handful of pork rinds. He leaned forward
and lowered his left hand with the treat while holding
onto the bar with his right hand.

"There you go, Morton. Well deserved after a day
of having to deal with Dev."

Morton devoured the pork rinds in less than a second, then sat in front of Louie with a mournful look on
his face.

"Not to worry, Morton. You'll get more when it's
time to leave."

Morton's tale was wagging and pounding against
the bar. Mike, the bartender, suddenly appeared and set
a full beer mug in front of me.

"Compliments of your partner," he said.

"Morton bought me a beer?"

"Yeah, you just keep thinking that way, Dev."

"Thanks, Mike," I said and raised the mug in his direction.

"So you learn anything this afternoon on this Chill
pox guy?" Louie asked.

"Yeah, two things. First, his name is Chillcot. Alex
Chillcot. Second, I'm pretty sure he bought a mansion
up on Summit Avenue for about a third of what the normal price would be."

"And you know this how?"

"Well, I called a sometime friend, or former friend, and she looked up the sale of this house on Summit Avenue. The sale price was listed at about six hundred grand. Oh, and the buyer was listed as Alpha Publishing Company."

"Back up for a second. A place on Summit sold for six hundred grand? That can't be right."

"That's what we both thought, but she was reading it on her screen. That seems to be the price. I know she triple-checked the price, and the buyer was listed as Alpha Publishing."

"Yeah, you already mentioned that."

"Well, the whole thing seems crazy."

Louie shook his head. "Sounds like whoever this guy is, he seems to have a lot of power. How in the hell could he pull this off? Didn't you say the owner was a state legislator?"

"Yeah, Senator Delvin Durkin."

"Durkin? That guy? He doesn't do anything unless it benefits himself. He wouldn't sell his home for a third of its value."

"Well, apparently, he did just that. I've got a call in to Tom Bishop. He was wondering about Chillcot coming to town, and now this sale is going down and sold to a company, no less. Wouldn't you think that is exactly the sort of deal that would lead you to ask for a higher price? Instead, the guy drops the price? It's crazy. I mean, I could have bought the thing for that much, maybe."

Louie shook his head. "You going to mention this to Tubby Gustafson?"

"Yeah, I'll gather all the information I can and present it to him in a written document at the end of the week. But I'm not going to put my name on it."

Louie shook his head just as my phone rang. I pulled the cell out of my pocket. "Oh, guess who? Bishop. I'm gonna take this outside. Keep an eye on Morton for me." I stepped out the side door and leaned against the building. "Hi Tom, thanks for returning my call."

"Sorry it took so long to get back. Dealing with a pal in another department. You said there were movers at that mansion on Summit?"

"Yeah, but I've got an update for you." I went on to tell him about the sale price of the mansion. I mentioned Alpha Publishing and Sarah Debbens, the realtor.

"Well, it certainly sounds like State Senator Durkin isn't playing with a full deck. Do you know how long he's lived in that house?"

"Not exactly, but it has to be at least fifteen years. He was there when I moved into my place and probably a lot longer."

"I'll have to check it out," Bishop said. "You find out anything else?"

"No, but I'm going to keep checking. Do you have any suggestions?"

"Not really. It would be interesting to see what you can find out on that Alpha Publishing company. The other thing is, if they were actually moving furniture out of that place last night, that suggests Mr. Chillcot is going to be arriving any day. He might even be here now."

"Speaking of him. Would you be able to send me an up-to-date image of the guy? I think you said the photo I had in that file was ten years old."

"At least ten years old. Yeah, I'll email one to you. I appreciate you keeping me in the loop. If you see anything that suggests Chillcot moving in, let me know."

"Yeah, I'll be happy to. I'll keep an eye out for that updated image."

"Coming your way in the next few minutes," Bishop said and disconnected.

"Everything okay?" Louie asked when I stepped inside.

"Yeah, just giving Bishop an update on the sale of that house. He seemed genuinely surprised. I get the feeling he might be doing a little checking on Senator Durkin."

Louie gave Morton another handful of pork rinds before we left. I had to run the windshield wipers to get the soot from Louie's exhaust off so I could see out the windshield. On the drive home, I went past Durkin's house. The semi-truck was gone. All three floors had lights on in a number of rooms, but somehow, it just gave off the sense of being empty.

I parked in the garage and went in the back door. I hadn't even taken my jacket off when my cell phone rang. Layla.

"Dev Haskell residence, how may I direct your call?" I answered. Then, after a long moment, "Layla?"

"God, I didn't know what to say. Hey, I'm out with some friends. Just wondered if it would be all right if I stopped by for a glass of wine on the way home?"

"I'm counting on it. Don't worry about the time. Whenever you get here is just fine."

"See you later," she said and disconnected.

I looked at my empty wine rack and headed out the door to Solo Vino, the wine store up the block.

Six

The news had put me to sleep when the doorbell woke me. Ever the watchdog, Morton remained asleep on the floor. The doorbell rang again, and I hurried out to the entryway. I waved at Layla and opened the front door.

"Oh, gee, it's about time. I thought I was going to freeze to death out there," she said, then grinned, wrapped her arms around me, and gave me a probing, wet kiss that lasted a good minute. Once she pulled away, I admired her skirt and blouse and made note of the fact it was ten degrees outside, and she didn't have a coat.

"Can I get you a glass of wine?" I offered.

"You think I need another one?"

"It couldn't hurt," I grinned. She took hold of my hand as we wandered into the kitchen. I had three bottles of Sean Minor Sauvignon Blanc chilling in the refrigerator. I filled the two glasses on the kitchen counter. We clinked glasses and took a sip. Followed by another passionate Layla kiss.

Thirty minutes later, I'd opened up a second bottle of wine, and we were heading upstairs to the bedroom. Layla left her shoes in the kitchen. She draped her silk blouse over the newel post on the staircase. She stepped out of her skirt as she entered the bedroom and kicked it into a corner. She pulled the covers back on the bed, adjusted the pillow, climbed in, leaned against the headboard, and blew me a kiss. I handed the wineglass to her just as Morton wandered into the room.

"Hold that thought. I'm going to let him outside. Back in a half-minute," I hustled Morton out of the bedroom. We hurried down the stairs and into the kitchen. Morton took his time. I let him outside and waited, then waited some more. He finally was up on the back porch. I let him inside and hurried back upstairs.

Layla's red bra and lacy red thong were on my pillow. Her wine glass was empty, and she was on her side with her back to me, snoring. I debated trying to wake her but decided it might be better if I waited until morning. Morton wandered in, and I led him into the guest room. I pulled the covers up over Layla, brushed my teeth, and when I stepped back into the bedroom, she was still snoring, only louder.

I was vaguely aware of her hurrying out of bed sometime in the middle of the night. Her snoring woke me just before 6:00 in the morning. I showered, shaved, dressed quietly, and was downstairs on the computer searching for Alpha Publishing when Morton wandered into the kitchen with what was left of a lacy red thong in his mouth. I took the remains of the thong and let him out the back door.

Twenty minutes later, I heard the toilet flush and the shower turn on. Layla appeared in the kitchen a half-hour after that. "You have any aspirin?"

"Right there on the counter, along with that sugary glass of orange juice to help your headache."

"Oh, thanks. I'm sorry, did we, umm—"

"No, it seemed sleep was a bigger incentive."

"You mean passing out. Oh, you perv, you brought my thong down here?"

"No, actually, Mor—"

"What the hell?" she said, holding up what was left of her thong.

"That wasn't me. Morton was the one who did that."

She looked over at Morton. He hung his head and turned away.

"Well, he gets it from you, Dev. Sorry about last night. All of a sudden, I needed to sleep, I guess."

"I think it's called passing out."

She shook her head. "I was out with the Santa's Workshop gang last night. We had a great time. God, I should have taken a taxi home. We're starting up in a week. Unfortunately, Arthur Soto is going to be Santa again."

"Is this the guy you said was drinking on the job?"

"Yes. Hopefully, he'll be on his best behavior this year, if he even knows how to do that."

"I hope it works out for you, Layla. I know you like doing it."

"I do. It's hard work, but it's so wonderful to see all the kids excited and happy. They're all smiles and usually on their best behavior. Well, I better get going. I'm already late for work. Did, umm, did I have a coat?"

"No, as a matter of fact, you didn't."

"Hopefully, it's in my car. God, thanks for putting up with me. Sorry about passing out. Raincheck?"

"I'd love it."

She kissed me on the cheek, and I walked her to the door.

"Thanks again, and thanks for the aspirin," she said. "Oh God, brrrr," she groaned and hurried toward her car parked almost crossways in my driveway. I watched her from inside the house moving her car back and forth in an effort to get unstuck. I was just about to head outside when she made it out of the snow, backed her car down the driveway into the street, and drove off.

Seven

Morton hopped into the backseat of the car, and we backed out of the driveway. On a whim, I drove past the former Durkin residence. A red Buick Enclave was parked in front of the house with the rear door raised. Two suitcases were lined up in the back of the car. The front door leading into the house was propped open by a brick. As I pulled to a stop behind the Buick, a woman who looked in her mid-fifties stepped out of the house. She was carrying two powder blue suitcases. She set one next to the front door and carried the other down the six front steps, nearly falling twice. Once she made it down the steps, she extended the handle on the suitcase and pulled it out toward the car. The front steps and sidewalk hadn't been shoveled, and she nearly fell again.

I quickly climbed out from behind the wheel and called, "Mrs. Durkin, I'm Dev Haskell, a neighbor. Here, let me help you. It's slippery, and you don't want to fall." I pushed the front gate open and hurried over to her.

"Oh, my goodness. Thank you. You've no idea. I'm getting too old for this sort of nonsense," she said and let go of the suitcase. I pushed the handle back into place and picked up the suitcase. "I'll just get the other one, and—"

"No, ma'am, leave it there. I'll grab it. You don't need to fall on those steps," I said, then stepped out of the front yard, across the sidewalk, and set the suitcase in the back of the Buick. I hurried up the front steps and grabbed the second suitcase.

"Oh, you've no idea. Thank you so much."

"Not a problem. Sorry to see you're moving. I had no idea the house was even for sale."

"Yeah, it was a surprise to a number of us," she said, and if looks could kill.

I carried the suitcase and placed it next to the other three. "Do you have more luggage going?"

"Just two more, but I can get them."

"Be a shame to break a leg when you're almost finished. Let me get them for you."

"Oh, that's so kind of you, but you don't have to. I can—"

"Please, I insist. It will just take a minute."

"Well, if you wouldn't mind."

"No trouble at all. Lead the way," I said and followed her up the front steps and into the house. The front hallway was paneled with a six-foot-high walnut wainscot. The wall above it had a reddish wallpaper with small, velvety-looking, eight-pointed stars. At the end of the hallway was a massive staircase with ten steps that led up to a landing where it made a hundred-and-eighty-degree turn, and ten more steps led up to the second floor.

The three rooms on either side of the first-floor hallway were a den, a library, and a dining room. Each room had a large fireplace and was completely empty. As we walked toward the staircase, our footsteps seemed to echo in the hall.

"I forget what you had hosted, but I was in here a few years ago," I lied.

"Probably some wretched fundraiser for Delvin," she said, not sounding happy as she started up the stairs. "God, the work I put into this place, and to have it end like this. Lord save me. Both suitcases are in the master bedroom," she said as we reached the top of the stairs. "Or what used to be the master bedroom. Damn it."

I followed her down the hallway and into a large empty room with more walnut woodwork, an antique brass chandelier in the middle of the ten-foot ceiling, and three large windows that looked out on the street. A king-sized bed on a steel frame with wheels had been pushed away from the wall. There was no headboard, no dressers, nothing but the bed with sheets, a white duvet, and two open suitcases on the floor next to the bed.

She bent over, arranged some items in the suitcases, and then closed them. Both suitcases were dark blue with what looked like white leather trim around the edges. They had to be at least sixty years old. There wasn't a raised handle or a set of wheels on either one, just a worn white leather handle to carry them.

"Anything else besides these two?"

She slowly glanced around the empty room and shook her head. "No, this was my last night here. I so love the place. So proud. It was good to us, to me. Damn it." She took a deep breath and said, "All right, now can I carry one of these?"

"No, I've got them both. One in each hand will keep me balanced," I said, raising both suitcases. They were obviously fully packed but not too heavy. I headed out the door toward the staircase. She remained in the room, just looking and thinking. I heard a sniffle or two as I headed down the stairs.

I placed the suitcases in the back of the Buick and pressed the button to lower the door. Once it was closed and I heard the lock click, I glanced at my car. Morton was lying in the back seat, personally involved with a bright green tennis ball, so I headed back into the house. Mrs. Durkin was just coming down the stairs.

"Is there anything else you need carried out?"

"Oh, you are so kind. No, I'm afraid that's the last of it. I'm headed to my sister's up in Hibbing. Looking forward to settling back with family. One more thing before you go. Let me make you a coffee."

"Oh, thank you, but you don't have to—"

"No, follow me. I insist. Now not another word."

"You're the boss," I said.

"Well, at least you know that," she said, then pushed open a swinging door, and we stepped into a pantry with white cupboards and six-panel glass doors on the upper cabinets. All the cupboards appeared to be empty. We stepped into a modern kitchen with lovely dark-stained wooden cabinets, brass handles, and a center island with a granite top. "Unfortunately, there's nowhere to sit, but Delvin's coffee machine is still here."

She set a white mug labeled 'HIS' in front of the coffee machine, placed a plastic pod in the top of the machine, and pressed a button. Coffee began to fill the mug a moment later. Once the mug was full, she handed it to me and then repeated the process using a mug labeled 'HERS.'

When the coffee was finished, she took her mug and raised it toward me. "Here's to you," she said, and we clicked steaming mugs. "Now, tell me your name again, please. It seems I've already forgotten."

"Haskell, Dev Haskell. I live almost straight through on Selby Avenue."

"Oh, so you really are in the neighborhood."

"Oh, yes, ma'am, been here for a lot of years. And speaking of forgetting, please tell me your name."

"Edith. Edith Durkin, although right now, I'm thinking of going back to my maiden name. This is so damn stupid."

"This is such a lovely home. Did you find it too big?"

"Oh, believe me, I had nothing to do with this move. That is all on Delvin, and it was just the latest straw in a number of last straws."

"Oh, I'm sorry to hear that."

"You're not a reporter, are you?"

I shook my head, "No, I'm a private detective. I've been doing that for a number of years."

"Do you carry a gun?" she wondered, looking at my belt.

"No, I mean, I have one, but most of what I do involves verifying employment records. You know, for when folks fill out job applications. Once in a while, I may be looking for someone that's been missing or checking into a car accident or something. It's not like on TV where they're shooting bad guys."

"Mmm, too bad. I've got a list."

"So you sold this house. I never even noticed a for sale sign."

"You're not the only one. No one was more surprised than me that the house was up for sale, let alone that it sold. Fortunately, I'll be able to leave without having to deal with the media."

"I can't imagine."

"Oh, you don't know the half of it. It can be really awful. They'll have a field day when this story breaks. That's why I'm moving in with my sister."

"Sorry to hear that. Will your husband join you?"

She studied me for a long moment, then shook her head and said, "No."

I finished my coffee, thanked her, and she thanked me back. I climbed in the car, and Morton and I drove down to the office. Louie's car was parked in my usual spot, so now there were three areas of soot on the boulevard snow. I pulled in front of his car and parked.

Eight

By way of greeting Louie said, "Well, it's about time. I was beginning to wonder. I had to make my own coffee this morning. You have another wild night with Layla?" We stepped into the office. Morton still had the tennis ball in his mouth and headed for his pillow.

"Believe me, nothing happened," I gave him an update on Layla's visit last night.

He laughed, "So much for having an affair with Mrs. Santa Claus."

"Oh, apparently, she's Santa's elf, which reminds me, she mentioned that Arthur guy was going to play Santa again this year. Thanks for saying something. I need to make a phone call," I sat down and turned on my computer. I Googled Santa's Workshop, got their phone number, and called.

"Santa's Workshop. How may I direct your call?"

"Hi, I'm calling about playing Santa Claus."

"One moment while I connect you to Human Resources."

The phone rang three times, and a woman answered, "HR department."

"Hi, I'm calling regarding your Santa Claus position."

"I'm sorry, sir, but that position has been filled."

"I was afraid of that. Is there a list of backups? Guys who would fill the position if your man can't make it?"

"There is. I can add your name to the list. One moment please."

She was back on the line a minute later. "All right, sir, your name please?"

I proceeded to give her my name, phone number, and email address. I listed Layla and Louie as references and gave her their phone numbers as well.

"Do you want to write out a script I should follow in case they call looking for a reference?" Louie suggested once I hung up.

"No, just tell them how wonderful I am. Don't worry. They're not going to call. The position is already filled. I just wanted to have my name on the list. Layla is bound to see it since I listed her as a reference, and she'll think I'm a nice guy and want to help out."

"How nice that you care, Dev," Louie said, and we both laughed.

I checked my email, and sure enough, there was a message from Tommy Bishop. I opened it and clicked on the file folder. A more recent image of Alex Chillcot appeared. I printed it off and placed it in the file from Tubby.

Later that afternoon, Louie headed across the street to The Spot. I took Morton on a brief walk, and we joined Louie in the bar. I behaved myself and only had two beers, then headed home. I was hoping Layla might have been feeling some remorse after last night and would call me, but it never happened. Morton and I headed up to bed just before 11:00. I think I woke up twice, just long enough to wish Layla was there, and then went back to sleep. I slept until almost 7:00 the next morning. Morton was waiting for me in the kitchen when I made it downstairs. I let him outside. He was scratching at the back door ninety seconds later.

After a breakfast of coffee and two pieces of toast with blueberry jelly, we drove down to the office. We'd gotten close to an inch of snow overnight, which wasn't much, but it was enough to cover the soot left from Louie's car. I pulled into my usual spot then moved ahead another ten feet, making sure there was enough room for Louie to park behind me.

I was watching two women in the apartment building across the street as they applied their morning makeup when Louie pulled up. Fortunately, he parked behind me, so all the debris from his exhaust pipe landed on the freshly fallen snow. He climbed out of his car, then shuffled across the street, never raising his feet from the icy surface. I was filling his coffee mug when the staircase began to creak and groan. I placed his steaming coffee mug on his picnic table desk and was turning on my computer when he opened the office door, gave me a wave, and headed for his desk chair.

After a few minutes and a number of slurps of coffee, Louie said, "You do anything after leaving The Spot last night?"

"Yeah, I watched the news and went to bed. A wonderfully boring night. What about you?"

About the same. I was home no more than an hour later. There was a guy who stopped in and was asking about you. You remember Ronnie Whitman?"

I seemed to think for a bit. "Is he a blonde-haired guy who has a bunch of tattoos?"

"Not sure about the blonde hair. His head was shaved. But he had ink on his neck. He was asking about you, just general stuff. Were you still investigating, that sort of thing?"

"What'd you tell him?"

"I told him you were still at it, and you were awfully jammed. He seemed nice enough, but I always like to play it cautious. You never know with some of these guys."

"If I recall, he ended up doing a year or two on illegal gambling charges, I think. He was running numbers for someone doing sports betting. Can't think of who that was, but he was one of a number of people caught up in it. You remember? They were running things out of a house over on the east side. I think four or five guys went down. Whitman was one of them. He seemed like a nice enough guy, at least from what I can remember. I knew of him but didn't really know him."

"Well, he might try to get in touch. I didn't give him your phone number or anything, and he never asked for it. He was still at the bar, talking with Mike when I left."

"Thanks for the heads up. I'll keep an eye out."

"Probably nothing," Louie said then picked up his phone and made a call.

I went on the computer searching for anything on Alex Chillcot and Alpha Publishing. There wasn't much. A few newspaper articles mentioned him as a person of interest in an ongoing investigation out in New Jersey, but the most recent article was dated August of 2019. I placed a call to Layla and left a message telling her I was just checking in. Louie was in court that afternoon, and I took a nap at my desk for about forty minutes. Louie was back in the office just after 4:00.

I was on a walk with Morton when I got a text message from Louie. We were on our way to The Spot, so I never did open the text. I figured whatever the message was, I was going to see Louie in a couple of minutes. We stepped into the bar, and I took three or four steps when two rather large guys stepped away from the bar and blocked me from moving any further. I tried to go around them, thinking maybe they were just jerks. One of them grabbed me by the arm. He had curly black hair pulled back in a ponytail and said, "We wanna talk with you, Haskell."

Morton continued to strain on the leash. Things weren't looking good at the moment, and I was thinking I could grab the curly-haired guy's wrist and snap his arm at the elbow, but that still left the bald-headed guy. Thankfully, he said, "Back off, Dizzy. Haskell, my name's Ronnie Whitman. We met a few years back. We'd like to talk to you, private like. Don't mean no trouble."

I looked at the jerk named Dizzy and then at his hand, squeezing my arm. He nodded slightly and released his grip.

"Yeah, Ronnie, long time no see. When did you get out?"

"Eighteen months ago. Look, we're just looking for some information. Don't mean no disrespect. You got a couple of minutes? Happy to buy you a beer."

"Let me just take my pal Morton here, to the end of the bar. Louie's down there, and he'll watch him. I'll be back in a minute."

"Don't think you can—"

"Shut up, Dizzy," Whitman said, then looked at me, nodded toward Louie, and said, "Go ahead, but don't take too long."

Morton pulled even harder as we moved toward Louie. We turned around the corner of the bar. Louie leaned down with a handful of pork rinds, which Morton quickly devoured. "Everything okay? I sent you a text message," Louie said.

"Yeah, I got it. I just didn't read it."

"Jesus Christ, it said 'emergency' in capital letters."

"Yeah, I guess I missed that part. You mind keeping an eye on Morton? Those two just want to talk. Probably some questions about Tubby or something. It should only take a minute or two."

"Everything all right, Dev? I saw those two," Mike, the bartender, said. He lifted his shirt and showed what looked like the wooden handgrip on a Colt .45 tucked into his belt.

"Thanks, but not to worry, Mike. I'm gonna talk to them in just a moment. I'm leaving Morton here with Louie."

Mike pulled a bag of pork rinds from the rack and tossed it on the bar. "On the house, keep Morton happy. Any problem, you just give me a nod," he said and walked back down the bar.

"I'll watch Morton. You mind yourself," Louie said.

"Thanks, Louie." I nodded and headed back down the bar. The conversation level in the place had definitely dropped, and I had the feeling everyone was watching me as I walked back toward Whitman and dumb shit Dizzy. "Why don't we step outside and talk," I said.

Both men nodded. Whitman led the way, I followed, with Dizzy behind me, looking over his shoulder a couple of times until we stepped outside. The stress seemed to dissipate once the door closed behind us.

"We're just parked across the street. You comfortable talking in the car?" Whitman said.

"What's this about?"

"There's a guy coming to town, and we're picking up some bad vibes."

Nine

The backseat of the white Range Rover seemed less than inviting. I waited for Dizzy to try and climb in next to me. If he tried, I planned to slam the door on his thick skull a couple of times just to get his attention. Fortunately for both of us, he settled into the front passenger seat. Whitman gave him a look that suggested something along the lines of 'Shut the hell up.'

"Appreciate you letting us interrupt your evening," Whitman said once he turned the car on. My first thought was to jump out, but he quickly added, "I'm just turning the heat on. You warm enough back there?"

"I will be. How can I help you?"

Whitman was staring at me in the rearview mirror. Dizzy was half-turned in the passenger seat, more or less facing me.

"Word on the street is you're somehow involved with this guy coming to town."

"I don't have the slightest idea what in the hell you're talking—Wait a minute. Does this have anything to do with this Alex Chillcot person?"

"Well, for not knowing who we were talking about, you seemed to pull his name out of your ass pretty fast," Dizzy said.

"Oh, man. Okay, here's the deal. You know Tubby Gustafson?"

"Yeah, of course we do. What's he got to do with Chillcot?"

"He had two of his guys pick me up and take me to his place on the River Boulevard. He gave me a week to find out as much as I can on Chillcot. Anything and everything. He gave me a so-called file on the guy, but all it had was an out-of-date picture of him that was at least ten years old and three sentences of not helpful information. I've been checking the guy out ever since. You probably already know this, but there is little or no information available out there on this guy. I've talked to some guys in the police department, and they gave me some info. They told—"

"You talked to the cops?" Dizzy half-shouted.

"Let him talk, Diz."

"Yeah, I talked to the cops. I'll talk to anyone who has information on the guy. Don't forget. I got Tubby Gustafson breathing down my neck."

"Good luck with that," Dizzy said.

Whitman shot him a look.

"Here's what I know so far." I went on to give them a brief version of what Tommy Bishop and Aaron LaZelle told me. I made a point of stressing the information Chillcot apparently has on everyone and how, if anything should happen to him, the information would go public, and a lot of people could be in trouble. "So you see, with all these guys out east, it's in everyone's interest to make sure nothing happens to Chillcot. That's why he's able to come out here and supposedly retire. Now, Tubby Gustafson doesn't think he's going to retire. He didn't say this, but my sense is he's worried the guy is going to come in here and start competing for business, and with the contacts Chillcot has and everyone wanting to keep him happy, that seems to be a legitimate concern."

Both of them were quiet for a moment. Then Whitman said, "So then, what were you doing helping that dipshit Durkin move?"

"Helping Durkin move? I wasn't helping. Oh, you gotta be kidding. I drove past their place the other morning and saw his wife carrying suitcases out of the house. I offered to help her. Told her I was a neighbor, which, actually, I am. But I thought I could maybe get some information. I talked to a realtor who was shocked that the place sold for six-hundred-and-fifty grand. She said it should go for three times that."

"Twelve million?" Dizzy said.

Whitman and I looked at him for a long moment before he said, "No, Diz, more like one-point-eight million and change."

"Oh, yeah, I guess."

"Anyway, it was Durkin's wife. Turns out he's a soon-to-be former state senator. I got a feeling Chillcot had some pretty serious dirt on the guy and forced him to sell for six-fifty. His wife told me she didn't even know the house was for sale. She's leaving the guy. I can't say I blame her. Moving in with her sister up in Hibbing. All I did was carry some suitcases out to her car. The house was completely empty except for a bed up in the master bedroom and a coffee machine in the kitchen. Everything else had been stripped down to the bare walls. I never did see Durkin. He seems to be keeping his distance from the wife, which is probably the smart thing to do. She seemed ready to strangle the guy."

"So you're not working for or with Chillcot?" Whitman said.

"Nope, never even heard of the guy until Tubby Gustafson got me involved."

"Shit," Whitman said.

Ten

Mike gave a yell from behind the bar when I walked back into The Spot. "Everything go okay, Dev?"

"Yeah, not a problem, but thanks for the offer to help."

"Louie poured down two drinks while you were gone, and I think he's fed Morton three bags of pork rinds."

"Oh, great. I better get both of them calmed down," I headed toward Louie at the far end of the bar.

"Thank God you made it back in one piece. You all right?" Louie said.

"Yeah, they just wanted information on Chillcot. I told them everything I know, which isn't much. They somehow had the idea I was working for the guy."

"Interesting. They may not be the only ones thinking that. You'd better be careful."

"I intend to. You want to head up to Roosters or down to Shamrocks and get something to eat? I'll buy."

"Yeah, thanks, but you can relax. I'm starting to calm down now that you're back. Those two guys had me worried. Who are they working for?"

I shook my head and said, "I don't know, and I figured tonight was not the time to ask. Obviously, they know about Chillcot coming to town, and I got the impression they're pretty stressed out about it. I'm sure the two of them and Tubby aren't the only ones worried about what Chillcot intends to do."

"Any idea when he's actually going to arrive?" Louie asked and drained his glass.

"No idea. I would think it could be sooner rather than later, although moving here from halfway across the country can't be fun at any time, let alone during a Minnesota winter."

"Here, Dev, on the house," Mike said, setting a beer down on the bar.

"Thank you, Mike. Very kind of you. I take back some of the awful things Louie was just saying about you."

"There's a long list of folks like that. Get you another, Louie?"

"No, I better take a pass. But thanks, Mike."

"I'll be playing it safe for the rest of the night, just in case," Mike said and raised his shirt to expose the pistol once more.

"Those two left, and I don't think they'll be coming back anytime soon."

"I'm still playing it safe," he said and walked down the bar to pour another round.

We chatted for a good half-hour. I finished my beer, walked Louie to his car, and then Morton and I headed home. I drove past the former Durkin house. All the lights were on in the place, and I could make out four male figures standing in the master bedroom up on the second floor. I figured the best thing to do would be to head home. I pulled into the garage, and we went in the back door. No sooner had I tossed a biscuit to Morton than my cell phone rang. Layla.

"The doctor is in," was how I answered.

"I'm feeling the need for an up-close examination. Do you have anything planned for the rest of the evening?"

"That sounds like the perfect ending to an otherwise crazy day. I'm just in the door. You want me to order a pizza or something?"

"No, in fact, I was thinking of swinging by Cecil's Deli. I'm in the mood for corned beef and bagels. Do you need some wine?"

"I've got a chilled bottle in the refrigerator, and I'll walk up the block and get two more bottles for backup."

"Don't feel you have to do that. After my less-than-stellar performance the other night, I'm limiting my intake."

"I'll see you when I see you, and thanks for the call."

I hung up and then hurried out the door and up to Solo Vino, anyway. I grabbed two more bottles of Sean

Minor Sauvignon Blanc and placed them in the refrigerator. I set the kitchen counter for two, then started a fire in the front room fireplace. I had some nice background music playing on the radio, and the fire was going nicely when Layla pulled into the driveway.

I opened the door and watched her as she climbed the steps onto the porch. She looked gorgeous, dressed in jeans and a knee-length brown leather coat. I took the Cecil's bag from her and got a kiss in return as she stepped into the house. We headed into the kitchen. I placed the bagels, coleslaw, potato salad, and corned beef in the refrigerator and took out the chilled bottle of wine. I filled our glasses, and we headed out to the front room.

"Oh, Dev," Layla said after a sip of wine, "this is lovely. Just what the doctor ordered. By the way, I got a call this afternoon from the HR department at Santa's Workshop. Thank you for signing up to play Santa Claus."

"Oh, my pleasure. The way you described it, I just felt the urge to participate," I lied. "Of course, they told me, and you said the same thing, that the position was already filled. I just thought it was a good idea to get my name on the list. Just in case. You never know."

"That's so sweet. Hopefully, Arthur will do something stupid again this year, and you can fill in. The kids are so fun and well, especially with your craziness. It's a chance to be part of something that's really important. You know, whatever you say to the children and their reactions, it's something that will be with them for the rest of their lives. Do you remember Christmas when you were a kid?"

"I remember we were up at like 3:00 in the morning on Christmas Day, running downstairs to the room with the Christmas tree to see what Santa Claus had left us. My father came down and told us to go back to bed."

She laughed and said, "Oh, that is hilarious. I can just see you. One of my brothers was snooping around our Christmas tree a few days before Christmas. My folks were starting to put gifts under the tree. Our house was the designated Christmas Eve location for my father's extended family. So, we had aunts, uncles, and grandparents in attendance. Anyway, my brother finds a gift with his name on it. It was a small square box gift wrapped with a ribbon and a bow. No one was around, so he picked up the box and shook it. The box started to move back and forth and make a noise. He set it down, and it kept moving back and forth and making this grinding sound."

"So what did he do?"

"He did what every little boy would do. He ran into another room and quickly unwrapped the gift. It turned out to be a little bank where you would place a coin in a slot, and the lid on the box would open up, and this hand would automatically come out, grab the coin, and deposit the coin inside the box."

"So, did he rewrap the thing?"

"No, one of my sisters caught him and told my mom. He got sent to his room, and to make matters worse, he had to attempt to go through the motions when the gift was rewrapped and it was time to open presents. He had burned out the motor on the thing, and it never worked again. After all that, he had to write a thank you note. He kept it in his bedroom for years as a reminder."

"Oh, that's great. I could see me doing that."

"Yeah, no doubt."

We ate dinner in front of the fire, had another glass of wine, listened to the music, and just chatted. Eventually, we wandered upstairs to bed. Morton slept in the guest bedroom, and when Layla got undressed, she placed her bra and thong in a dresser drawer just in case Morton somehow made his way into the bedroom.

I was up before the alarm went off. I turned it off, showered, shaved, and dressed downstairs. Morton wandered down around 7:00, and I let him out. I heard the shower running a few minutes later. I set the kitchen counter for breakfast and made preparations for French toast. When I heard Layla on the stairs, I placed the first two pieces in the frying pan and poured her a coffee.

"Mmm-mmm, it smells wonderful. Pancakes?"

"No, French toast with real maple syrup."

"Oh, God, I can't wait."

"Here, take a seat and have some coffee. How'd you sleep?"

"Well, let's see, dinner in front of the fireplace, some wine, great sex, yeah, I slept pretty soundly. Thank you. What time were you up?"

"The usual, a little before 6:00."

"I'll never understand that."

"Just the way I am. I think it might be something I learned in the army that I'll never be able to shake."

"Well, thank you for your service, especially last night," she said and laughed.

Eleven

When Layla headed out the door it was close to 9:00. I put Morton in the car, and we drove past the former Durkin house. Six different guys were working on the windows in front and I slowed down to check out the activity. Four trucks from a glass manufacturer with all sorts of sheets of glass leaning on racks in the back of the trucks were on the street. Another guy appeared to be changing the locks on the massive oak front door. By all indications, Alex Chillcot was going to be moving in sooner rather than later. I pulled to the curb two houses up the block and made some quick notes on the back of an envelope listing the number of men working and the name of the company installing the new glass in the windows.

I decided to clip the leash onto Morton's collar and walk past. We slowed our pace as we approached the house. There were four sawhorses set up on the sidewalk with sheets of plywood on top, creating two temporary workbenches leading up to the house. Sheets of glass were on both workbenches. We turned at the corner and walked along the sidewalk, looking at the east side of the house. A workman opened the wrought iron side gate and climbed into the back of a truck with more sheets of glass. He was using a tape measure to check the size on various pieces.

"Are there a lot of broken windows in that house?" I asked.

He looked up, smiled, and shook his head. "No, we're replacing all the windows in the place with bullet-proof glass."

"Bulletproof?"

"You'd be surprised how many homes have it. We did another home just around the corner last year. Bulletproof glass, security cameras, alarm systems, you can never be too careful."

"That's got to cost a fortune."

He smiled and said, "If you have to ask, you can't afford it." He measured another sheet of glass, pulled it off the rack, and headed back to the front of the house.

We turned at the alley and walked past the three-stall garage. A guy was back there installing a keypad at each door. He gave us a friendly nod as we walked past. All the workers seemed very happy. I figured they must be making a small fortune on the project. We walked up the alley, back to the car, and headed down to the office.

Louie was seated at his picnic table desk, talking on the phone. He gave a wave as we stepped in. I had taken only two steps into the office when the smell of burnt coffee hit me. I glanced at the pot. The burner was on, and there wasn't enough coffee to cover the bottom of the pot. I turned the burner off and dripped the remnants into the sink.

"Oh yeah, sorry 'bout that. I meant to make a fresh pot."

"Not to worry, I'll take care of it."

"You think those two guys from last night will come back to The Spot?"

I shook my head as I rinsed out the coffee pot, then filled it with six cups of water. "No, they were looking for information on Chillcot. I didn't have any, or the little I had was of no value. There are other places and people they can check out. They probably know some guys working for Tubby, which would be a good place to start. Oh, and get this. On the way to work this morning, I drove past the house he bought. There were all sorts of guys working on the windows. Four trucks were parked around the place with different-sized sheets of glass in racks in the back of the trucks."

"Did someone break a bunch of windows last night?"

"No. I asked one of the guys what was up, and he told me all the windows were being replaced with bulletproof glass. God, I can't imagine what that's going to cost." I poured the water into the coffee maker, then set a filter in it, and began to fill it with coffee grounds.

"They're replacing all the windows with bulletproof glass?"

"That's what this guy told me, and he was one of the people doing it."

"Incredible," Louie said.

I turned the coffee pot on. A moment later, water began running over the fresh coffee grounds and dripping into the pot.

"Did you try to reach Delvin Durkin?"

"No. I thought about it for a minute, but honestly, Louie, there's no point. The guy's a politician. If he did talk to me, there'd be about a one percent chance he'd be telling me the truth. And if he ever did decide to talk, I have to believe he'd be talking to a newspaper reporter or one of the news stations rather than talking to the likes of me. She never came out and said it, but reading between the lines, his unhappy wife is probably going to divorce him or, at the very least, leave him for a while, if not forever. She was one unhappy camper yesterday."

Louie shook his head and said, "I can't believe he basically left over a million bucks on the table. Either he's going to work for Chillcot, or the guy has a lot of dirt on Durkin and isn't afraid to use it."

"Yeah, my thought is on the latter. You know, a politician. Chillcot probably has him by the short hairs. Be interesting to find out what it is, but like I said, at the end of the day, Durkin is a politician. They're all crooks."

Louie nodded.

The coffee was finally finished. I poured a fresh mug for Louie and filled my mug. I wasted the better part of the day looking into mob business out in New Jersey and New York. Chillcot's name was mentioned occasionally, but he was never in any way directly tied to specific mob undertakings. I took Morton for a walk at the end of the day, and we met Louie in The Spot for a drink and a handful of pork rinds.

Both TVs above the bar were on in anticipation of the pregame show before the Minnesota Wild hockey game. At the moment, the local nightly news was on, but the sound was off. I happened to glance up at the TV just as the banner headline in red letters flashed across the screen. DOUBLE MURDER MOB RELATED.

That struck me as strange. Violent crime in town was definitely up, like in so many other cities, but the words Mob Related seemed like a bit of a stretch. I was probably the only guy in the place that even caught it. The bar was crowded, but mostly with people in hockey jerseys meeting for a drink before taking the bar bus down to the Xcel Energy Center to attend the Wild game. There was no point in asking Mike to turn up the sound.

Five minutes later, my phone rang, Tommy Bishop. I turned toward Louie. "Hey Louie, I gotta take this call. Can you keep an eye on Morton for a minute?"

"No problem. You want another beer?"

"Oh, I better hold off until I see what this call is about. Shouldn't be more than a minute or two." As I stepped outside, I swiped my finger across the screen and answered. "Hi, Tommy, what's up?"

"Hi, Dev. Sorry to bother you. Something's come up, and I wondered if you wouldn't mind coming down to the station. Hopefully, you can help us out with some general information."

I thought for a moment. This suddenly didn't sound like a social call. Then the TV screen with DOUBLE MURDER MOB RELATED flashed in my mind. "Yeah, Tommy, be happy to. I've got my dog Morton with me, so I'm going to run him home, and then I'll be down. Shouldn't be more than twenty minutes, thirty at the most."

"Much appreciated, Dev. Just ask for me at the front desk, and I'll have someone run down and bring you up."

"Not a problem, Tommy. See you shortly."

I stepped back inside. Louie looked at me and said, "I'm getting the sense that call didn't go the way you expected."

I shook my head. "Not exactly. Tommy Bishop," I said and went on to give Louie the short version of Tommy being in Special Investigations and the news blurb about a double murder.

"Well, good luck, Dev. You need anything, just call."

"Thanks, Louie. Come on, Morton. I'm afraid we've things to do." I drove home, let Morton in through the back door, tossed him a biscuit, and headed down to the police station.

There were three vans from different TV channels parked in front of the station with cameramen and report- ers standing on the sidewalk. I parked in the lot across the street and walked around them.

"Excuse me, sir. Are you involved in the double homicide investigation?"

I shook my head, said, "I don't know anything about that," and entered the building.

Twelve

There were two officers standing guard just inside the entrance. One of them gave me a nod and said, "Anything we can help you with, sir?"

"I got a call from Detective Bishop, Special Investigations. He told me to ask for him at the front desk, and he'd send someone to bring me upstairs."

"Sorry to slow you down," he said and nodded toward the front desk

"How can I help you?" the sergeant seated behind the desk asked.

"I got a call from Detective Bishop, Special Investigations. He asked me to come down here. My name is Dev Haskell."

"Oh, yeah, I thought I recognized you. You do a lot with Lieutenant LaZelle, don't you?"

"Yeah, although he'd probably say I just make things more complicated."

He chuckled and picked up the phone. He pressed three keys and a moment later said, "I have a Dev Haskell down here at the front desk for Detective Bishop. Yes. Okay, thank you," he said and hung up.

"They're sending someone down. Should be just a minute."

"Thanks, I'll grab a seat," I walked over to an area with four rows of black plastic chairs. I was the only person there, and I hadn't sat for more than a minute or two when the security door opened, and detective Tony Olson stood there and called, "Dev Haskell?"

"Right here, Detective," I said as I hurried over to him.

"Nice to see you again, Dev. How are things going?" he said as he held the door for me. We took the elevator up to the third floor, walked down the hall to the Homicide section, and Olson entered the code on the keypad next to the door.

Only half the desks in the section were occupied at this late hour and most of the officers were on the phone. Olson led me through the open area and into Aaron LaZelle's office. As I stepped in, Aaron said, "Thanks, Tony. If you'd close the door, please."

Tommy Bishop was in the office along with Detective Sergeant Norris Manning. I'd had a negative relationship, which is putting it nicely, with Manning until about eighteen months ago. I'd helped him out on a problem with his son, and that seemed to move our relationship onto a different, more positive track. That said, I planned to remain overly cautious around him.

I smiled and gave a nod to Manning and Aaron then said, "What's up, Tommy?"

"We have a double homicide on our hands, Dev, and your name came up."

I automatically shot a quick glance at Manning. Fortunately, he was looking at Bishop, and he didn't catch it. "I think I know about this only because I saw a headline flash across the TV screen at The Spot. The sound was off, and your call came through almost at the same time. Was it someone I know?"

"Someone you interacted with recently," Manning said, still not looking at me.

"Jesus Christ, don't tell me it's Layla. Oh please, don't tell me it's her."

Now Manning looked up at me like I was crazy. "Layla? What the hell are you talking about, Haskell? Who's Layla? And no, it's not some woman."

"Well then, who?"

"You have any recent interaction with Dixon Gillespie?" Bishop asked.

"I don't believe I know anyone by that name."

"What about Ronald Whitman?"

I shook my head. "No, I—wait a minute, Ronnie Whitman? What'd you say the other guy's name was? Dixon?"

"Yes, Dixon Gillespie," Aaron said.

"They're the two murder victims?"

"So, you do know them?" Manning said.

"Well, I know of Ronnie Whitman. Don't know him that well. He and another guy I didn't know got in front of me last night at The Spot."

"Got in front of you?" Bishop said.

"Yeah, I was walking in with Morton. He's my dog. They were at the bar and purposely stepped in front of me. Clearly blocking my way. They said they just wanted to talk with me. I left Morton with Louie, my office mate, and stepped outside with Ronnie Whitman and the other guy. I'd never seen the other guy before. Whitman referred to him as Dizzy a couple of times. That's why I didn't pick up on his name, but that last name Gillespie must be where the 'Dizzy' comes from."

"So, you left with them. Where'd you go?"

"Nowhere. I mean, we walked across the street, Randolph Avenue, and sat in their car and talked. Couldn't have been more than five minutes, maybe closer to three. They were asking me what I knew about Alex Chillcot. He's apparently moving into town from somewhere in New Jersey. From what I've read, he's mob connected. As a matter of fact, they thought I might be working for him."

"You ever meet him?" Manning asked.

"Chillcot? God no. In fact, I was given an out-of-date image of the guy by Tubby Gustafson, and Tommy, you gave me a more current picture. I told you Tubby Gustafson wanted me to find out everything I could on Chillcot. That's what I've been trying to do. It's just that there isn't much out there. I do know that he apparently bought a mansion on Summit Avenue and—"

"Did Whitman or Gillespie say where they were going after talking to you?"

"No, once they found out I didn't know much about the guy, and Tubby Gustafson gave me a week to find stuff out, that pretty much took the wind out of their sails. When were they killed?"

"Late last night, they were shot in the car. Whitman's car."

"A white Range Rover?"

"Yes."

"That was the car we were in. Those two were in the front seat. I was in the backseat. Where were they when they were shot?"

"In the parking lot of The Trough, you know it?"

"Yeah, I've been in there a couple of times, but the last time was three or possibly even five years ago. The place was pretty much of a dive if I recall."

"Nothing's changed. They were killed in the parking lot, automatic weapons fire. It appears to have been over a hundred rounds fired. Autopsies are scheduled for tomorrow," Aaron said.

"Any suspects?"

All three shook their head.

"I can tell you I was in the house that Chillcot purchased. He paid way below the going rate. He—"

"Yeah, we looked into that. Nothing short of amazing," Bishop said.

"I spoke to his wife. She suggested the sale and the move were a big surprise to her. In fact, she told me she's heading up north and moving in with a sister in Hibbing.

I had the impression she was leaving Durkin, her husband."

All three nodded.

"Any other questions? I'm sorry I don't have more information, but I don't. Just about everything I know about Chillcot I got online. Oh, I can tell you one other thing I learned. There were crews at the house he bought on Summit this morning. I talked to one of the guys working there, and he told me they're installing bulletproof glass in every window of the house. Plus, they're adding security cameras and alarm systems."

Manning looked at Aaron LaZelle and shook his head.

"Thanks for coming down right away, Dev," Aaron said.

"Am I free to go?"

"Yeah, go on home and enjoy the rest of your evening," Bishop said.

"Wish I had more to tell you, but I don't."

"Appreciate you making the effort," Manning added.

"Give a call if I can be of any help," I said and stepped out of the office, closing the door behind me.

Detective Olson was up and out of his desk chair as I stepped into the hall. "You all set?" he asked.

"Yeah, I was little or no help."

"Good you came down anyway. Come on, I'll escort you down to the front desk, and you can get back to whatever you were doing."

We took the elevator down to the main floor. He held the security door for me as I stepped into the lobby. I gave the sergeant at the front desk a nod and headed out of the building. As I stepped out onto the sidewalk, I had a bunch of questions hurled at me from the news people.

I held up my hands and said, "Sorry, fellas, but I was just in there going over a car insurance problem. I don't know anything you're asking about."

They went back to leaning against their vans and looking bored. I crossed the street, climbed into my car, and headed home. I ignored the idea of driving past The Trough or Chillcot's house on Summit.

Thirteen

Since Layla wasn't over, I slept through the night. Morton and I drove past Chillcot's house around 7:30 the following morning. No work crews were in sight. Other than a stack of sawhorses, footprints, and ladder markings in the snow around the house, there was nothing that suggested work was being done. From what I could tell, the windows that I knew had been worked on looked just fine.

We were down in the office before Louie. I made a fresh pot of coffee and printed off my report for Tubby Gustafson. I still only had bits and pieces of information, although I added my brief meeting with Ronnie Whitman and Dixon 'Dizzy' Gillespie along with my interview, such as it was, with the police last night.

Louie wandered in just after 9:00 and was busy doing final preparations for an 11:00 court appearance when my phone rang. "Haskell Investigations."

"Yeah, dumb shit, we're parked out in front of your dumpy office building. Expect you down here in two minutes, or we're coming up to get you," Fat Freddy said.

"Be right down," I said and hung up.

I grabbed my five-page file. All my notes were double-spaced and in 14-point type. At least to the untrained eye, it looked like there was a good deal of information.

"Wish me luck, Louie. I'm heading to my meeting with Tubby Gustafson on Chillcot coming to town."

"Thanks. I was thinking of complaining to myself about my court appearance this morning. Now that you mention it, I've got nothing to bitch about."

"Good luck in court," I said, stepped out of the office, and hurried down the stairs. Fat Freddy was in the front passenger seat, and a thug I didn't recognize was behind the wheel.

As I climbed into the car, Freddy looked at me and said, "Gee, right on time. Maybe you can teach a stupid dog new tricks."

"I'll take that as a compliment, Freddy. How are things going for you guys?"

"Same day, different shit."

"I think you meant to say different day, same shit," I said.

"Yeah, whatever," he said and shot me a look.

With the exception of Fat Freddy's fifteen-second call announcing we were on our way, we drove the rest of the trip in silence. The Cadillac Escalade pulled to a stop just opposite the front door of Tubby's mansion. I noticed that there were four guys lingering outside the front door instead of the usual two and wondered if this might be the new normal with Alex Chillcot coming to town. I stepped out of the car. A guy patted me down then led me into the mansion, where I was patted down again. Today, there were two guys who appeared to be standing guard in the entryway.

After I was patted down and got the all-clear, one of the thugs led me down the hall to Tubby's office. Another guy I'd never seen before was wearing a suit and tie, sitting in a chair that was leaning against the wall. He lowered the chair as we approached and stood.

"He's here to see the boss," the thug who led me down the hall said. "This is Haskell."

The suit and tie knocked on the door as he opened it and said, "A Mr. Hassell to see you, sir."

"Oh, God, not far from the truth," Tubby laughed. "All right, show him in and then stay near the door in case I call for help."

The suit and tie stepped into Tubby's office and held the door for me. Once I was in the office, he closed the door behind me on his way out.

Surprisingly, Tubby was dressed in a gray pin-striped suit, and a starched white shirt with a red tie. He was seated at his desk with a number of files in front of him. There was no sign of his massage table or, unfortunately, the two lovely, nearly naked women who gave him his massage.

Tubby leaned back in his chair and said, "All right, Haskell. So what did you manage to find out?"

"Well, sir, first and foremost, there is little to no information out there on Alex Chillcot. He seems to have run just beneath the surface in New York and New Jersey. I did learn that, over the years, he has garnered a good deal of private and personal information on anyone and everyone. His strength appears to be the fact that everyone knows he has this information, and if anything should happen to Chillcot, this very private, personal information will be available within minutes. It will be sent to mob bosses, the authorities, spouses, anyone and everyone, and that apparently makes Chillcot virtually untouchable."

Tubby thought about that for a long moment and said, "How does one gain access to this list of Chillcot's?"

"I've looked and looked and never found anything concrete to suggest it actually exists. All I know is, everyone back east is playing it safe and doing everything in their power to make sure it's never released."

"So, you don't know if the information is kept in a safe, in his home, or even in a safety deposit box?" Tubby said.

"Correct, sir, or, for that matter, kept up in the cloud somewhere with a program set up to release the information automatically. It strikes me as being rather ingenious, and he has everyone from out east really over a barrel."

"Interesting."

"I did some investigating of his purchase of a home on Summit Ave. Recent rough estimates of the value of the place run from one point four million to one point nine and some change. State Senator Delvin Durkin sold the home on Summit Avenue to Chillcot for the princely sum of six hundred and fifty thousand dollars. That leads me to suspect Chillcot had information that forced Durkin to sell the place at a loss. The fact that the home was sold, and at that price, was a complete surprise to Durkin's wife, Edith. When I spoke to her, she suggested she may be divorcing Durkin."

"You spoke to his wife?"

"Yes, sir, I wanted to find out everything I possibly could and report it to you. Other than a bed in the master bedroom, the home was completely empty. I carried her last two suitcases out to her car. She told me she was thinking of going back to her maiden name. She was about to drive up to Hibbing and move in with her sister."

Tubby studied me for a moment. "What else did you learn?"

"The next day, I went past the place, and there were a number of people working, installing alarm systems, security cameras, and bulletproof glass in all the windows."

"Bulletproof glass? How in the hell did you find that out?"

"I asked one of the workmen what they were doing, and he volunteered the information."

"Anything else?"

"Yes, sir. There was a double homicide the other night. To my knowledge, no suspects have been identified at this point, but the two victims had spoken to me earlier that evening and wanted to know what I knew about Chillcot."

"Who were they?"

"Two guys, one named Ronnie Whitman and another with the last name Gillespie. He was called Dizzy. They were in their car in the parking lot of a bar called The Trough. Whoever killed them, and I think there were at least two people, they used automatic weapons. The cops told me there were over a hundred rounds fired into the car."

Tubby nodded but didn't comment and then asked, "So what did you tell Whitman and Dizzy?"

"They thought I may have been working for Chillcot because I was checking things out for you. It was pretty obvious that wasn't the deal. We didn't talk for more than five minutes, if that. Next thing I know, they had the hell shot out of them. Do you know much about them? Were they working for someone or on their own?"

"Mmm, they were available on a contract basis. Pay them to do a job. Not the brightest bulbs on the tree. What else do you have for me?"

"Everything I told you I've got in this file, along with an up-to-date image of Chillcot. My sense is he'll be moving into that house on Summit sooner rather than later. I don't know anything about his staff. I have absolutely no proof, but if he was somehow connected to the shooting the other night, it wouldn't surprise me. The final thing is to mention again that there just is not much information on the guy. A lot of speculation, but that's about it."

"You know, Haskell, once in a great while, you catch me by surprise. I appreciate the information. Keep your ear to the ground. If you learn anything else, I'll expect to hear it immediately."

"Yes, sir."

Tubby picked up his cell phone and punched two numbers then set the phone down. A moment later, the door opened, and the suit and tie guy stepped in.

"Escort him to the entry. Thank you, Haskell. Mind yourself."

Apparently, I was dismissed. No threats, no negative comments. It was one of the nicest meetings I'd ever had with Tubby. Obviously, he was focused on Chillcot and didn't have the time to degrade me.

Fourteen

At the end if the day I had a beer in The Spot with Louie. It tasted so good I had a second, and then Morton and I headed home. We drove past Chillcot's place on Summit Ave, and I pulled to the curb. The work crews were gone, but the front windows on the first floor had black wrought iron burglar bars with a scrolled pattern over the windows. I got out of the car and walked around to the side of the house. Same thing. All the first-floor windows were covered with the same wrought iron pattern. I checked the back of the house, more of the same.

"Can I help you," a voice called from behind me. I turned to see a muscular guy with a crew cut. He was wearing a black leather jacket and blue jeans and looked way too young to be Chillcot.

"Oh, hi. I'm a neighbor, Dev Haskell. Just admiring the burglar bars you've installed. I've been thinking about doing the same thing myself. Are you the new owner?"

"No."

"Did you do this work? It's really nice."

"No."

"Okay, well, thanks," I said and headed back to my car. As I pulled away, I saw him in the rearview mirror, watching me until I disappeared. Once home, I made a grilled cheese sandwich and fooled around on the computer until 10:00. I pulled on my jacket and walked over to the Chillcot house. Other than the front porch light, the first floor was dark. A light was on up in the master bedroom, but the shades were drawn. I went around the block and down the alley. As I passed the garage, a motion detector light flashed on. That suggested there were probably motion detector lights mounted on the house as well.

I headed home, caught some news on YouTube for a half-hour, and went to bed. Morton woke me around 3:00 a.m. I tried to calm him down, but something was bothering him. I opened the drawer on the bedside table and took out my Glock. I slipped on my jeans, left the lights off, and made my way downstairs.

No one appeared to be on the front porch. I walked back to the kitchen. The back porch was empty, but the gate was partially open, and I always close it. I glanced out the windows in the back of the house. I didn't see anyone, but along with Morton's paw prints, there were footprints in the snow. I hadn't been back there since it snowed. I thought back to the jerk with the crewcut at Chillcot's house. Could he have taken my license number and gotten my address?

I double-checked the back and front doors. I wedged a chair just beneath the doorknob of each door and went upstairs to bed. Morton, apparently comfortable, was stretched out on the bed. I slept fitfully for the next two and a half hours and finally got up. Morton joined me in the kitchen an hour later.

Once we finished breakfast, we headed down to the office. I didn't drive past the Chillcot place on the way. Louie wandered in just after nine. Apparently, I had dozed off because, when he opened the office door, I suddenly jerked awake.

"Oh, sorry," he said and then cleared his throat a couple of times. "Didn't mean to wake you."

I got up, filled his coffee mug, and set it on the picnic table. After a few minutes and a number of sips, he said, "So, late night with Layla?"

"I only wish," I said and filled him in on someone poking around my place in the middle of the night.

"Sounds like it could be that guy from Chillcot's. Interesting, he would have gotten your address and checked you out."

"Yeah, but it's one thing to drive past and look at the house. It's quite another to come into the yard and look around at 3:00 in the morning."

"Isn't that what you did at Chillcot's? Looking around at those burglar bars?"

"No, not really. First of all, it wasn't three in the morning. Second, I didn't go in the yard. I was just standing on the sidewalk looking around. Of course, the other thing is, I never actually saw whoever was checking my place out. Maybe it was just some local half-wit and not the guy from Chillcot's."

"That's possible, although under the circumstances, I'd rate it as slim to none," Louie said then drained his coffee mug. He waddled over to the pot and poured a fresh mug. "Be interesting to see if there was any more activity at your place today."

"Hopefully, whoever it was decided I wasn't worth it."

Fifteen

My day was spent reading everything I could find on the murders of Ronnie Whitman and Dizzy Gillespie. I left a voice message for Tubby Gustafson telling him about Chillcot's wrought iron burglar bars and took Morton for a walk at the end of the day. We joined Louie at The Spot for a drink. Morton had inhaled a handful of pork rinds from Louie, and I was halfway through my beer when my phone rang. The call was identified as 'caller unknown,' and usually, I would just let it go, but for some reason, I answered, "Haskell Investigations." At the moment, the jukebox was playing Garth Brooks on the second verse of 'Friends in Low Places.' I had the cell phone up against my right ear. The index finger on my left hand was in my left ear, and I gave Louie a nod and headed out the side door, so I could hear whoever was calling.

"Sorry, please hang on for just a moment. I've got someone singing next to me," I said as I stepped out the side door.

Two guys were leaning against the building on either side of the door. I stepped outside and said, "Hello, are you still there?"

"Right next to you, dumb shit," one of the guys said, and suddenly, he and his partner grabbed me from behind. I dropped my cell phone as they hustled me into the open trunk of the car parked at the curb.

"Hey, hey, what the hell are you doing? Wait, stop, stop. Don't do this," I shouted, not that they paid any attention to what I had to say.

They tossed me into the trunk. I bounced once or twice and then started to sit up and said, "What in the hell are—" The lid of the trunk suddenly slammed into my forehead, and things went dark.

When I came to, the car was moving, and I was shivering it was so cold in the trunk. I could hear some music coming from the front seat, and I shouted, "Hey, I think you made a big mistake. I'm not the guy you want. Just let me out, and I won't tell anyone. Hey, did you hear me? Hello? Hello? You got the wrong guy here. Can you hear me?"

The music on the radio suddenly grew louder, and the bass began to vibrate through the vehicle. I curled up, closed my eyes, and placed my hands over my ears.

It felt like we'd been traveling for a couple of hours, but it was probably just ten or fifteen minutes. My head was pounding. I was freezing and visibly shaking from the cold. The bass was still vibrating through the vehicle, and I wondered how anyone could stand it. The car suddenly slowed and took a right turn. A moment later, the music stopped, and I heard what sounded like a garage door opening. The car moved ahead a few feet, stopped, and two car doors opened and closed. I could hear voices just outside of the trunk but couldn't make out what was being said.

The lid to the trunk suddenly opened. I had to close my eyes from the bright light shining in, and suddenly, a pair of hands grabbed my shirt and yanked me out of the trunk, none too gently.

I blinked my eyes open and looked at the two figures in front of me. We were in what looked like a double garage. Both men were wearing ski masks. One of them turned and headed toward the front of the garage. The larger of the two shoved me and shouted, "Get your worthless ass in gear and follow him, dumb shit."

I followed the guy to the front of the garage and through an open door. Another guy was standing in a passageway that was connected to the house. He wasn't wearing a ski mask. My first thought was, *Thank God it was warm.* My immediate second thought was *If he's not wearing a mask, does that mean they're going to kill me?*

"Bring him into the basement," the guy without the mask said.

"Hey, look, guys. I think you made a mistake and—"

"Are you that piece of shit, Dev Haskell?" the guy behind me asked.

"Yeah, but I—"

"There's no mistake. Now get your dumb ass into the basement," he said just as the first guy opened the basement door and stepped to the side.

I looked at him, and he nodded toward the basement stairs. Suddenly the guy in back shoved me, and I stumbled down the first couple of steps and then grabbed onto the handrail and stopped my fall. I pulled myself back onto my feet and picked up my pace just to get a few feet of distance between me and the idiot who shoved me.

The basement looked like it had been redone fifty or sixty years ago. Wood paneling was on the walls, and there was a fireplace in the corner of the room. There were lights in the ceiling, but they were turned off, and the room was illuminated by two table lamps on either end of the couch. A wood fire was burning in the fireplace.

"Take a seat, Haskell," someone said. I headed for the couch, and the same voice said, "Get your ass down on the floor in front of the fire."

I settled down on the floor and fought off a dizzy spell as I bent my head and apparently moved too fast. The three of them sat down on the couch opposite me. The two with ski masks pulled them off, which didn't exactly encourage me into thinking everything was suddenly going to be okay. One of the guys had a tattoo of a vine with red flowers running down his neck.

Sixteen

My thought was I could explain my way out. "Look, fellas, I don't know what this is about, but I'm sure if we can just talk, you'll see you're dealing with the wrong guy. I'm more than willing to help you in any way I can and—"

"Are you Dev Haskell?" the larger of the three asked.

"Yeah, I told you that. It's just that I haven't done anything that—"

"Shut up for a minute and just listen. You'd better answer some questions like your life depends on it, because it does."

"That's why I think you might have made a mistake and—"

"For God's sake, would you please just shut the hell up for a minute?"

"Okay, okay, my lips are sealed," I said and pinched my lips, indicating just that.

The big guy looked at the other two and shook his head.

The guy in the middle of the three, the one who hadn't worn a ski mask, said, "Haskell, friends of ours, very good friends, met with you the other night. You had them followed and—"

"First of all, I'm not sure who you're talking about. Second, I didn't have anyone followed, anywhere."

"Are you telling us you didn't meet with Ronnie and Dizzy?"

"That's what this is all about, Ronnie and Dizzy? Yeah, they got in touch with me the other night at The Spot bar. We talked for all of about three minutes in Ronnie's car, a white Range Rover. He was in the driver's seat, and Dizzy was in the front passenger seat. They were asking me questions about Alex Chillcot. In fact, they were thinking I worked for the guy."

"And do you?" the driver of the car asked.

"No. I'll tell you the same thing I told them. Tubby Gustafson contacted me. He told me to find out everything and anything I could on Alex Chillcot. I'd never heard of the guy until Tubby mentioned him. A detective in Special Investigations gave me some information, I looked up some things online, and I was told Chillcot purchased a house on Summit Avenue. I checked the place out. Do you know the house I'm talking about?"

Two of the three nodded. I went on to tell them about the sale price, the wrought iron burglary bars, the bulletproof glass, Durkin's wife, and the little I knew about Chillcot."

"So you're telling us you haven't spoken to Chillcot lately?"

"Spoken to him? I didn't even know the guy existed until Tubby Gustafson got me involved. Now, suddenly, it seems like there are a whole bunch of folks not all that happy about him moving here. I've never met Chillcot. I told Tubby everything I learned about Chillcot, and I'm pretty sure most of it was news to him."

"Tell us what you learned," the guy sitting in the middle said.

I told them about Chillcot's list of people, finishing up with, "It's basically his get out of jail free card. No one wants to touch him because all that information will get sent to individuals, cops, the FBI, the DEA, everyone. Suddenly, they're all working to make sure nothing happens to Chillcot and that he leaves town."

They seemed to think about that, and then the jerk who tried to push me down the stairs asked, "So when is he coming to town?"

"I don't know. But based on the work being done on the house and the fact that they've got the motion detector lights, security cameras, bulletproof glass, and the burglary bars installed, I've been telling everyone it looks like he's going to be here sooner rather than later."

"Have you talked to him?"

"I already told you, no. I didn't even know the guy existed until maybe a week ago. In fact, there's a big guy who I think might work for Chillcot staying in the house now. At least, I think he is. I also think he tried to get into my place last night around 3:00 in the morning. I never saw him, but there were footprints in the snow, and my dog woke me up."

They looked at one another. The guy in the middle half laughed and said, "That was us."

"You guys tried to break into my place?"

"We were just checking you out, Haskell. How long have you been on Gustafson's payroll?"

I debated how to answer that and decided the truth would probably be the best way. "We go back a number of years. By the way, I'm not on his payroll. He's never paid me, ever. Truth is, he doesn't really like me, but we exchange information from time to time."

"And you didn't tell him about talking to Ronnie in his car?"

"Not until the day after. I think whoever killed Ronnie and Dizzy did it sometime after midnight. The cops brought me in for questioning on that. I told them the same thing. We only talked a couple of minutes out in Ronnie's Range Rover. In fact, the cops told me over a hundred rounds were fired into Ronnie's car, which means there were at least two guys doing the shooting. You hear anything on the autopsies?"

They all shook their heads.

"I'll check in with the police tomorrow and see if I can get any information."

The big guy shook his head. "What information do we need? They're dead. Enough said."

"Might be nice to know what kind of weapon was used, maybe two different ones, which would confirm my thought that there were two guys doing the shooting. Do you know, were Ronnie or Dizzy regulars at The Trough?"

"They were there from time to time. It's not a surprise they were there the other night. Whoever the shooter was, he may have been waiting there for hours."

"Is there anyone else, besides someone with Chillcot, you could think of who would have done this?"

They seemed to think for a long moment and then shook their heads. "Maybe a couple of irate husbands but no one who would have killed both of them in the parking lot and certainly no one with that type of firepower."

"Did Ronnie make his feelings on Chillcot known? Did he talk to other people besides me?"

"He was a man on a mission when it came to Chillcot. To be honest, we all are, and from what you say, so is Mr. Gustafson. Once the guy gets here, he's going to screw the business we've all worked so hard to build. We'll have to get real jobs or worse."

"Anything else I can help you guys with? I'm sorry you lost your friends. Really, I am, but I don't work for Chillcot. I've never met him. Never talked to him on the phone, and if the murders of Ronnie and Dizzy are any indication of what the world's going to be like when he comes to town, I'm not looking forward to it."

Seventeen

At least when they drove me back to The Spot, I wasn't tossed into the car trunk again. I'd like to say they kept me blindfolded until we got there, but they'd actually placed a pair of plaid boxer shorts over my head. Fortunately, they'd been washed. They pulled up to the side door and stopped. "Get your dumb ass the hell out of the car, Haskell," the big guy in the passenger seat shouted.

I didn't have to be told twice. I tossed the boxers on the floor, got a quick look at the driver with the red-flowered vine tattoo, and hopped out of the car. They took off down the street before I could even close the door. It was a winter evening, and as they sped away, I couldn't tell if the car was dark blue or black. As far as the make went, I had no idea. I spotted my phone still on the sidewalk next to the side door. I picked it up and went into the bar.

Louie had a glass up to his lips. He glanced at me, drained his glass, and set it on the bar. Morton was lying at his feet, and he gave me a quick look. Two empty pork rinds bags were on the bar in front of Louie.

"That must have been one hell of a phone call. Hey, you all right?" Louie asked as he focused in on my forehead.

"Thanks for asking. No, I'm not all right. I was kidnapped. The idiots slammed the trunk lid on my forehead and took me someplace, thinking I was involved with the murders of Ronnie and Dizzy," I said and proceeded to fill him in.

When I was finished, he said, "Wow, who knew?"

"Well, apparently no one," I said, then picked up my half-empty beer mug and took four large swallows of warm beer. "Hey, Mike, can I get a cold one here?"

He was at the opposite end of the bar, nodded, and started to fill a mug.

"You know who they were?" Louie asked.

"Not really. I suppose I could try to find out, but I don't want to stir the pot any more than it already is. Everyone seems to be going crazy over this Chillcot coming to town, and I want to stay as far away from that as possible."

"Sounds to me that, like it or not, you're already right in the middle. At least as far as these characters know."

"Yeah, I'm afraid you may be right."

Mike set the fresh beer mug down in front of me then stared for a moment before he said, "What the hell happened to your forehead? Your brain working on a problem it can't figure out?"

"No, just bumped it. Thanks for the beer."

"I put it on Louie's tab."

"Thanks, Mike. Things are starting to look better already." I talked with Louie for another thirty minutes. He tried to talk me into calling the police, but I just wanted the entire event to go away. I said good night, put Morton in the backseat, and we drove home. We didn't go near the house on Summit Avenue.

Once we were home, I wedged a chair beneath the doorknob on the front door and then checked the back door. The chair was still in place. I opened the refrigerator, pulled out some leftover pizza, took two aspirin, and settled down in front of the TV. We wandered up to bed after the 10:00 news. I examined my forehead in the bathroom mirror. I had a large red bump, close to four inches long, across my forehead just below my hairline.

I woke with a throbbing headache around 4:00, took two more aspirin, and fell back asleep. Morton woke me just before 8:00. I let him out the back door, grabbed a shower, and nibbled on some toast for breakfast. At least my headache was gone, although the welt had grown from red to more of a purple. Just in case, I placed a half-dozen aspirin in an envelope, and we drove down to the office. Louie's Ford Fiesta was already there, so I pulled in front of it and parked.

Amazingly, Louie had made a fresh pot of coffee, and I poured a cup. My headache hadn't returned, so I decided not to take any aspirin.

"How'd the rest of your night go?" Louie asked.

"I've had worse," I said and let it go at that. Louie left for the courthouse just after 10:00, and I dozed off in my chair. A knock on the office door woke me. I opened my eyes just as Detective Tommy Bishop stepped into the office.

"Oh, sorry if I'm interrupting," he said as I opened my eyes and stretched.

"Just checking my eyes for light leaks. What brings you in?"

"I had a text message from a pal in the DEA. Apparently, Alex Chillcot boarded a plane an hour ago, and he's on his way here."

"You going to meet him at the airport?"

"Oh, God, no. Not my problem, at least not yet. The FBI may have a tag on him, but that's about it. What the hell happened to you?" he said and nodded at my forehead.

"Oh, umm, really banged it on the top of a door frame last night. I was on a chair getting a box off the top shelf of my closet. It's a little better today, although it looks a lot worse. At least the headache hasn't come back."

He nodded and didn't ask any other questions.

"I haven't been past that house in a couple of days. Do you know if the moving van with furniture has arrived?"

"No idea. We're picking up all sorts of bad vibes from the locals. There was another shooting late last night. Does the name Clitis Morehead ring a bell?"

"No, never heard of him."

"Well, he'll make the news tonight. He was found in his car this morning around four a.m. His name was just released."

"Someone killed him?"

"A single round to the head. I'm sure it will be ruled as death by natural causes, based on the business he was in."

"You think this is related to the arrival of Alex Chillcot?"

"Let's just say we're keeping that option open. Things seemed to have kicked up a notch or two in the past couple of weeks. The two murders the other night and now this. Interesting, so far, it's been no one in Gustafson's crew. It's a smaller group, a number of loose cannons, independents."

"And you're thinking Chillcot is involved?"

"It's one of a number of thoughts. We're guessing he has a few people here, but we haven't identified anyone yet. It would be the logical move, go after the independents, the loose cannons, and get somewhat established before you aim at the main man."

"Meaning Tubby Gustafson?"

"Exactly."

"What about the guy I thought was already staying in Chillcot's house?"

"As far as last night's shooting, he was in the house the entire night, so it wasn't him pulling the trigger."

"Is he out there dealing with people? Checking things out?"

"He's out and about but keeping a low profile. He's getting the lay of the land, and based on the areas he's been, the east side, Lower Town, Rice Street, University Avenue, he seems to know his way around the better areas for street sales."

"The one time he talked to me, I was looking at the work done on the Chillcot place. I didn't recognize him and didn't pick up anything like an East Coast accent."

"You're one of the few who have actually heard him speak. We've got him monitored and have a tracking device on his car. Chances are he's aware of the device, but as long as he's just driving around town, there's really nothing we can do. Since he is leaving the device on the car, if nothing else, it provides him a certain degree of protection. If he got into it with someone, our guys would call for a squad car, or, if things got really serious, they'd have to get involved."

"What a mess," I said. "Hey, how are things going with that foster child, a little boy, if I recall?"

"Yeah, I think things have settled down. He's back with his parents. They were both out of work which led to a lot of problems, financial and otherwise. The wife was sorry to see him go, and so was I, for that matter. Hopefully, things will work out for them."

"Anything on the horizon, another kid in need of help?"

"There's always that, but nothing on our list. It's nice to get a couple of days off, but we'd like to get another one. The wife really misses being a mom, and she's damn good at it."

"Well, I hope someone else washes up on your shore. God bless you both for doing it."

"Thanks, Dev. Listen, you pick up anything from Gustafson or anyone else regarding Chillcot, let me know."

"I will, Tommy. Thanks for stopping by."

"My pleasure. Watch yourself in the closet, now," he said and headed out of the office.

Eighteen

I thought about Bishop stopping by the office. He really had nothing to say other than Chillcot was apparently on a flight heading toward the city. Well, and the shooting of Clitis Morehead, whoever that was. I wondered if he hoped I'd pass the information on to Tubby Gustafson.

I thought about calling him or maybe sending an email to Fat Freddy, but if the business competition was going to be ratcheted up a notch or two, I didn't want any email or phone records showing I'd contacted Tubby or Fat Freddy. That left only one other option. I clipped the leash onto Morton's collar, pulled on my jacket, and we headed out to my car.

I made the drive to Tubby's in about fifteen minutes. It surprised me how pleasant the route was. I guess largely because I was in my car as opposed to riding in the back of Tubby's Escalade with Fat Freddy giving me a hard time.

As I pulled onto the circular drive leading up to Tubby's mansion, the four guys around the front door immediately spread apart and had their weapons at the ready. But then again, I was driving my car. A vehicle some of them had never seen before. It was simply second nature that they would be on the alert. I pulled to a stop opposite the front door. Two of the guards had their weapons already placed loosely against their shoulders. They'd be able to fire accurately in a half-second if need be.

I lowered the window and said, "Hi guys, Dev Haskell, sorry to bother you. I wanted to see Mr. Gustafson for a moment. I don't have an appointment, but I have some Important information for him."

No one said anything for a long moment, and then one of the guys I didn't recognize said, "Pull into a parking space, and we'll take it from there."

The parking area was straight ahead, just beyond the circular drive, as it began to curl around and head back out onto the street. I parked my car, climbed out, and locked it. Morton remained stretched out in the backseat chewing on his tennis ball.

Two guys walked toward me. They were six feet apart and playing it careful. I didn't recognize either one of them. "Why don't you assume the position against the trunk of your car, and we'll check you out," one of them said.

I turned around, spread my arms and legs, and then leaned forward and rested my hands on the trunk of my car. The younger of the two patted me down while the other guy kept his AK pointed at me.

"Okay, you can stand up," the younger guy said. "He's good."

The guy pointing the AK at me turned, gave a wave toward the door, and said, "We'll just wait here for a moment. No point in walking over there if they're not going to let you in."

I placed my hands in my jacket pockets and waited, then waited some more. It was a sunny day and a balmy 5 degrees Fahrenheit. I was about to get back in my car and turn on the heat when one of the guys waved us forward. I took the two steps up onto the front stoop, and the door opened for me. I quickly stepped inside to the warm entry. I was patted down again and then had to hang my jacket on a coat rack before a guy led me down the hall to Tubby's office.

Just like the other day, the same guy in a suit and tie was in a chair leaning against the wall. Today he was reading a book. He closed the book, set it on the floor, and stood.

"Haskell to see Mr. Gustafson," my escort said.

"Yeah, I recognize him," the suit said, then knocked on the door as he opened it and said, "Sir, Hassle to see you."

I followed him into Tubby's office. As soon as I walked past him, he stepped back into the hall and closed the door. That was fine with me. Things seemed to be back to normal, at least in Tubby's office. He was lying face down, stretched out on the massage table with his eyes closed. A large white towel covered his fat ass. At least thirty pounds of Tubby's fat hung over the side of the table. Two topless Asian women were massaging his hairy back and dimpled shoulders. I noticed that they were wearing latex gloves today.

"So, Haskell, an unannounced visit. Let me stop you right there. If you're looking for a job, the answer is no, absolutely not."

"Oh, no, sir, quite the opposite. I've received some information and thought you might be interested."

"Information?" Tubby said, suddenly opening his eyes and raising his head just enough to stretch his triple chins into one large, wobbling, fat sack. "Let's hear it."

"Two bits of information, actually. The first, an individual, by the name of Clitis Morehead, was found dead early this morning. He'd been shot. The authorities are looking at this as possibly another shooting in an effort to establish an area of operation for Alex Chillcot."

"Chillcot? Good lord, when is this going to end? Will he even end up here? I'm beginning to wonder."

"I believe your question is about to be answered, sir. Apparently, he boarded a flight this morning and is heading this way as we speak."

Tubby groaned, swore, raised his shoulders, and dismissed both women with a wave of his hand. They bowed and took three or four backward steps, then turned and quickly hurried to the door in the back corner of the room. Tubby swung his legs over the side of the massage table and lowered himself to the floor. The table creaked, shook, and rattled but somehow managed to stay together. I looked off into the distance rather than watch him wrap the white towel around his massive waist. He walked over to his desk, picked up what was left of a cigar from the ashtray, and stuck it in his mouth. His stomach appeared even more massive than usual. He had to have at least a seventy-inch waist.

"You said Chillcot is on a flight to the twin cities?"

"Yes, sir, that's what I've been told."

"And this person who was shot last night, tell me the name again."

"Morehead, sir. Clitis Morehead."

"And did you know him?"

"No, sir. At least not that I can recall. The name isn't ringing a bell."

"Interesting, very interesting. Anything else?" Tubby asked as he opened a desk drawer and took out a lighter.

"No, sir. That's all I know."

"Mmm-mmm, not surprising. All right, thank you again, Haskell." He picked up his cell phone and tapped the screen twice. A second or two later, the office door opened.

"Yes, sir?" the man in the suit said, stepping into the office.

"Show Haskell out, Dennis."

"Thank you, sir," I said and hurried out of the office before Tubby lit his cigar or summoned the unfortunate women to continue his massage. I followed Dennis down the hall, where he turned me over to the two thugs reading comic books at the front door.

One of them gave me a disgusted look, reached over, and pulled the front door open. I grabbed my jacket from the coat rack and hurried outside. The door slammed closed behind me, and I quickly walked to my car. Morton was still involved with his tennis ball. On the way back to the office, I stopped at Solo Vino and purchased two bottles of Sauvignon Blanc wine. Louie's car wasn't at the office, so I parked in my usual place. I left the bottles of wine to chill in the car, and Morton led me up to the office.

Louie returned early in the afternoon. I was on the phone with Layla when he stepped into the office.

"I was thinking you might want to come over for dinner tonight if you can fit me in."

"Well, I'd love to, Dev. But I'm working at Santa's Workshop tonight until 7:30."

"Actually, that sounds perfect. I've got a busy afternoon," I lied. "I can work late and cook dinner. Plan on coming over once you're finished. Don't bother to change. Just come over, have a glass or two of wine, and relax. I'm sure you're going to be tired after dealing with kids all day."

"Yeah, not to mention, pain in the ass, Arthur. He's his normal, awful self. It's our first day, and he's already crabby. Besides, I think he's drinking again. I can smell it on him. He's ruining the idea of Santa Claus for all the children. I wish you were Santa this year."

Thank God I'm not, I thought then said, "Let me take care of you tonight. You don't have to bring anything except yourself. Besides, I'd love to see you in the elf costume."

"Oh, that's so sweet of you, Dev. I know you're going to love the costume. I'll see you tonight. It's probably going to be closer to 8:00 before I can get there. Are you sure that's going to be okay?"

"It's going to be perfect, Layla. I'll see you then," I said, and she disconnected.

"Sounds like you're going to be busy tonight," Louie said.

"One can only hope."

Nineteen

Morton and I headed home just before 5:00. I stopped at the grocery store and picked up things for dinner, including a package of six chicken breasts that were twice as expensive as they'd been just two weeks ago. Once home, I grabbed the groceries and the two bottles of wine from the backseat. I tossed Morton a biscuit and got the crock pot out. I followed a favorite recipe for white chicken chili, using four of the chicken breasts and putting everything in my crock pot.

I changed the sheets on the bed, cleaned the bathroom, vacuumed the front room, and arranged the fireplace. I shaved and hit the shower at 7:00. A half hour later, I was dressed and watching out the window for Layla. She arrived forty-five minutes later. It was worth the wait. She climbed out of the car wearing a long, red wool coat and red high heels. I opened the door for her as she climbed the steps to the front porch.

"Oh, man, what a day. I could use a glass of wine." She gave me a kiss on the cheek, stepped back and said, "What happened to your forehead?"

I gave her the same closet line I told Tommy Bishop.

"Oh, you poor thing. You're going to get some very special care tonight."

"Thank you. I need it. Come on, sit down in front of the fire, relax, and let me serve you. How'd things go today?"

"Oh, the kids were wonderful, just like always. Arthur was a real pain," she said and stopped in the entryway. I helped her remove her wool coat and draped it over the newel post leading up to the second floor. She was dressed in a silky white blouse with the top two buttons undone displaying a bit of cleavage. The red velvet outfit covered her shoulders and arms, and went down to the middle of her thigh with white furry trim around the wrists and the bottom of the dress.

"I had no idea Mrs. Santa Claus could look so sexy," I said.

"She doesn't, and she's twenty years older than me. Remember, I'm one of Santa's elves. There are always two of us there just to make sure creepy Arthur doesn't try to grab us while we're working. God, it would be just like him."

"Was he drinking again?"

"He sure smelled like it, but we were watching him, and I never saw him take a drink, ever. I don't get it. Anyway, the kids were wonderful. A lot of them were dressed up in their Sunday outfits to come and see Santa. They were all on their best behavior. A couple of the real little ones were crying, and their folks were taking all sorts of pictures. That happens every year."

"Well, come on into the front room and settle in front of the fire while I get you a glass of wine." I led her over to the fireplace. The fire was going, and I'd moved the two upholstered chairs a little closer for warmth. I'd placed a small table between the chairs and had a platter of cheese and crackers and a bowl of chips and dip waiting.

"Oh wow, you really went all out," Layla said and giggled, looking at the chips and crackers.

I couldn't tell if she was serious or joking. "I'll be back with the wine in just a moment."

I'd say we chatted for the next forty-five minutes, but really, I just listened as she told me stories about the families and, every once in a while, something about Arthur. I brought the bowls of chili out along with a basket of bread, and we ate in front of the fire. I made sure her wine glass was never empty, and we headed up to bed just before eleven. I got Morton settled in the guest room, and thankfully, Layla was still awake and smiling when I stepped back into the bedroom.

I was wide awake the following morning and knew better than to wake her. I dressed, went downstairs, and brought the morning edition of the newspaper up on my laptop.

There it was on the front page. A headshot of the big guy who had attempted to push me down the stairs the other night. The caption below the headshot read, 'Clitis

Morehead Murdered. The city's forty-sixth homicide victim.'

Tommy Bishop had mentioned him just yesterday when he'd stopped by, but since I didn't know the guy's name, it never registered. I told Tubby about the murder, but I never in my wildest dream thought it would be this guy. A part of me thought good riddance, but then I immediately thought of Alex Chillcot arriving yesterday and was afraid this wasn't going to be the last. The article was brief, just two short paragraphs. Morehead's body was found in his car parked downtown. He had been shot in the head at close range. The police were asking anyone with information to contact them.

Morton wandered down a half-hour later. I let him outside and filled his food and water dishes. It was 5 degrees below zero outside this morning, and he was scratching at the back door ninety seconds later. He inhaled his breakfast and then settled onto his pillow in front of the radiator.

I heard Layla upstairs just after 8:00 and set the kitchen counter for breakfast. She entered the kitchen wearing my green plaid terrycloth bathrobe. She gave me a passionate kiss, and I handed her a mug of fresh coffee. Morton stepped over and thrust his nose between her legs.

"Oh, yikes. Cold nose, puppy, cold nose," she said and climbed onto a kitchen stool. Morton wandered out of the kitchen.

"Did you close the bedroom door? No doubt Morton's heading upstairs to see if your thong is available."

"I think I did, and if I didn't, don't worry. I put my undergarments in one of your dresser drawers and placed my elf costume and heels in your closet, so there's nothing he can get."

"Good, not that I don't believe you, but I'm going to run upstairs for a moment and check just to be safe."

"Mmm-mmm," she said as she sipped some coffee. "Do whatever you want, baby."

I hurried upstairs. The door to the bedroom was closed, and Morton wasn't up there. I went downstairs and found him in the front room, lying in front of the fireplace.

"Was the door closed?" Layla asked as I stepped back into the kitchen.

"Yes, it was. Can I talk you into some French toast with real maple syrup?"

"God, I thought you'd never ask. It's the only reason I came over last night."

I shot her a look, and she laughed out loud. We ate breakfast and then went back upstairs to the bedroom. It was close to 10:00 when she left, and Morton and I headed down to the office. I purposely took a different route, so I didn't drive anywhere near Chillcot's house. I parked in front of Louie's Ford Fiesta, and we hurried inside.

"Well, to what do I owe the pleasure?" Louie said as we entered the office.

"Sorry, just some things I had to attend to this morning."

"Those things wouldn't happen to have something to do with Layla, would they?"

"What makes you say that?"

"The lipstick on your cheek and the faint scent of perfume."

"Oh, yeah, well, I guess I missed that," I said, rubbing both cheeks.

"Dev, I was kidding."

"Oh." I glanced at the coffee pot. There was only enough for half a cup in the pot, which means it was the remnants of yesterday morning's coffee. I turned off the burner, dumped the coffee down the sink, and made a fresh pot.

"You see this morning's paper?" Louie said.

"Yeah, I did. You referring to the shooting?"

"Yeah, I'm blanking on the guy's name, Lesshead, or something like that.

"Clitis Morehead."

"Sounds like you knew him."

"Not really. Remember my story about the two guys grabbing me the other night?"

"Yeah."

"He was one of them. Tried to push me down the stairs. There's no way to prove it at this point, but I'm wondering if this is related to Chillcot supposedly arriving yesterday. I need to call Aaron LaZelle and let him know about my experience."

"You didn't tell him?"

I shook my head. "I didn't want those idiots coming after me. They told me not to tell the cops and that Morehead jerk was a loose cannon. Anyway, that problem is apparently solved, so I'm going to have a coffee and then call Aaron."

I phoned Aaron and, at no surprise, left a message. "Hi Aaron, Dev. Hey, I had a run-in with this Clitis Morehead guy who was found in his car yesterday morning. Give me a call when it's convenient. Thanks."

I had a second cup of coffee, debated calling Tommy Bishop, and decided not to. Aaron returned my call toward the end of the afternoon.

"Yeah, Dev. Got your message. We're a little bit jammed down here with the third murder in three days. You got anything current regarding Morehead?" He said something to someone in the office and came back, "Sorry, go ahead."

"Yeah, I had a run-in with Morehead and two other guys two nights ago. They basically kidnapped me, took me to someone's house, and accused me of working for Chillcot. Fortunately, I was able to convince them I wasn't working with him and had never met or interacted with him."

"You knew it was Morehead?"

"No, I didn't know it was him and didn't know his name until I saw the newspaper article online this morning."

"You said he was with two other guys?"

"Yeah, he and another guy grabbed me outside of The Spot, took me to some guy's house, and questioned me. Apparently, I passed because they took me back to The Spot."

"You need to get down here and see if you can identify the other two guys. Can you come down now, or do you want me to send someone to give you a ride?" That was Aaron's way of nicely telling me to get my dumb ass down there, or he was going to send a squad car.

"I'll head down there now," I said.

"Thanks," he said, not sounding very happy, and hung up.

"No need to tell me. I'll watch Morton. If we're not here when you get back, you know where we'll be," Louie said without looking up from the file in front of him.

"Thanks, I better get a move on. He didn't sound pleased."

Twenty

They had me seated in Interview Room Three. At least I wasn't chained to the table. No doubt they'd want me to identify the other two who'd been with Clitis Morehead. I didn't have a problem doing that. At the moment, I was telling myself how stupid I had been for not reporting them right away. Of course, if Morehead hadn't been murdered, I wouldn't have known he was one of the dumb shits that had kidnapped me for ninety minutes. I was screwed either way.

The door opened, and Detective Manning walked in, followed by Tommy Bishop. Aaron brought up the rear and was carrying a laptop. They didn't look tired, they looked exhausted, and I guessed they'd probably been going nonstop since whenever Morehead's body had been discovered yesterday morning.

"Dev, we have a series of mug shots," Aaron said. "We'd like you to take a look at them and give us the details. Does that lump on your forehead have anything to do with this?"

"Yeah, it does." I looked over at Bishop. "Sorry I gave you a line about it, Tommy. At the time, I didn't know who Clitis Morehead was. I just knew I didn't want them coming near me again, so I gave you the line about banging my head in the closet. They tossed me into the trunk of a car and slammed the lid down just as I was attempting to sit up. I was knocked unconscious, but I don't know for how long. Could have been a minute or five minutes. All I knew was the car was moving when I came to."

"For the record, I thought I could trust you up until I heard your bullshit. So why don't you tell us the truth now and see if you can ID the other people involved? When we're done here, you might want to get that bruise checked out by a doctor. We have someone here who can do that," Bishop said.

Ouch. Not bad, I'd ruined my friendship with the guy, and it had barely even started. I sat down, Aaron sat next to me, and Bishop and Manning sat on the other side of the table. After we went through the basics of knowing that the interview was being taped, and I was there of my own free will, Aaron lifted the lid on the laptop. The computer sent out a musical chord, and the screen came to life. Aaron input a password, and suddenly two images appeared, a front view and a profile image of a guy.

"We've assembled a file of known Morehead associates," Aaron said. "You can push the right arrow key to bring up the next individual or the left one to go back. While you're looking through the images, give us the details on your assault and kidnapping."

I nodded and began telling the story as I glanced at the images. I started off with the phone call from the unknown number, stepping outside The Spot, and dropping my phone as they hustled me into the trunk of the car.

"You get the make of the car?" Manning asked.

"No, it all happened too fast. When they dropped me back at The Spot, they took off before I was barely out of the car. All I really know is that it was a dark blue or black four-door."

I continued talking as I looked at the images. A couple of them were close to what the guys looked like, but no match. I was telling them about pulling into the garage and how I was freezing when I stopped on an image.

"I believe this is Clitis Morehead," I said and turned the laptop toward Aaron.

He nodded and said, "Let the record show Mr. Haskell has identified Clitis Morehead." He then read off a file number that was in the upper right-hand corner of the screen.

I went on to tell them about Morehead almost pushing me down the staircase and the questions they were asking regarding the murders of Ronnie Whitman and Dizzy Gillespie. I stopped at a second image. I was looking at the driver of the car that kidnapped me. His red-flowered vine tattoo was visible in both images.

"This guy was driving the car," I said to Aaron and turned the computer toward him again.

He nodded and said, "Let the record show Mr. Haskell has identified Jessie Grimes," then followed up with the file number.

I went through maybe seven more images and there was the third guy. "They took me to this guy's house. He never wore a ski mask and seemed to be in charge, although Morehead was clearly a loose cannon."

"You're sure?" Aaron asked.

"Yeah, it's definitely him."

"Let the record show Mr. Haskell has identified Michael Irons," he said and followed up with the file number.

I finished my story with the fact that the entire event, from the moment they grabbed me outside The Spot, to when they dropped me off, couldn't have been more than an hour and a half.

They seemed to suppress a laugh when I told them that Louie didn't even bother to check and see what was taking me so long. I told them I had informed Tubby Gustafson that Chillcot was on a flight yesterday morning and mentioned that I had purposely not gone near the house he bought since my kidnapping. "That's pretty much it. Is there anything else you want to know?"

They seemed to think for a moment, and then Aaron said, "Bishop was right. You should get that thick skull of yours checked out. Look, Dev, I don't think calling us after this happened would have made a bit of difference as far as Morehead's murder is concerned. But it still would have been nice to know. The association of these three with Whitman and Gillespie forms a pattern. It would appear that Chillcot has either linked up with locals or has sent people in ahead of him, possibly both. I'm just glad you managed to survive and that you finally shared this information with us."

"Thanks, I'm sorry I waited. I just hoped it would all go away."

"Did Gustafson give any indication of what he planned to do?" Bishop asked.

I shook my head and said, "I had the sense he had no idea of what he was going to do. I think he may be waiting for Chillcot to arrive and see where things go from there. If I wanted to make a cold assessment of things as they stand, the murders of these three really haven't done anything to hurt Tubby's organization. In fact, they may have eliminated a potential problem or two."

All three of them nodded then Aaron said, "Anything else?" as he looked around at everyone.

Bishop and Manning shook their heads. I didn't say anything. "Okay, Dev, you're free to go. I think for the rest of us, it might be a good idea to head home and climb into bed."

"I might just sleep in my car," Bishop said as he stood, and everyone laughed. Aaron led the way out of the room, I followed, and Manning and Bishop brought up the rear. Manning headed into the restroom, and I slowed down until Bishop came alongside.

"Hey, Tommy, I want to apologize again for not be-ing straight with you. I was just hoping the whole thing would go away."

"Yeah, I get it, Dev, but thanks for saying that. We still friends?" he offered and held out his hand.

"Absolutely, I'm counting on it. Once things calm down, I hope we can get together for lunch or dinner. I'll buy."

"Good. I'll pick out some expensive place. Come on, I'll escort you downstairs, just to make sure you leave the station," Bishop said, and we both laughed.

Twenty-one

Louie's car was still on the street and I pulled in front of it. The lights were off up in the office, so I went into The Spot. "Beer?" Mike asked as I stepped in the door.

"Yeah, and you better get another round for Louie, too. Thanks," I headed down the bar toward Louie. There was an empty bag of pork rinds on the bar, and Morton was seated at Louie's feet, gazing up expectantly. "Oh, I see he's pretending to be well-mannered. Everything go okay?" I said.

"Yeah, no problem. We've only been here for about twenty minutes. More importantly, how did things go for you?"

"Pretty well. I was able to ID the three guys from the other night. I apologized a couple of times for not telling Aaron or Tommy Bishop right away. We were all friends again by the time I left."

"Good. They say anything about Chillcot?"

I shook my head. "No, and to be honest, I didn't expect them to. They all looked like they'd been working thirty-six hours straight without a break. Probably all on their way home now, and they'll be sound asleep five minutes after they step inside."

After chatting with Louie for a half-hour, Morton and I left for home. Since it was dark, I figured there wouldn't be a problem just driving past Chillcot's place. I slowed down as I passed his house. There was a large moving van in front. This time, three guys dressed in gray slacks and jackets were carrying chairs up the front sidewalk and into the house. It looked like all the lights were on inside, and I saw two guys in the living room talking with drinks in their hands. Both looked too young to be Chillcot. I drove around the block, and as I came alongside the house, I passed a burgundy Chevy Traverse with a New Jersey license plate parked on the street. For a brief second, I thought it would be funny to slit two of the tires just to welcome who ever owned the car. Instead, I repeated the six-digit license number, then stopped two blocks away and wrote the number on the back of a receipt from the grocery store.

A bowl of leftover chili went in the microwave for dinner, and I settled in front of the TV to watch the evening news with my fingers crossed. Fortunately, there wasn't any report of someone being shot. I wedged chairs underneath the front and back doorknobs again, and Morton and I climbed the stairs to bed. One of the pillows had a slight perfume scent from Layla, and I slept through the night on her side of the bed.

My alarm woke me at 6:00 the next morning. I watched the news online while sipping coffee. Once again, just the usual reports of idiots doing idiotic things, congress doing nothing, and thankfully, no shootings in town overnight. As soon as Morton finished his breakfast, we headed down to the office. I drove past Chillcot's place in the process. The burgundy Chevy Traverse was exactly where it had been last night, and the moving van was gone.

I parked in my usual spot, and Morton and I headed up to the office. At no surprise, Louie had neglected to turn off the coffee pot last night. I poured what was left down the sink and made a fresh pot.

When Louie pulled up, I'd been watching two women through my binoculars in the apartment across the street. Unfortunately, they were both wearing bathrobes and spreading peanut butter on toast. He parked behind my car, waited for a bus to pass, and then shuffled across the street. I filled his coffee mug with fresh coffee as the stairs creaked and groaned.

He entered the office red-faced and gasping for air after the ten-step climb. After a half-dozen deep breaths, he took his wool coat off and attempted to hang it on one of the hooks on the wall. He did something wrong because the coat fell to the floor. He groaned, looked at it for a moment, but didn't bother to pick it up, and headed for his desk.

I gave a final look through the binoculars, but since nothing was happening, I tossed them in my desk drawer. "What time did you get home last night, Louie?"

He slurped another sip of coffee and said, "It was a quiet night, so Mike shut things down early. I was home before 11:00."

God, I'd been asleep for a good half-hour before Louie even made it home. "I checked out the Chillcot place on my way home last night. There was a moving van with guys hauling in furniture and a car with New Jersey plates parked on the side street. Looks like Chillcot has arrived. Thankfully, there were no news reports this morning of anyone killed last night."

"You really think things are going to be that bad?"

"I hope not, but I fear that might be wishful thinking."

"God, I hope you're wrong," Louie said.

"Yeah, me too," I agreed just as my cell phone rang. Aaron LaZelle.

"Good morning, Aaron. What's up?" I asked, thinking my fear of more murders was about to be confirmed.

"Nothing's up, which is just fine. I wanted to call and thank you for smoothing things over last night with Bishop. Very much appreciated, and thanks again for coming down. We were all exhausted and just wanted to get home."

"You finally got some sleep?"

"I woke up this morning, and I was still half-dressed in a t-shirt and trousers. I hit the bed and apparently went out like a light."

"Well, you all needed it, and thanks for being a gentleman last night. You could have read me the riot act, and you would have been correct."

"It worked out. Actually, that's why I called, wondered if you might have time to grab a quick lunch at Mickey's Diner today."

"I can do that. As long as you let me pay."

"Yeah, that will work," Aaron said and laughed. "How does 1:00 sound? That way, we can be at the tail end of the lunch crowd."

"Sounds perfect. I'll see you there. Say, I was going to give you a call this morning."

"You don't have to apologize again, Dev."

"Good, because I wasn't going to do that. But I did want to tell you I drove past Chillcot's place last night. There was a moving van with guys hauling furniture into the place. A burgundy Chevy Traverse with New Jersey plates was parked on the side street. I got the license plate number right here if you want it."

"Yeah, give it to me, and I'll check it out."

I gave him the plate number, and we disconnected.

"Everything okay?" Louie asked.

"Yeah, just getting together for lunch today."

"Good move," Louie said.

I headed down to Micky's Diner twenty minutes before we were going to meet. It was just a five-minute drive from the office, but I wanted to try and score the only booth in the place. The diner was built back in 1937 to resemble a railroad dining car. Today it's listed on the

National Register of Historic Places. Fifty feet long and ten feet wide, Mickey's has distinctive red and yellow porcelain-enameled steel panels and Art Deco style lettering on the exterior. A row of 10 train-style windows graces the front of the place. The interior features floor-mounted round stools along a well-worn counter. The menu consists of eggs, pancakes, hash browns, hamburgers, milkshakes, ice cream floats, and malts. It's open 24 hours a day, 365 days a year.

There's a small parking area just next to the diner, and I was able to score the last parking place. I hurried inside and walked toward the back of the diner. A hand-written sheet of paper was on the table with the word RESERVED written in black marker.

"You'll have to grab a stool at the counter, honey," a woman behind me said. She held a coffee pot in her hand and two mugs.

"Oh, I'm meeting a pal down here, and I was hoping to get the booth. When's the person coming for the booth?"

"He's due any minute, and he's a cop, so I'm afraid you're out of luck."

"A cop? It isn't Aaron LaZelle by chance, is it?"

"Yes, as a matter of fact, it is."

"You're meeting up with him?"

"Yeah, we're pals."

"Well, grab a seat there. He just called, said he was on his way. You want a coffee or a malt?"

"I better stick with the coffee, black," I said as an image of Tubby Gustafson wrapping the towel around his gigantic waist the other day flashed in my mind.

"I'll be with you in a second," she promised and stepped behind the counter.

Twenty-two

She had just placed silverware and two paper placemats with an image of the diner on the table and was in the process of filling two coffee mugs when Aaron stepped in the door and headed toward the booth.

"Good afternoon, honey, right on time. So far, your friend has behaved himself."

"No one is more surprised than me, Gretchen. I'll have my usual."

"I guess I'll have the same," I said.

"You know what I order?" Aaron asked once Gretchen stepped away.

"Yeah, I think so. A bacon cheeseburger, hash browns, and a slice of apple pie for dessert?"

"Oh, you do know."

"Hey, were you able to run a trace on that New Jersey license plate?"

Aaron nodded and took a sip of coffee. "Yeah, owned by a guy named Michael Rossi. Everyone apparently calls him Mickey."

"He got a record?" I asked.

"The guy's an attorney, Chillcot's attorney, actually. I talked to a couple of Jersey guys out there on the gang squad. From what they said, Rossi is very much like Chillcot, smart, low profile, and doesn't make waves. Suspected of being involved in illegal gambling but only suspected, never charged with anything."

Gretchen was back with our food a few minutes later, just as a squad car rushed past with lights flashing and the siren wailing. Aaron poured catsup on his cheeseburger and had just taken a bite when his cell phone began playing the theme from Jaws. "Oh shit," he said and answered. "Yeah, what's up? Ok. Where? Who? Oh, no. Okay, I'm on my way." He disconnected and shoved his phone back into his pocket. "Sorry, I gotta run. Officer down," he said and hurried out of the diner. A moment later, his car zipped past with lights flashing.

"Oh, dear. You want me to box that up for him?" Gretchen asked.

"Yeah, I guess you better, and I'll take the check whenever you have a minute."

She was back with a Styrofoam tray and the bill. I glanced at the bill and said, "Gretchen, you only charged me for one meal."

"Lieutenant LaZelle eats for free here. He stopped a robbery a few years back. Crazy man was going to shoot all of us. LaZelle talked the nutcase down, and fortunately, no one was hurt. He'll never be charged a dime while I'm here."

"That's nice and no surprise. I'm still going to pay for his meal. You keep it as a tip if you want." I ate my cheeseburger, most of the hash browns, and all of the apple pie. I placed Aaron's meal in the takeout tray, paid the bill, and headed back to the office.

"I thought you were having lunch with Aaron? You got takeout?"

"He got called out on an officer down emergency. I just hope everything is going to be okay."

"Just from what you said, I doubt that's going to be the case."

"Yeah, well, no point in this going to waste. You interested in a cheeseburger and some apple pie?"

"Happy to help," Louie said as I handed him the box. He devoured the meal in just a couple of minutes. At no surprise, he cleverly managed to hit both his white shirt and light blue striped tie with a drop of catsup.

Louie left for a court appearance at 2:00. I was on my laptop checking for breaking news on the 'Officer Down' call Aaron had responded to and hadn't found anything when my cell phone rang. Layla.

"Hey, how's it going today?"

"Oh, one of those days. Lots of kids. Arthur is crabbier than usual, and I'm exhausted."

"Why is he crabby?"

"Who knows? He's just a real pain in the butt. I don't know why they keep hiring him."

"Sounds like you could use a long back massage and maybe a glass or two of wine in front of the fire. You interested in coming over tonight?"

"Oh, thanks, Dev, but I don't think I'd be very good company. Arthur has put me and everyone else in a really bad mood."

"How about this? The door is open if you want to come. I'd be happy to fix you dinner and—"

"Were you listening? It's not been the best day. Look, Dev, I'm sorry. Arthur's made me crabby, and once we're finished, I'm going to grab a wine with one of the girls and then go home. Don't take it personally. I just need some downtime. Okay?"

"I get it. Not a problem, Layla. Might be good to go out with one of the girls, and you can both rant and get it out of your system."

"Thanks for understanding. Chat tomorrow?"

"If you feel up to it."

"I'm sure I will. Thanks, bye, bye."

I couldn't remember when the last time was that Morton and I were in The Spot before Louie, but that was what happened. I gave Morton his handful of pork rinds and had a beer. I debated ordering another but then decided it might be a better idea just to head home. We drove past the Chillcot house on our way home. Nothing was happening outside the place. The Chevy Traverse was now parked in front. Lights were on in a couple of the first-floor rooms, but I couldn't see anyone through the bulletproof windows.

When I got home, I parked in the garage. For dinner, I had another bowl of chili. I really liked the stuff, but this was the third night in a row, and there was still enough left for a small bowl tomorrow. I warmed my bowl in the microwave, dumped the remnants into a container, placed it in the refrigerator, and soaked the crock pot.

We settled in front of the TV, and I clicked on the news just in time to catch the lead story, a shooting late this morning of an FBI agent and his wife downtown. The story was sketchy. The victim's names were being withheld pending notification of next of kin. The reporter on the scene said that four shots had been fired, and as he was talking, I spotted Aaron in the background speaking with three other officers. I think Tommy Bishop walked past at one point, but he was far enough away to be out of focus, so I couldn't be sure.

I thought about calling Layla just to check in then decided it was too soon after her call and that maybe a night off from me was just what she needed. I scanned one of the cable film sites for thirty minutes and didn't find a movie that caught my interest. I ended up reading a couple of chapters in a Civil War book I hadn't opened in over a year.

The 10:00 news had a little more information on the shooting, but still, no names of the victims and, apparently, no arrest had been made. Morton and I went up to bed, and I thought about Layla for ten or fifteen minutes before I drifted off to sleep.

Twenty-three

The next morning I was up before the alarm went off. Showered, shaved, and pulled on jeans and a sweatshirt from the Summit Beer Brewery. I checked the morning news on my laptop. The names of the victims in yesterday's shooting were the lead story. Robert and Catherine Hogan, husband and wife. Hogan was an FBI agent, and his wife was a schoolteacher. Apparently, she was pregnant, and they had just left her obstetrician's office. I shook my head and wondered how things could get any worse. A pregnant woman and her husband? I'd gladly pull the trigger on whoever did this.

We were down in the office before Louie. I made a fresh pot of coffee and was enjoying the view through my binoculars. One of the women, a redhead probably in her mid-twenties, was applying makeup with a towel wrapped around her waist. Out of the corner of my eye, I caught Louie's Ford Fiesta pulling in behind my car. I watched the makeup application for ten more seconds, then put the binoculars back in the drawer.

I had a steaming mug of coffee waiting on the picnic table when Louie stepped into the office. At least today, when he hung his coat on the hook, it didn't fall to the floor. He gave me a nod and settled into his chair. Eventually, he asked, "Did you hear about that dreadful shooting downtown yesterday?"

"How could I miss it? It's been the lead story for almost the past twenty-four hours."

"Did you know him, this FBI agent, Hogan?"

"No, at least not that I can recall. But the two of them, a husband and wife, murdered downtown in the middle of the day. This has got to stop. I know Aaron and his team are doing everything they can, but things are really getting crazy in this town. Some idiot shoots a pregnant woman. I hope the cops pull out all the stops and get whoever is responsible."

"You think this has anything to do with Chillcot coming to town?"

"I've been wondering about that. I haven't heard it from anyone, but suddenly, in less than a week, we've had five murders in the city. In some way, shape, or form, it's all drug related. Three lowlifes and now an FBI agent and his wife. You do have to wonder if Chillcot arriving on the scene doesn't have something to do with this."

I skipped lunch and worked through the afternoon. I think I checked the news for updates on the murders just about every hour, but there was nothing. I took Morton for a walk at the end of the day. It was sunny, and the temperature was up around 15 degrees Fahrenheit. An improvement over the last couple of days. We covered the full three-block distance on our walk and then met Louie in The Spot.

"Get you a beer, Dev?" Mike called as we entered. I was about to say yes, but then I remembered Layla might be calling in the next hour or so and decided I would take a pass. "Afraid not, Mike, but pour Louie another and put it on my tab."

Morton strained on his leash as we headed down the bar. Louie was ready with a handful of pork rinds as Morton came around the corner of the bar.

"Oh, Morton, well done. You made it through another day of keeping Dev on the straight and narrow. Here's your treat," he said, then leaned down with Morton's treat.

Morton inhaled them in just a second or two. As fast as he ate them, it never ceased to amaze me that not so much as one pork rind ever hit the ground. Morton licked Louie's hand clean, then sat almost at attention, staring up in the hope there was more. Mike arrived with a fresh drink for Louie. I pulled the last bill from my wallet, a ten, and told Mike to keep the change.

"You're not having anything?" Louie asked.

"Keeping my fingers crossed that Layla calls in an hour or so. She finishes up around 7:30, and I'll try to entice her with dinner."

"Yeah, you said she enjoys the job."

"Oh, yeah. Loves dealing with the kids. They're all on their best behavior for Santa Claus. Unfortunately, she doesn't like the guy who's Santa. She says he's crabby and not very nice to the kids. She's convinced he's drinking on the job, but no one can catch him. Apparently, the city hires him back every year."

"Did you check him out?"

"What do you mean, check him out?"

"Well, think about it. If he's not happy being Santa Claus, that probably means there is a laundry list of complaints on the guy. The people he's working with think he's drinking on the job. At the end of the day, why isn't whoever's in charge paying attention to all that?"

"Interesting. Me investigating Santa Claus. That could pay some unexpected dividends with Santa's elf, sexy Layla."

"Sounds like a good idea to me."

I glanced at the clock. Santa's Workshop would be open for another fifty minutes. "I think it might be a good idea to check on Santa and see how things are going."

"You want me to keep an eye on your friend?" Louie said and nodded at Morton, still sitting at attention and staring up at him.

"No, I'll drop him off at home. It's on the way."

Louie nodded, emptied the bag of pork rinds into his hand, and reached down to Morton. Of course, Morton devoured them, and we headed out the side door. I was still in the habit of quickly checking left and right for anyone lingering around the door. Fortunately, no one was there. I dropped Morton off at home and headed downtown to Santa's Workshop.

Twenty-four

Santa's Workshop was located on the first floor of what used to be Dayton's department store. The store had closed back in 2013. Since then, the building had gone through a number of vacant periods along with various business schemes that never seemed to work.

Signs in the former store windows directed me to the Workshop entrance. Inside was a college kid who looked like he'd rather be anywhere else. He was dressed in a green vest with a large candy cane design on either side of the vest and a cap with a plastic candy cane stuck in the hatband rather than a feather. His gold name tag read Oliver.

"Ticket for one?" he asked without looking up from some kind of textbook in front of him.

"Yeah, I come every year," I lied. "What's Santa like this year, Oliver?"

"Same as the last couple years, not much fun. That'll be five dollars," he said.

I spent the last of my money at The Spot and so I used my credit card.

He didn't react and handed me a three-by-five-inch red ticket that read:

Ho! Ho! Ho!
Santa's Workshop

There was a barcode along the bottom edge of the ticket. I walked toward the door labeled 'Enter' and held the barcode just below the device next to the door, a red-colored light illuminated the ticket. As I moved the ticket slightly so that the light was on the barcode, the sliding door suddenly opened. I followed a winding path past sleds, Christmas trees, and a cardboard fireplace with stockings hanging from it.

Suddenly Santa was just ahead, seated on an ornate-looking throne with a large wooden candy cane on either side. Next to the throne was a large bag with all sorts of toys and a couple of dolls sticking out.

Santa's red nose and cheeks appeared to be natural as opposed to makeup. He looked very bored as the little boy, around six years old, sat on his lap and explained which tablet and computer game he wanted. Two more anxious-looking kids waited in line ten feet away. Layla was there in her sexy elf costume, talking to the kids in line. She looked up as I entered, gave me a quick nod, and went back to asking the kids if they had been good this year. Both kids, a boy and a girl nodded and prom-ised they had been very good.

"All right, next," Santa suddenly called and pushed the little boy off his lap. The two kids Layla had been talking to held hands and approached cautiously.

"Well, come on, hurry up. It's getting late," Santa called and then grabbed a handful of what looked like raisins from a dish next to his throne.

Layla took the boy's hand and led them to Santa.

The boy held up his arms to be lifted onto Santa's lap, but Santa ignored him and took another handful of raisins. Layla lifted the little boy onto Santa's left leg and then set the little girl onto his right leg. They both stared wide-eyed at Santa.

"Well, come on. I haven't got all night. What do you want for Christmas?"

The little girl said, "I would like the American Girl Doll, Truly Me, please, Santa."

"A Barbie would be better," Santa said.

"But I want the American Girl, Truly Me," she said.

"Take what you can get, kid. What about you? What do you want?" he said to the little boy.

The kid just stared wide-eyed, apparently too afraid to speak.

"How 'bout a lump of coal. Would you like that?"

"I...I want a Stuntosaurus Monster Truck."

"What? Never heard of it. Go home and think of something else."

A woman barged past Layla, apparently the mother, and said, "Benjamin, Amelia, come on, we're leaving. This isn't Santa Claus. He's a bad elf pretending to be

Santa. Let's go home, and we can write a letter to Santa, and tomorrow we'll bake cookies to leave for Santa when he comes to our house on Christmas eve."

"Maybe I won't come to your house on Christmas Eve," Santa half-shouted.

Layla stepped forward, "You were right, mom. This is a bad elf pretending to be Santa. Why don't you come with me? We have candy canes for you, and when Santa comes back, I'm going to tell him what you want. Bad elf, you had better stay in that chair until I get back, or I'm going to use my magic powers on you."

"Your magic powers?"

"I mean it, bad elf," Layla said in a vicious tone.

"You know what I think?" Santa slurred as Layla hurried the children and their mother away.

"You heard the elf," I said and stepped toward Santa. His eyes were bloodshot, and he appeared to have trouble focusing. Definitely intoxicated. As he looked over at me, his head wavered from side to side. Layla, the children, and the mother were far enough away that they wouldn't hear. Santa's Workshop was going to close in fifteen minutes, and no one was in line to see this jerk.

"Let me give you some advice," I said. "You'd better get your act together and fast. I hear you treating another kid like you did those two, and I'm not going to report you. I'm going to kick your dumb ass. You understand what I just said?"

"You can't talk to me like that. I'm going to call security."

"Your choice. You can either go home or spend the night in the emergency room."

"All right. Hope you're happy, but I'm leaving. No one threatens me, ever."

"That wasn't a threat, you idiot. That was a promise," I said as he stood up from the chair. He weaved back and forth for a moment to get his balance. He staggered four or five feet around me and headed toward a door marked 'Employees Only.' I quickly pulled out my phone and began to film him as he staggered away and disappeared through the door.

I walked over and looked at the contents of the bowl he'd been eating from. They were definitely raisins. I picked up the bowl and smelled the raisins. Gin. That was it. He soaked the raisins in gin and ate them all day. He wasn't drinking. He was eating gin-soaked raisins.

Twenty-five

Layla hurried up the path past the cardboard fireplace with Christmas stockings. "Where did he go?" she gasped.

"He left through that door marked 'Employees Only.'"

She shook her head. "You see what I mean? He's just awful. Talking like that to those poor kids, their mother is absolutely furious. Who can blame her?"

"I'm surprised someone hasn't punched him in the nose."

"Oh, believe me, more than one father has threatened to do just that. I tell you, he has got to be drinking. I mean, he's just so obnoxious and downright mean. Did you hear what he said to those little kids? That's going to be with them for the rest of their lives. He has single-handedly ruined the Christmas experience for so many children that I've lost count."

"And you've reported him?"

"We've all reported him countless times. They just tell us they can't find any bottle. Our attendance has been down by almost half year to year for the past two years.

I mean, look at it three years ago, before Arthur started, there would have been a line here with ten minutes left to go, and we'd work an extra half hour just so everyone got a visit. Now, we have long spaces of no one coming in, and it's all due to Arthur and his horrible personality."

"Well, I think I may have found one of your problems."

"Oh great, Arthur isn't bad enough. Now you've found another problem?"

"Yeah, here's the thing. Arthur is definitely intoxicated, and he's a crabby drunk. But he's not drinking."

"Well, then how—"

"This is what he's doing. Here, smell one of these, eat one," I said and held the raisin bowl in front of Layla. She sniffed the bowl and immediately jerked back.

"Oh. My. God. That's where he's getting the alcohol—from his raisins. He eats them all the time, non-stop." She picked one up, put it in her mouth, and then spit it out. "Oh, that tasted absolutely awful."

"Yeah, a hundred-proof raisin. That's where he's getting the liquor. He's soaking these raisins in gin for a day or two, and then they're probably the only thing he eats all day. Hundred-proof raisins."

"No wonder we haven't been able to catch him drinking. He's been eating these stupid things," she said. She sniffed the bowl once more and jerked her head away.

"Take these and turn them in tomorrow. They'll prove he's been under the influence, and you certainly can't have that when there are children involved."

"I can try, but there have been so many negative reviews on the guy, and he's still here every season. I just don't get it. None of us do, and like I said before, he's ruined our customer base."

"Report it tomorrow and use these as your evidence. Does he park in the customer parking area?"

"I think so, up on top of the building. We get a pass for free parking up there. I can't believe he'd pay to park in the lower levels of the ramp."

"Good. I'm going to hurry outside, grab my car, and hopefully catch him coming out of the ramp." I gave her a kiss on the cheek and hurried out the door. My car was parked around the corner and at the end of the block. I didn't run, but I wasn't wasting any time getting down to my car. After 7:30 on a winter's night downtown, the streets were pretty empty.

I jumped in and drove halfway up the one way street to the exit of the parking ramp then pulled to the curb and waited. And I waited some more. I was just about to call Layla and ask her if she wanted to come over for dinner when a lime green Chevy Spark suddenly came out of the parking ramp exit and turned right. Arthur was still wearing his Santa beard and the red hat with white fur trim. Fortunately, there wasn't any traffic because Arthur didn't so much as slow down to see if anyone was coming.

I pulled away from the curb and followed him as he went straight for a couple of blocks, then took a left onto West Seventh Street. He finally pulled into the parking lot for DiGidio's Bar. I drove past the entrance to the lot, turned at the corner, and parked on the side street.

Arthur was just opening the driver's door of his car. As the door opened and he stood, I heard the sound of breaking glass. He staggered toward the bar's back door. I walked over to his car, looked at the broken half-pint bottle on the ground, and headed for the front door. When I stepped inside, Arthur was at the opposite end of the bar, waiting while the bartender was pouring his drink. It looked like a gin martini with a lemon twist.

What I found interesting was that usually, if someone came into a bar dressed as Santa, there would be a lot of joking going back and forth, probably a couple of pats on the back. It wouldn't be uncommon for someone to say they'd pay for the drink and tell Santa they'd like a new car or something for Christmas.

Nothing like that happened. In fact, I had the distinct impression anyone who was a regular kept their distance from Arthur. Once he paid for his drink, he settled onto a bar stool. The couple who were next to him took one look and immediately got up and moved to the opposite end of the bar. I looked around the room. It wouldn't be unusual to see a few folks laughing or smiling at Santa. But with Arthur, a few heads were shaking, and one woman in the booth directly behind him flashed her middle finger for a long fifteen seconds.

"What can I get you?" the bartender asked.

"I'll have a Summit IPA. Hey, what's with Santa Claus? No one seems to like the guy."

He looked back over his shoulder and shook his head. "Oh, yeah, Arthur Soto. Probably the most worthless Santa Claus you could ever meet. He's been doing it for a couple of years now. Ruining Christmas for families at Santa's Workshop downtown. I think once you take your kids there, you're liable to spend the rest of your life helping them recover."

"How can he play Santa for that long if he's so awful?"

"You ever hear of Melody Soto?"

"A politician, isn't she?"

"Yeah. In fact, she represents a district on the city council. Let me tell you. You don't want to end up on her bad side. I'll be back with that beer in just a minute."

I took my time drinking the beer. It was almost 8:30 when I left. Arthur had finished a second martini and was ordering a third. The place was a little more crowded, but no one was sitting near Santa. I drove home, and Morton met me at the back door. I let him outside and fried up a pork chop. We watched the 10:00 news. No one had been arrested in the murders of the Hogan couple. Information on the murders seemed to be sketchy at best.

It dawned on me that I hadn't heard anything from Aaron or Tommy Bishop regarding charges or, God forbid, an arrest of Jessie Grimes or Michael Irons, the two remaining suspects in my ninety-minute kidnapping. But then, between Alex Chillcot coming to town and the Hogan murders, I figured Aaron and Tommy probably had their hands full.

Twenty-six

We were in the office right around 7:30 the following morning. I had been on my laptop for a good hour and a half checking out articles on Melody Soto, Arthur's sister on the city council. Louie had just pulled in behind my car. I didn't see him park, but I heard the explosion when he turned his car off and glanced out in the street just in time to see the cloud of soot and grime from his exhaust system settle onto the snow.

I filled his coffee mug with fresh coffee and set it on the picnic table as I heard him making his way up the stairs. After he caught his breath and drank the better part of half the mug, he asked, "So, did you check out that Santa character last night?"

"Yeah. He was just as bad as Layla told me. Turns out his sister is Melody Soto."

"That battle ax on the city council is his sister? That might explain a lot. No one wants to end up on her bad side."

"You know, Layla mentioned that the attendance at Santa's Workshop is down from what it had been just a couple of years ago. I wonder if the sister is the reason all the complaints have been ignored and the customer numbers are down."

"Based on what you witnessed yesterday, if you had kids, would you take them back to see that guy? God, you'd probably warn all your friends and tell all the parents in your kid's class not to go." Louie shook his head and said, "Yeah, it's a real shame." He headed over to the courthouse an hour later.

I took Morton on a short walk, and once we were back in the office, I phoned Aaron LaZelle and ended up leaving a message. "Hi Aaron, it's Dev. Just wondering if there's anything happening regarding Michael Irons or Jessie Grimes and my kidnapping. I realize you guys are most likely jammed after the Hogan murders. If there's anything I can do to help, please let me know. Thanks."

I did some more online investigation of Melody Soto. She seemed to have been able to position herself as the key vote in a number of tight situations between the two parties on the city council. She'd been instrumental in getting various provisions adjusted, rewritten, or voted down over the years. She voted for and against either side to such an extent that she was labeled as an independent. Interestingly, one of the articles I read suggested that her district was always the first to get its streets repaired and plowed. Restaurants, bars, trash haulers, and businesses courted her support for licenses and bypasses to existing city ordinances. It took a while, but I was able to find her address.

I left Morton in the office and drove over to Melody Soto's residence at 86 Mississippi River Boulevard. Her home was a large, single-story rambler with an attached three-stall garage and what appeared to be an unattached, two-story rental unit in her backyard. The thing was right behind her house, no more than six or eight feet behind the single-story rambler and in direct violation of a number of city codes. I pulled down the alley and drove past the unit behind her house. It basically took up the entire backyard. A double garage was on what would have been half of the first floor of the place.

I found it interesting that large wooden fences in the neighbor's yards on either side, as well as on the property across the alley, blocked any view of the unit looking in or out. It would appear the neighbors weren't all that happy with the structure behind Soto's house. I copied down the addresses of the three homes with the fences and headed back to the office.

With some searching through county property tax records, I was able to get the names of the people who owned the homes on either side and across the alley from Soto's home. I called the state Department of Motor Vehicles and asked for my pal Dennis Glazier.

The phone rang three times before he answered, "Dennis Glazier, Motor Vehicles."

"Oh, hi, Dennis. Dev Haskell calling. I'm sorry. Did I wake you?"

"Very funny, not. How are you doing, Dev?"

"Life is good, Dennis. Hey, I'm wondering if you can help me out. I got a neighbor thinking of building a rental unit in their backyard. They're going to have to get all sorts of city ordinances bypassed to do this, and I have the addresses and names of three people who went through a similar situation a few years ago and lost. If I gave you the names, could you get the phone numbers for me?"

"Not a problem, Dev. Be happy to do so. What night were you planning to buy me dinner down at Shamrock's?"

"Just about any night you want."

"Perfect, give me those names."

I gave him the first name, James McDiarmid, and could hear him running his fingers across the keyboard.

"I've got three individuals with that name. You have an address?"

"The River Boulevard in St. Paul."

"Yeah, here we go. You got a color crayon to write down the number or a responsible ten-year-old nearby who can help?"

"I've got a red color crayon and a blank spot on the wall," I said. He gave me the number, and we went through the process two more times. When he'd finished, I thanked him, and he promised to be in touch for a dinner engagement.

I phoned the McDiarmid number. A woman answered after six rings. From the sound of her accent, I guessed she was originally from either North or South Carolina.

"Hello."

"Hello, my name is Dev Haskell. I'm hoping you can help me. I have a next-door neighbor asking the city for permission to build a rental unit in their backyard. It would be in violation of a number of city codes, but I'm afraid the city might grant permission. I happened to drive past your home today, and it looked like you may have dealt with a similar situation, and I—"

"All I can tell you is it was dreadful. We're all law-abiding taxpayers, and the city voted against us each and every time we appealed the process. They're all criminals if you ask me. We've lived here for almost forty years, and to have them do this, violate their own laws and statutes, it's ruined any support I may have given them. Of course, the woman next to us is one of their own, Melody Soto. It's dreadful, absolutely dreadful, and we're the ones who followed the rules. None of our neighbors wanted to see that ridiculous eyesore built, and the city ignored each and every law and statute on the books. So much for the rule of law when it comes to someone on the city council."

"The house next to you is owned by Melody Soto?" I tried to act surprised.

"Please, don't get me started. We didn't have a chance. The three of us, the family on the other side and the neighbors across the alley, spent thousands in legal fees, and at the end of the day, it was all for nothing. I wish you the best of luck, but you're going to find yourself in an uphill battle."

"That doesn't sound too promising."

"I wish I could sound more positive, but it was an absolute travesty. Ruined our neighborhood. Melody Soto lives an isolated life. No one talks to her. She's never invited to our holiday get-togethers like Christmas or the Fourth of July, and we certainly won't ever vote for her. We plan to send a hundred dollar check to whoever runs against her, regardless of the party they represent."

She went on for another few minutes before she disconnected. The next two calls had a similar response. Basically, the people followed all the rules and were screwed because Soto was on the city council and wielded a lot of power. It suddenly became clear why Arthur Soto was able to ruin Santa Claus's reputation year after year.

Twenty-seven

The time was almost 5:00 when I glanced out the window. Louie was just stepping out of his car and heading into The Spot. I clipped the leash onto Morton's collar, pulled my jacket on, and was about to head out on our walk when the phone rang. "Haskell Investigations."

"Hi, Dev, Aaron, returning your call."

"Oh, thanks for calling me back, Aaron. I'm sure you've got a lot on your plate, and I just—"

"We're jammed. The murder of the Hogans has brought federal agents into town, and I don't have to tell you what a pain in the ass that is. We haven't been able to follow up on Grimes and Irons. As you know, we're short-staffed, to begin with, and at the moment, it's all hands on deck working the Hogan murders."

"God, I just can't believe that happened, but then given the state of things, maybe it isn't a surprise. Any leads?"

"Nothing. The feds are insisting the murders were actually carried out by a mob crew. We're not prepared to disagree, but that doesn't bring us any closer to solving the case."

"Anything I can do to help?"

"Yes, there is. Don't get involved. We're meeting in about an hour, and hopefully, we'll be able to iron out some of the difficulties we've been facing. Are things going okay for you?"

"Yeah, trying to help Layla and the folks down at Santa's Workshop get rid of the guy playing Santa this year, actually the same guy who's played Santa for the last couple of years."

"Oh, yeah, you mentioned that. Where does it stand?"

"In the mud. Despite continued complaints from employees and customers regarding the current Santa and a pretty severe drop in families showing up over the last two years, he's still there. Get this, Layla has been convinced the guy is drinking on the job, but they've been unable to catch him in the act. I stopped by there yesterday around 7:00 and heard him be a complete jerk to three little kids. He was so mean to a little boy and girl that their mother got involved, and the guy, Santa, told the kids he may not come to their house this Christmas."

"Oh, God, that's pretty bad."

"You aren't kidding. Layla thinks he's been drinking, but no one has ever caught him. Then, last night I'm watching the guy, and he's eating all these raisins."

"Raisins?"

"Yeah, he left after he told the kids he may not come to their house, and I suggested he leave before I put him in the hospital. Anyway, I checked the raisins he'd been eating, and they had been soaked in gin. That was how he was getting the alcohol."

"I have to say that's pretty clever. Did you report it?"

"Layla was going to do that today. The problem is, his sister is Melody Soto."

"The city council rep for Ward Two?"

"Yeah."

"She rules with an iron fist. I think folks in that district like her."

"Probably, but she's kept this jerk brother of hers playing Santa Claus for the past two years, much to the dismay of everyone involved." I went on to tell him about following Arthur Soto, dressed as Santa Claus, to DiGidio's and how everyone kept their distance.

"Too bad. Hopefully, Layla will have better luck with the bowl of soaked raisins. Hey, I better ring off. We got a ton of stuff happening, not to mention the meeting with the FBI and a half-dozen other agencies. Talk to you later."

"Thanks for the call, Aaron," I said, but he'd already hung up.

We went on our walk and covered the entire three-block area in about fifteen minutes, then hurried into The Spot. Morton nearly yanked my arm out of the socket, straining on the leash to get to Louie.

"How'd things go in court this afternoon?" I asked as Louie reached down to Morton with a handful of pork rinds.

"Very well, the judge ruled on a nice settlement, which means I'm buying the first round," Louie said just as Mike approached.

"What'll it be, Dev?"

"Well, since Louie is buying, I think I'll have a pitcher of beer," I said and winked at Mike.

"Anything for you, Louie?"

"Thanks, I'm good, and change that pitcher to a mug."

We all laughed, and Mike headed back down the bar.

"Any news from Layla?" Louie asked and took a sip of his drink.

"No, and I didn't expect any. With this Arthur Soto playing Santa Claus, she's got an uphill fight on her hands to get rid of the guy. That said, you'd think essentially drinking on the job, even if it is eating gin-soaked raisins, would be enough to finally get the guy fired."

Louie shook his head. "Tough deal. It's such a shame. What else is cooking?"

"Not much. Trying to keep on Layla's good side."

"How's that working?"

"Oh, you know, the usual."

"Sorry to hear that," Louie said just as Mike set a mug of beer down in front of me. "Well, there you go,

Dev. Looks like things suddenly appear to be improving."

Twenty-eight

Morton and I had just stepped into the house when my cell phone rang. Aaron LaZelle. "Hi Aaron, everything all right?"

"I think so. We had a little meeting after our get-together with the feds. Would you have time to come down to the station? We've got some things I'd like to go over with you, and I would like to do them in person rather than on the phone."

"Have I done something that—"

"No, Dev, surprisingly, this isn't about something you've screwed up, but if you're willing, we could sure use your help."

"I'll head down there right away," I said.

"Thanks, Dev. I knew we could count on you."

I tossed Morton a biscuit and hurried out to the garage. I ran through two yellow lights on the way down to the police station. Something was up. I had no idea what, but Aaron had never, ever been so secretive. It wasn't lost on me that he said *'we'* could sure use your help.

I pulled into the parking lot across the street from the station. The potholes were filled with packed snow, and since it was just after 8:00 p.m., I was able to get a parking place right in the front of the lot. I hurried into the station and headed toward the front desk. The desk sergeant saw me walking into the lobby and picked up the phone. As I stepped in front of him, he was completing his conversation. "Yeah, he just stepped in. I'll escort him up personally," he said and hung up. He turned to the officer next to him and said, "I'll be back in five minutes, Jimmy. Anyone asks, tell 'em I went to the can. Haskell, you come with me," he said and stepped out from behind the desk. I followed him through the security door and over to the elevators. He didn't say anything, and once we stepped inside, he pressed the button for the fourth floor. The Homicide division, Aaron's office, was on the third floor. I was about to say something but then decided against it.

When the elevator got to the fourth floor, the doors opened, and Tommy Bishop was standing there. "I'll take it from here, Sarge, thanks. Follow me, Dev," Bishop said and headed down the hallway. He stopped at the door labeled Special Investigations, input a code on the keypad next to the door, and once the door buzzed, we stepped inside.

The office was similar to Homicide, although there weren't as many desks. Two guys were at their computers going over something in hushed voices. Neither one looked up as we walked past. We walked to the end of the room and then down a hallway past an interview room and entered the next one. Aaron was seated at a table along with Detective Manning and two other officers I recognized but couldn't remember their names.

Aaron nodded and said, "Thanks for coming down, Dev. Grab a chair. You remember Gary Peterson and Denny Jackson. They were in Homicide until sixteen months ago and then transferred into Special Investigations."

"Yeah, good to see you again," I said as I pulled out a chair next to Manning and sat down.

Both men smiled and gave me a nod as Bishop settled into a chair across the table from me. Aaron said, "Dev, sorry for all this secret bullshit, but we're just trying to play it safe. Some things have come up. Bishop, why don't you take it from here."

"Thanks, LT," Bishop said. "Dev, we had our meeting with the FBI. They are officially heading up the investigation into the Hogan murders. We will fully cooperate in whatever way we can. Among a variety of subjects that were discussed in the meeting, it was brought to our attention that the mob is suspected in the murders."

"The mob? I guess that maybe makes sense since Hogan was with the FBI. I'm just curious, five murders within the space of a few days. Does this have anything to do with Alex Chillcot coming to town?"

Bishop looked over at Aaron, who nodded. "Yeah, we think it does. No definitive proof as of now, but I think we can state it's highly likely."

"I would add it would be a shock if Chillcot is not involved. The mob is involved in New York and New Jersey. Images of the two men who committed the Hogan murders were captured on security tape, and they've been identified as members of the New Jersey mob."

"Do you want me to investigate them?" I asked.

"No, but there's a problem we think you can help us with."

"Okay, yeah, sure, happy to help," I said.

Bishop looked over at Aaron, who nodded again. "So, here's the deal," Bishop said. "The Hogans have three children, ages four, six, and eight. The two older children are boys, and the little girl just turned four last month. Here's our concern. The history of the Jersey mob is that, with murders such as this, they eliminate not just the parents but the family as well. Specifically, the children."

"But four, six, and eight years old? These kids aren't going to do anything. They're kids, for God's sake."

"Yeah, that's right, but killing them will send a message to everyone. You screw with the mob, you cross them, and there will be a major price to pay. A price far beyond just the murder of whoever they viewed as the problem."

"So what would you like me to do?"

"Here's where we are, officially, we have the children in a hotel with twenty-four-hour security. We've put out the word that they're confined to a suite with FBI officers inside and outside the suite."

"But what if there's an attempt? What if four or five of these thugs attack? Or what if they plant a bomb? What if they poison the food? What if—"

"That's where you come in, Dev."

"What? You want me to test the food?"

"No, we want you to take the children."

"Take the children?"

"Yeah, as of now, they've actually been hidden at my house," Bishop said. "My wife, Christine, is watching them. We have agents in and outside the house. But here's the problem. With just a little bit of information, my wife and I would be a logical place for the children to be. It's not rocket science for the mob to put two and two together. If we've learned anything, it's that these bastards aren't stupid. What we want to do is hide the children in your home. My wife will be there to care for them. You carry on with your day as usual. Go to work, stop at The Spot, and visit your girlfriend Layla at her unit in the Blair House."

I wondered for a second how they even knew about Layla, let alone that she lived in the Blair House. "And you'll post security to protect them?"

"Absolutely," Bishop said. "Here's the thing, it's only going to be a matter of time before I'm checked out to see if the kids are with us. We knew the Hogans. In fact, they were over for dinner just the week before. It's also one of the reasons the kids are with us. It's not some strange setup where they're separated from one another or shuttled around to a different place every two or three days."

"When would you plan on doing this?"

"Tonight, if that works."

I thought for a half-second. "Yeah, it works. Of course. I'd be happy to help. I, I'd consider it an honor. I'll do whatever you guys want."

Twenty-nine

The kitchen counter was covered with a dozen grocery bags. I'd taken a half-eaten pizza, a BBQ pork sandwich, and takeout containers from four different restaurants out of the refrigerator and tossed them in the trash, well, except for the half-eaten pizza with extra cheese and sausage. I warmed that in the microwave and ate it as I put away the groceries. A Special Investigations officer, a redhead, named Tina, was upstairs getting the guest room set up for the three children. Toy trucks, Legos, battery-charged dinosaurs, two dolls, and a stuffed teddy bear were in the front room. My den had suddenly become home to stacks of games, a tricycle, and two battery-operated dinosaurs.

At the moment, Morton was in the kitchen gnawing on a new rawhide bone I used to eliminate the 'What the hell is going on?' look he gave me when I hauled in the groceries. Two Special Investigations officers, whose names I'd already forgotten, were setting up sleeping quarters in the basement. Another officer was setting up temporary security cameras throughout the first floor.

At 12:45 a.m., I opened the back door, and three officers carried the three sleeping Hogan children into the kitchen. One of my new basement residents led them upstairs to my former guest room, now the 'kid's room.' Tommy Bishop's wife, Christine, was already set up in the second-floor bedroom at the end of the hall. The room overlooked the backyard. The three officers who carried the sleeping kids wished me luck and left. One of the guys settled in the basement while his partner was out in the front room building something with the Legos and keeping an eye out.

Christine Bishop came down to the kitchen just as I'd put away the last of the groceries. "You getting settled in up there?" I asked.

She nodded and said, "Yeah, I just wanted to come down and say thank you for doing this, Dev. Those poor kids. Hopefully, this will be over soon."

"I don't think it will ever be over for them. To lose your folks at any time, let alone when you're so young and under these circumstances, it's really sad. No one deserves that."

Her eyes began to tear up, and she said, "Bobby and Cathy were a wonderful, loving couple. I'm going to miss them for a very long time, in fact, probably forever."

I gave her a hug and said, "Is there anything you need up in that bedroom?"

She shook her head and said, "No. You've already done more than enough with just letting us stay here."

"Everyone just wants you and the children safe. If you need anything, anything at all, please let me know. Oh, and the kitchen is open to you. Anything in the refrigerator or cabinets is yours. Do you drink coffee?"

"Yes, I do."

"I'll make up a full pot for tomorrow morning and set the timer for 6:00 a.m. Help yourself to whatever you want and let me know if there is anything you need."

"I just want this all to be over and the children to be safe," she said.

"We're halfway there. The children are safe. Tommy and the FBI will get this over just as fast as they can. Don't you worry."

"Thanks so much," she said and squeezed my hand. "If it's okay, I'm going to peek in on the children and then try to get some sleep."

"Good idea. I'm going to get things ready for breakfast and head upstairs myself."

I filled the coffee pot for ten cups and lined mugs up on the counter next to the pot. I placed three different boxes of cereal on the counter, along with three spoons and bowls for the kids. I decided I would set my alarm and get up before everyone else and make French toast.

Morton was upstairs asleep in front of the door to the kids' room. I decided to leave him there. He'd serve as a good alarm system should anything unusual happen in the middle of the night. I set my clock for 6:00 a.m. and was asleep once my head hit the pillow.

I woke a couple of minutes before the alarm went off. Morton was still stretched out in front of the kids' room. I showered, shaved, and went downstairs. The coffee was already on, and one of the men from the basement, Emmett, was sipping a cup at the kitchen counter.

"Did you get any sleep last night?" I asked.

"Sleeping bag on a cot. What could be better?" he said and smiled.

"I was going to make some French toast. Can I talk you into some?"

"That would be great, but please, don't go to any trouble. We've got MREs lined up in the basement."

"I'm familiar with MREs. Maybe try the French toast with real maple syrup from northern Minnesota. Besides, you probably need the sweetening."

"You're right about that," he laughed.

Christine Bishop was down twenty minutes later, wearing a white terrycloth robe and fuzzy blue slippers. She said, "Good Morning," and joked with Emmett for a moment, who she obviously knew. Once she filled a coffee mug, she headed back upstairs. Morton wandered down a little after 7:00. I let him outside, and he was scratching at the back door a minute later. He inhaled his breakfast, hurried back upstairs, and settled in front of the door to the kids' room.

"Your dog's name is Morton?" Emmett asked.

"Yeah, he watches out for me, well, unless someone has a treat to bribe him with, and then I'm on my own."

Emmett laughed and nodded. "Yeah, I know the routine. Is he home during the day?"

"No, not to worry. I'll take him down to the office with me."

"Well, if you wouldn't mind leaving him here, I think he'd keep a close eye on the kids, and he can give an alert well before we would be aware something was up. Besides, I bet they would love him."

"If you think it would make things safer, it's not a problem. I'll leave him here. He'll alert you when he has to go outside, and that cookie jar on the counter over there is filled with dog biscuits. Give him one, and he'll be your friend for life."

"I'll be sure to do that," he said.

I made French toast for Christine and Emmett and had just served them when Morton gave a couple of friendly yelps upstairs. Christine had told me their names, Rowan, eight years old, Kevin, six, and Bryn, who was four. By the time I hurried out to the front room, Morton was escorting the three kids down the staircase. Everyone got their faces licked as they stepped off the stairs.

"Hi, gang. My name is Dev. It's great to see you. This is Morton. He lives here, too. Can you help me and take care of him today while I go to work?"

The little girl, Bryn, wore pink pajamas emblazoned with a ballerina and a white swan. Kevin, the six-year-old, wore black pajamas with all sorts of Marvel cartoon characters on them. Rowan, who was eight, was dressed in red and black Spider-Man pajamas and said, "We'll take good care of him. Does he like to play?"

"That's all he likes to do. Come on, follow me into the kitchen, and we'll get you some breakfast, and I'll show you where I keep the treats for Morton."

We headed into the kitchen, and Morton followed.

"Well, good morning. How did you sleep?" Christine said as she hurried off her stool and gave all three children hugs and kisses.

"We're going to take care of Morton today," Kevin said.

"Oh, that is so nice of you to help out, and I know Morton will be very happy with you here. Now, how about some breakfast?"

Things went on from there. After breakfast, Christine took them into the den and showed them the toy trucks, Legos, dinosaurs, both dolls, and the teddy bear. Bryn immediately gathered up the teddy bear and held onto him.

I left for work a little after nine. I drove around the block twice just to make sure nothing seemed out of place. Everything looked fine, and driving past my house the second time, I passed a squad car parked at the curb three doors away. The driver was talking on his cell phone.

I thought for half a minute about driving past Alex Chillcot's house and decided that would be a bad idea. I didn't want him to know I existed in any way, shape, or form.

Thirty

When I got to the office, Louie's car was already there. I pulled in front of it and parked. "Well, look who finally decided to make an appearance," Louie said. "Late night with Miss Layla?"

"No, just taking care of some things. How was your night?"

"Oh, I was probably home forty-five minutes after you. I'm heading over to the courthouse in a few minutes. Walking a first-time offender through the process. I expect he'll be found guilty, pay the fine, and if he's smart, he'll attend the classes, and I'll never see him again, hopefully. You working on anything?"

"I'm going to see if I can learn anything else on this Alex Chillcot coming to town. I think—"

"Did you catch the news this morning?"

"No, why? What happened?"

"Another shooting early this morning. Actually, a deadbeat client I represented once some years back. A guy by the name of Leroy Ross. Someone shot him down on Jackson Street around 4:00 this morning."

"That name rings a bell."

"I probably mentioned him. He stiffed me for fifteen hundred bucks because he was found guilty of driving while under the influence. Nothing I could do but take him through the motions. I got him off with time in the workhouse, but apparently, that wasn't good enough, even though it was his second offense. Anyway, someone shot him earlier this morning."

"He was shot at 4:00 in the morning, and they already released his name?"

"No, I heard about the shooting on the morning news, but a friend at the courthouse called me with Leroy's name about twenty minutes ago. That lower Jackson Street area is where he operates, or rather it was."

"Interesting, that's downtown. Sounds to me like there's a possible turf war going on. And the person who called you was sure this Leroy Ross was the victim."

"That's what he told me. Ross was making his way up the illegal gambling ladder. He hosted high-price poker games and ran some betting operations. Hey, listen, I should probably head out. By the way, where's Morton this morning?" Louie said, looking around.

"Oh, he got a new chew toy and was having an up close and personal relationship with that this morning, so I left him at home. Besides, I might be running around later today, and I didn't want to stick you with him."

"Oh, he's never a problem," Louie said as he stuffed a file into his briefcase.

"Thanks, and good luck this morning."

"I already know how it's going to go," Louie said as he slipped on his coat. He gave me a wave as he headed out the door.

I emptied the coffee pot into my mug. The mug was maybe two-thirds full. I took a sip and shuddered. Clearly, the coffee had been made yesterday morning, which meant it had been on the burner for over twenty-four hours. I dumped it down the sink and made a fresh pot.

While the fresh pot was brewing, I debated for a moment and then picked up the phone and called Tubby Gustafson. I got the result I expected. A voice answered, "Hello." It wasn't Tubby. I was pretty sure it was whoever was in the security room watching the images on a dozen different screens from the cameras around Tubby's mansion. Based on what I'd seen the last time I was at the place, it was a pretty safe bet the security was operating at maximum level.

"Hi, this is—"

"Dev Haskell. Yes, we know that," the creepy voice said.

"I'd like to speak with Mr. Gustafson, please."

"What is this concerning?"

"It's concerning information I have."

"If you'd care to pass that on, Hassle, I'll make sure Mr. Gustafson receives it."

"No, I need to speak with him personally. This is information not yet public, and I believe he would find it very interesting."

After a long pause, he said, "Just a moment while I see if he has time to speak with you."

What a jerk. I'd spoken to this creep before, always with the same result. More than once, he ended up putting my call through when Tubby had been on the massage table while the two women provided relaxation. The same thing happened this time because, suddenly, there was a ringing sound on the line. After two rings, Tubby said, "Now what do you want, Haskell?" It was probably too early for his massage, which meant he'd be even crabbier than normal.

"Good morning, sir. Sorry to bother you, but I just received some information I thought you should know."

"So, if it's that important, why are you keeping me waiting?"

"Sorry, sir. There was a shooting last night downtown. On Jackson street."

"Oh, Haskell, once again, you find yourself two steps behind the rest of the world. I'm aware of the incident. It was on every TV station and public radio this morning. This isn't new information."

"The man shot was named Leroy Ross, sir."

There was a long pause before Tubby said, "Ross? Leroy Ross? How in God's name do you know this? The name of the victim was withheld pending next of kin notification."

"I have my sources, sir. Thought you should know immediately since Ross has been a bit of a problem for you in the past."

"Not sure what you're referring to, Haskell. But thank you all the same. Are you sure it was Ross? Was this at 463 Jackson Street?"

"Yes, I'm sure, at least as sure as I can be. My source would have no reason to provide false information. As to the address, I don't know anything about that. What's there?"

"Nothing I'm aware of," Tubby said, clearly lying to me. "I thought that was the address they mentioned on TV. Do you think Chillcot was involved?" Tubby asked, a rare occurrence requesting my opinion on something.

"I don't know anything for sure, but there appears to be a definite uptick in, umm, adversarial behavior in that particular marketplace."

"Haskell, I'm amazed. You almost sound like you know what you're talking about. Thank you for your call." Click

I found it interesting that Tubby asked my opinion regarding Chillcot. Things were going so well that I decided to phone Layla next. I ended up getting dumped into voicemail.

"Hi, Layla. This is Dev. Just checking in to see how things went with your turning in Santa's dish of gin-soaked raisins. Please give me a call when it's convenient." I got a call back from an unhappy Layla a half-hour later.

"Hey, how'd it go?" was how I answered.

"You don't have to tell me who you are when you call, Dev. It's on our caller ID and I recognize your voice."

"Oh, okay, I'll try to remember that. I was just wondering if anything was happening with Santa regarding the gin-soaked raisins?"

"No, and nothing will be happening because apparently someone stole them, and so the evidence is gone, missing, disappeared."

"Who did you give it to?"

"Give it to? There was no one to give them to. The office was closed, so I wrapped them up carefully and placed them in the refrigerator in the break room. By the time I got in today, they were gone. Someone took them."

"It must have been Arthur Soto. He's the only one who—"

"What difference does it make, Dev? They're gone. Now it's my word against his, and nothing is going to happen. I'll say he did it. Soaked all those raisins in gin and ate them throughout the day, and he'll deny it."

I thought for a moment. "Well, he may have gotten rid of the evidence, but that doesn't mean he'll change his ways. He's going to come up with a new way to get loaded. In fact, he probably already has. Maybe he's hidden a bottle in the men's room, or he's carrying half-pint flasks in his Santa Claus suit. But believe me, he's still going to be drinking on the job."

"You know what the bad news is, Dev?"

"What?"

"The bad news is you're right, and there's nothing we can do about it."

"There might be something we can do about it."

"Like what?"

"I don't know but give me some time to think about it, and I'll come up with something."

"I hope you're right," she said and disconnected.

Thirty-one

Louie was back in the office just before noon. He arrived with a couple of Big Macs, fries, and two chocolate shakes. "Thought you might need something to sweeten you up," he said, handing me the chocolate shake and a bag.

"Oh, thanks, Louie. You didn't have to do this, but it's very much appreciated."

"My pleasure, you're always running up to Roosters for BBQ pork sandwiches, so I thought this was the least I could do."

I opened the bag, pulled out the Big Mac and the fries, and took a long sip of the chocolate shake. "Mmm-mm, really good. Thanks again. Hey, Louie, your pal who called with the information on Leroy Ross getting shot, did he happen to give you an address?"

"An address? I think he was shot on the street. Not in a house or an apartment building. Why? Do you know someone down there?"

"No, just something I was wondering. These recent murders all seem to be linked in some way, shape, or form to illegal gambling. I just wondered if that was the case with Leroy Ross."

"Well, I don't know about the location, but yeah, Ross was a gambler. I know he'd tried some years back to get into the legal end of things, but his arrest record prevented that. He's one of those characters who has always been suspected but never charged with anything major. Of course, then, Hogan was dealing with RICO enforcement, wasn't he? That would certainly line up with illegal gambling."

"Yeah, it would. Umm, thanks again for lunch."

"My pleasure," Louie said and began to inhale his Big Mac.

Once I finished lunch, I checked out a couple of things on my laptop, then told Louie I was going to run an errand. I drove down to Robert Street, drove to the four-hundred block, and took a right to Jackson Street a block away and a one-way street. I parked around the corner from the address Tubby had mentioned. The building was on the edge of downtown. It was a two-story brick building with a peaked roof and a sign that read 'Sweeny's Auto Repair.' The first floor appeared to be a car repair place. There weren't any gas pumps in front, but there were three large garage doors facing the street. There was another garage door in the back of the building. Two stacks of torn and shredded rubber tires, a smashed car door, and a couple of bumpers were piled next to the door in the back. Based on the snow piled on top of the tires, they'd been there for a while.

I tried the glass door at the front of the building, but the place was locked, and there was a 'CLOSED' sign hanging on the door. There were no employees visible through the windows. Lights were on up on the second floor, but there was no way to see if anyone was there. Garage hours and a phone number were listed on the front door. I entered the phone number into my cell phone and walked back to my car.

Once in the car, I turned the heat on and called the number for Sweeny's. It rang twice, and then a recording played that said, "All our lines are busy at the moment. Please leave a message, and we will return your call as soon as possible."

I disconnected and drove down the street. On a whim, I drove past my house. Everything looked quiet. No signs of any trouble. I figured the best idea would be to not stop and check inside, thereby disrupting whatever the everyday routine was for the kids. Once again, I decided not to drive past Chillcot's place and headed down to the office. Louie was asleep in his desk chair, snoring softly.

I turned on my laptop and Googled the 463 Jackson Street address. The only thing that came up was Sweeny's Auto Repair. Not so much as a police report or a newspaper article reporting anything at the address.

Louie woke up a half-hour later. He stretched in his chair and then said, "Oh, been here long?"

"No, just a couple of minutes," I lied. "Hope I didn't wake you."

"I just closed my eyes for a second or two," he said.

I decided to take a pass on stopping in at The Spot at the end of the day and headed home just after five.

I pulled into the garage and went in the back door, just like I usually do. I stepped into a kitchen filled with a wonderful smell. Christine was at the stove stirring a pan. A large pasta pot was already on the boil.

"Oh wow, it smells delicious," I exclaimed just as Morton hurried into the kitchen to check out who had entered the house. He came over and gave me permission to scratch his head.

"Oh, thanks," Christine said. "I hope you don't mind, but the kids were hungry, and I thought if I cooked dinner, it would be one less thing you would have to do. I'm just boiling up some pasta, and I made a sauce based on things I found in your pantry. By the way, the kids really enjoyed your dog. He's very nice."

"Oh, believe me, Morton has his moments. Hey, I don't have a problem with you cooking, Christine. You've got your hands full, and I'm just trying to make it look like I'm keeping to my normal schedule, whatever that is. Did everything go okay today?"

She nodded and said, "Yeah, under the circumstances. A couple of arguments between the brothers, and Bryn wanted to see her mother, but all of that is to be expected."

"Did you let them outside?" I asked.

"No, there were a couple of times they could have used it, but children in your backyard would have been unusual, and I just wanted to play it safe. I spoke to Tommy on the phone. He's going to push foster care to place the children with us."

"Will that be a problem?"

"No, not at all. As a matter of fact, they'll probably welcome the offer. Three children are a tough placement, and under the circumstances, the parents being murdered and all, a lot of people won't want to be involved with that."

"That's really nice of you two."

"Thanks, and it's really nice of you to let us stay here. Tommy told me you didn't so much as blink when he presented the offer."

"That never would have even occurred to me. Three kids who just lost their parents, and they need to be protected. It's an honor to be involved."

"Yeah, that's how we feel, too."

"Anything from the guys?"

"You mean Emmett and Chuck? No, I've known them since they joined Special Investigations. They're very nice. Emmett Casey came from a big family, I think eight kids, and Chuck Steiner has three brothers. They're both used to kids and the craziness that comes with that."

"It seems pretty quiet right now," I said.

"Emmett's online in the den, and Chuck has the kids upstairs. He's reading a book to them. I can't tell you which one. A bunch of books were brought from their home along with the toys."

"There's no extended family?"

"No, Bobby had a brother who died of COVID sixteen months ago, and Cathy was an only child. Both sets of parents died at a young age, early sixties or maybe late fifties."

"Man, it just doesn't end."

"Helps to remind us to count our blessings," she said. She slipped a slotted spoon into the pasta pan and placed two pieces of rotini on a small plate. She picked one up and blew on it to cool it off before she placed it in her mouth. "Oh yeah, that's done."

I sat next to the three kids at the kitchen counter and ate pasta. Just as the kids finished their six-minute dinner, Emmett and Chuck came in. They told me everything had been quiet and there were no problems. While Christine directed the kids to pick up toys in the den and the front room, I loaded the dishwasher and cleaned the pans. Once the guys finished up the pasta, I laid out cereal boxes and bowls for breakfast and set the timer on the coffeepot for 6:00 a.m. Between 7:15 and 8:00, Christine put the kids to bed. Once they were all in bed, Morton took up his position in the hall in front of the bedroom door.

I poured Christine a glass of wine just before 9:00, and she went up to her room. I let Morton out after the evening news, and we went up to bed. Once again, he settled in front of the kids' room. I set my alarm for 2:00 a.m. I needed to check on something.

Thirty-two

The alarm woke me and I was out of bed and hit the alarm about two seconds after it went off. I pulled on jeans and a sweatshirt and headed downstairs. Morton was still stretched out on the floor in front of the door to the kids' room. He moved his head and opened one eye as I walked past. I heard him take a deep breath as I headed down the stairs. Chuck was on the couch reading a file as I stepped into the front room.

"Everything okay, Dev?"

"Yeah, not a bother. I'm supposed to check on a client's restaurant around 2:30 over on the west side. I should be back by 3:00. Can I get you anything from the kitchen before I leave?"

"No, thanks, but I'm fine. Kids are all asleep?"

"If they're not, they must be up to something because they're being awfully quiet. Morton's asleep just outside the room."

"Yeah, I like that."

"I'll see you in a bit," I said and headed into the kitchen. I pulled on my jacket, a black stocking cap, and gloves and headed out to the garage. When I turned on the car the radio came on just in time to hear the weather report. The current temperature was five degrees below zero. I let the engine warm for a minute before I backed out of the garage and down the driveway.

There was hardly any traffic at this hour. I made it through all the traffic lights without having to stop once, although I did slow down for one before the light turned green. I took a left off Kellogg Boulevard and drove down Robert Street until I turned a block away from the corner just before Sweeny's Auto Repair on the one-way street. As I turned, I noticed there were lots of lights turned on up on the second floor. As I drove past the back of the building, a guy with a two-wheeler was pushing a stack of four boxes up a ramp and into a moving truck. The truck was maybe twelve feet long. It was white, with a red logo on the side and the words 'IL GIARDINO DEI PIACERI'. I parked down the street and walked back to the alley behind Sweeny's.

I pulled a pen from my jacket pocket and wrote down the words on the side of the truck on my hand. I stood behind a dumpster across the alley from Sweeny's and watched as three guys continued to load the truck. At one point, two of them stepped out carrying what looked like a tabletop with a large hole. Just as they entered the back of the truck, the third guy stepped onto the ramp carrying a roulette wheel. It had begun to snow, and they were back a few minutes later with a four-wheeled cart and a large green felted craps table that they pushed up the ramp. They left the four-wheeled cart in the back of the truck. One of them raised the ramp and slid it into the truck, and then he pulled the rear door closed. I hurried back to my car.

I quickly climbed in and then prayed they would drive by soon so I could turn on the heat. While I waited, I copied the writing on my hand to the back of a receipt from the liquor store. It took maybe five minutes before the headlights on the moving truck flashed on, and they headed out of the alley and onto the one-way street past me. A black Mercedes followed. The guy I'd first seen pushing the two-wheeler was behind the wheel of the Mercedes. I waited until the car took a right at the end of the block before I turned on my car and drove down the street with my lights off. The Mercedes was just taking a right turn at the next corner, heading back to Jackson Street.

I kept my lights off and waited until I saw it take a left onto Jackson Street and disappear. I suddenly had an idea where they might be headed. I pulled up to Jackson Street and watched until the taillights were two blocks away. Once they were that far off, I turned on my head-lights and took a left. I followed them to Kellogg Boule-vard, where, at no surprise, they took a right. Now, I was almost positive I knew where they were headed.

I followed them up Robert Street. At this hour, we were the only vehicles on the street. At the top of the hill, they made a left-hand turn onto Summit Avenue, and now I was dead certain I knew where they were headed. Once I was past the St. Paul Cathedral and the curve in

the street, I pulled to the curb and turned off my headlights. I watched as they drove past the next four blocks
and their taillights almost disappeared from sight. I
turned my headlights on and followed their path.

There was just enough snow on the street for them
to leave a trail, not that I needed it. Sure enough, both
vehicles had turned right on Arundel Avenue and parked
on the wrong side of the street heading north. Not that it
made a difference at this hour. They were in the process
of pulling open the rear door of the moving van, and
three more guys were coming down the steps from the
side entrance of Chillcot's house.

The guy who drove the Mercedes was there holding
a painting in a gilt frame of two guys playing cards at a
table, one of them was smoking a pipe. One of the guys
said something to him, everyone laughed, and he hurried
into the house with the painting.

The roulette wheel, the craps tables, the poker tables
and chairs, all of it would be set up at Chillcot's place
before sunrise. No doubt they'd have a select list of customers they'd contact with the new address.

It would be work, but if they set the casino up on the
third floor, it would be way more secure than having it
on the second floor of Sweeny's Auto Repair. As I drove
past, one of the guys was in the process of pulling out
the ramp from beneath the moving truck. With six guys,
they could have the thing unloaded in about thirty
minutes. It was still circumstantial, but my guess was I'd
just seen the reason Leroy Ross had been murdered.

I headed home, pulled into the garage, and went in the kitchen door. Chuck was partially hidden alongside the refrigerator as I stepped into the kitchen.

"Oh, God, I just saw the headlights in the driveway. I was hoping it was you, Haskell, but we can never be too sure. Everything okay at your client's restaurant?" he said, shoving his pistol back into his shoulder holster.

"Yeah, everything appeared to be just as it should. Let me ask you something. I heard from an acquaintance yesterday that a guy named Leroy Ross was shot and killed downtown early yesterday morning. Do you know anything about him?"

"How did you hear that?"

"This guy I know told me."

"Told you yesterday?"

"Yeah, yesterday morning as a matter of fact."

"Damn it. There's a leak somewhere. That information wasn't supposed to be public until mid-day today."

"I looked him up online. There wasn't much information on the guy."

"He was smart and independent. Wanted to be his own boss and not have to report to anyone."

"Sounds like that thought process could put a target on his back."

Chuck nodded. "Yeah, depending on who you talk to. I'd met him a few times. He was a bit of a charmer, but being successful and independent are two reasons you'd be targeted."

"You have anyone in mind for the murder?"

"Oh, you know how it goes. There's always a laundry list of names, and half of them will tell you to catch them if you can. Right there, that should eliminate them from the suspect list. That's one thing that never seems to change with the business we're in."

"I'm not following. What's that?"

"It just continues to be crazy."

"Can't disagree with you there. I'm going to head upstairs and catch a few more hours of sleep. Hope the night remains quiet on your end."

"Yeah, me too. Sweet dreams."

"Good night," I said and headed up to bed. This time when I passed the kids' room, Morton raised his head and opened both eyes. As soon as he saw it was me, he went back to sleep. I tossed my clothes on the far side of the bed, crawled under the covers, and went to sleep.

I woke a little after 7:00. I took a quick shower, dressed, and headed downstairs. Christine was in the process of serving up pancakes to the kids. Chuck was putting his plate in the dishwasher. Emmett was pouring syrup over the stack of pancakes on his plate. Morton was gnawing on his rawhide bone and watching the three kids.

"Well, Dev, last one up. Can I talk you into some pancakes?" Christine said.

"You don't have to talk me into them. I'll definitely have some."

"Maybe grab yourself a coffee, and I'll have them ready for you in just a minute. All right, kids, is everyone going to be in the clean plate club this morning?"

Bryn grew a face and said, "I can't finish mine."

"You have to try, honey."

"I'll help her," Rowan said, placing his clean plate in front of her and sliding her plate over toward him. He finished what was left on the plate in three large bites.

"Oh, that was very nice of you, Rowan," Christine said.

"My plate is clean, too, and I did it all by myself," Kevin said.

"Very well done, Kevin," Christine said, which brought a grin onto Kevin's face.

The kids and Morton adjourned to the den. Chuck headed downstairs to sleep while Emmett did a quick walk around the outside of the house.

"Have you heard anything from Tommy?" I asked Christine as I placed the kids' plates in the sink and began to rinse them off.

She nodded and said, "Yeah, we chatted last night. You know how it is, very busy talking to people, asking questions, basically trying to put a puzzle together. A puzzle that's always missing key pieces."

"Yeah, unfortunately, I do know how it is, and that's a pretty good analogy." We chatted for a couple of minutes, and then I checked in with Emmett out in the front room. I said goodbye to the kids, gave Morton a

head scratch, and headed out the door after telling Christine to try to remain sane.

Thirty-three

Once again, I decided not to pass by the Chillcot house, although I wondered if I should refer to it as the house or the casino? When I got down to the office, Louie's car was already there, so I parked in front of it. Louie was seated at his desk, talking on the phone. He gave me a wave and pointed at my desk where a chocolate-covered doughnut was resting on a paper napkin.

I gave him a thumbs-up, poured myself a coffee from a recently made pot, and topped up Louie's mug. I turned on my computer and quickly checked the day's obituaries. No one I knew, and I wasn't listed, so it looked like I'd have to get some work done. Louie hung up the phone just as I took a bite of the doughnut.

"Mmm-mmm, thanks for this, Louie."

"My pleasure. Besides, you need sweetening. No Morton again this morning? You sure everything is okay?"

"Yeah, not to worry. I've got a friend staying over with a couple of kids. They like Morton, and he likes them, so it works out."

"A friend? Is everything okay with Layla?"

"Yeah, as far as I know. In fact, I'm going to give her a call in just a bit to see if maybe I could schedule some time with her. She's really working this Santa's Workshop gig, and she has to deal with the jerk who's Santa Claus."

"The Soto guy, right?" Louie said.

"Yeah. I want to check with her. See if she thinks he's still drinking. If he is, I'm going to find out how or where he stores his bottle. I've got a video of him staggering out of the workshop. I want to come up with some film of him actually consuming, and then maybe that will be enough to finally get him fired. What do you have going on today?"

"I'm mostly in the office, I think. I might have an appearance later this afternoon, but I haven't heard anything yet. If I don't hear anything by 10:00, I think I'm pretty much in the clear."

"Hope it goes your way," I said and did a brief check to see if there was any news regarding the former gambling establishment above Sweeny's Auto Repair. There was nothing, which didn't surprise me. Unfortunately, it seemed the newspaper had absolutely no idea there had been an illegal establishment on the second floor of the place or that Leroy Ross was involved. It maybe spoke to what had happened to the newspaper as more and more people had gone to getting their news online. Staff was cut and cut again. Now the joke was, if a reporter on the paper had to write a story of an incident on the east side, they would have to program their GPS to find their way over there.

Louie's phone suddenly rang. He shot me a look and said, "Oh shit," then answered. It was a short conversation. He apparently responded to a couple of questions. "Yes. Yes. No. Yes," then finished up with, "thank you for the call. I'll be there shortly."

"Appearance this afternoon?" I asked.

"I only wish. No, I'm due in thirty minutes. Damn it. I was hoping I could take it easy today. Don't wait up for me," he said as he tossed a file into his briefcase and stepped around the picnic table to pull his coat on. "See you later," he said and headed out the door.

I watched out the window as he crossed the street and climbed into his car. The black cloud of exhaust debris exploded from the back of his Ford Fiesta, and he headed down the street.

I picked up the phone and called Tommy Bishop. He answered before the phone barely rang. "Dev, everything okay?"

"Yeah, Tommy. Everything's fine. Christine and the three kids are doing well, and if she keeps cooking these delicious meals in short order, none of my clothes are going to fit."

"Yeah, she's great in the kitchen, well, and umm, elsewhere, too."

"Hey, I might have some information for you."
"Oh?"

"Nothing regarding Christine or the Hogan kids. Like I said, they're fine. This is tied to that Leroy Ross shooting the other day."

"What do you have?"

I went on to tell him about all the gambling equipment being moved in the middle of the night and taken up to the Chillcot house.

"You gotta be kidding me. I can't believe they even had access."

"I was down there early yesterday afternoon, right after lunch, and the place was closed and locked up. I just had a feeling something might be happening, and if so, it most likely wouldn't be done during the daylight hours."

"Yeah, you were right on that count. Tell me the name again on the truck."

I read the name, 'IL GIARDINO DEI PIACERI' off the liquor store receipt. "Pardon my pronunciation. I'm not at all familiar with the place. Does it ring a bell with you? Maybe it's some kind of high-class place where I wouldn't be allowed in. You think it might be a taco place?"

"It's Italian, Dev. Hang on just a second. Let me translate it. Oh yeah, not sure it's a restaurant, but it means The Gardens of Pleasure."

"Yeah, it could be anything from a massage parlor to a high-buck restaurant. Interesting, I better write that down."

"You said there were a half-dozen guys at Chillcot's place?

"Yeah, that's what I saw. I'm guessing they could have had that truck emptied in twenty or thirty minutes. They had a two-wheel dolly and a four-wheel cart that the craps table was sitting on. All those guys, once they get the stuff inside, I'm sure there's a wide staircase, and they could get everything up to the second or third floor with no problem. Have you seen the place?"

"Yes, well, I mean, I've been past it. We got floor plans of the house from the state historical society. I think the place was built back in 1890. That's a hundred and thirty-two years ago."

"I've been past it a million times over the years, but I've pretty much stayed away once Christina and the kids arrived. I don't want Chillcot having any idea who the hell I am."

"Thanks, Dev, I appreciate that. And thanks for opening your door and letting them stay."

"Glad to be able to do it. Any idea what's going to happen?"

"With Chillcot? No, but this information you just provided will go a good way in focusing on the guy. It could have taken a year or more to learn about this, and because you saw what was going on last night, we know about it before he's even up and running."

"If I hear anything else, I'll let you know."

"Thanks again for having Christine and the Hogan children."

"She's doing a great job."

"You're doing a great job taking care of everyone, Dev. Thank you."

I disconnected with Tommy and called Tubby Gustafson. I went through the same routine again with the creepy voice guy in the security room, but he finally transferred my call to Tubby.

"What is it, Haskell?" Tubby answered. In the background, I could hear two female voices. I guessed it was the same two women giving him a massage, apparently a daily activity. I actually felt sorry for them having to deal with Tubby's lard ass and—"Did you hear me, Haskell? I asked you what you wanted. Hello? Haskell, are you there?"

"Yes, sir, thank you for taking my call. I was thinking—"

"For God's sake, Haskell. I'm, I'm working. What is it you want?"

"I just wanted to pass on some information, sir." I went on to explain everything I'd just told Tommy Bishop, although I couldn't see any point in telling Tubby I had informed someone in Special Investigations. When I gave him the name on the side of the truck, he said, "What the hell does that mean?"

"It's Italian, sir. It means "The Gardens of Pleasure."

"The name doesn't ring a bell with me, interesting. I'll have someone check it out. You mentioned there were six individuals emptying the truck?"

"Yes sir, six that I saw. There may have been more in the house. I have no idea, and at that hour, if I drove past a few more times, I was afraid I would have drawn their attention."

"Surprisingly, you made the wise move, Haskell. Interesting, very interesting. They had access to the building."

"Sweeny's? It certainly appeared to be the case. As I mentioned, it was closed when I was there earlier in the afternoon, and that just got me thinking."

"Humpf, imagine, you thinking, that in itself is strange. Very good. I appreciate the phone call. Anything else?"

"No sir, that's all I have at the moment."

"Very good. It pains me to say this, Haskell, but thank you," Tubby said and hung up.

Thirty-four

After lunch I phoned Layla. Based on the way she answered, things didn't seem to have really improved. "Dev? Well, what do you know, surprise, surprise, you're really not dead. How nice to finally hear from you."

"Hi, Layla. I thought I'd just give you a break after the raisins disappeared. I know that couldn't have made you very happy."

"Couldn't have made me very happy? Are you kidding? I wanted to put Santa in his sleigh and push it off the Smith Avenue Bridge."

"Do you think he's still drinking?"

"No, Dev. I don't *think* he's still drinking. I *know* he is. He's an even bigger jerk than usual. When he talks to the children, he's slurring his words. He's drinking so much he's running to the bathroom about every twenty minutes."

"To the bathroom? I bet that's it, Layla. That's where his bottle is. I'll be over later this afternoon. I'm going to want to film him, and we'll have positive proof regarding what he's up to."

"You really think so?"

"I think we've got a pretty good chance. I'll call you before I come over."

Louie arrived back in the office just after 3:00. Things were apparently going well, under the circumstances, up until his client started calling the judge names and telling her in no uncertain terms that 'her head was up her ass.' As one might imagine, that quickly brought the proceeding to a close. His client was taken away in handcuffs and given a week to review his claims. Louie had remained in the judge's chambers, filling out paperwork for another hour.

"Do you think he'll learn his lesson?" I asked.

"Probably not," Louie said.

I phoned Layla and left a message then headed over to Santa's Workshop just after 4:00. No one was more surprised than me to see a line of ten or twelve kids waiting to see Santa, but then this was the final week before Christmas. Everyone seemed to be on their best behavior except for Arthur Soto, the meanest Santa ever.

He'd just sent a little girl away in tears, and Layla was dealing with an irate mother when Santa stood and announced, "Back in a minute. I need to pee."

Two mothers took their children's hands and hurried out of the Workshop. Layla was attempting to calm down the mother with the crying little girl. I followed Santa through the 'Employees Only' door. He staggered down the hallway and into the men's room. I waited thirty seconds and entered. There was Santa standing in front of the paper towel dispenser. A handwritten note in black sharpie was taped to the front of the dispenser 'Out Of Order.' The top of the dispenser was open, and Santa had a half-full mason jar up against his lips.

He took one look at me and said, "It's mouthwash, and I'm not sharing."

"That's okay. I wasn't going to ask." I pulled out my phone, took three quick pictures of him drinking from the jar, and left. When I stepped back into the Workshop, Layla was all by herself.

"Where did everyone go?" I asked.

"Come on, Dev. Would you want your kid exposed to that creep?" she said as a tear ran down her cheek.

"Maybe this will help," I said and pulled out my phone. "Take a look."

"Oh, God, look at him. You just took these, didn't you?"

"I did, and I've one more thing left to do, but I have to wait until Santa comes out and—"

"Where in the hell did everybody go?" Santa said and then let off a very loud belch.

"They left. They don't want their kids exposed to a drunken fool like you. I'm calling the cops on you, and they're going to lock your ass up. You're a disaster waiting to happen," I said.

"You can't talk to me like that. I'm...I'm Santa Claus."

"You're an idiot, and you should be locked up. You've ruined Christmas for countless families. You've single-handedly destroyed Santa's Workshop, the most popular Santa visit in town."

"I think I'm going to go back and pee again. I want your dumb ass gone by the time I get back."

"Not to worry, I'll help the cops put you in the back of the squad car."

"We'll see about that," he said as he staggered back through the 'Employees Only' door.

"What are you going to do?" Layla asked.

I pulled out my phone, called 911, and said, "I'm calling the cops. They'll lock him up, and then whoever is in charge will have no choice but to fire his worthless ass, no matter who his City Council sister—"

"St. Paul Emergency 911."

"Yes, I would like to report an intoxicated individual at Santa's Workshop. He's harassing employees, children, and their parents."

"Your name, sir?"

"My name is Devlin Haskell. I'm a private investigator in the city of St. Paul."

"Can you describe this individual?"

"Yes, his name is Arthur Soto. He's dressed as Santa Claus. I have a video of him drinking in the men's room. He's intoxicated, staggering, shouting at people, frightening children, and he needs to be arrested for drunk and disorderly conduct before he physically assaults someone or harms a child."

"I'm dispatching a squad now. Will you remain on site?"

"Yes, and I'll be happy to assist the officers in any way I can."

"Officers are on their way. You can expect them within the next four minutes."

"Thank you," I said and disconnected. "The cops are on their way. Will you wait here for them? I'm going in to grab Arthur in case he tries to make a run for it."

"Oh, be careful, Dev."

"I'll be fine. He's probably in the men's room drinking," I said and made my way back through the 'Employees Only' door. I hurried down the hall to the men's room. I took a deep breath and pushed the door open. The place was empty. I checked all three stalls. He wasn't there. I lifted the top of the paper towel dispenser and peeked in. There it was, the mason jar. Now, three-quarters empty. I left it where it was and hurried back out to Layla just as two police officers walked up the path past the Christmas trees and the cardboard fireplace with the Christmas stockings.

"You called reporting an intoxicated Santa Claus," one of the officers said to Layla.

"I called," I said. "He was here a moment ago but fled the scene. He's really drunk. If he gets behind the wheel, there's no telling what the damage will be."

"He has a car here?"

"He parks up on the top floor. Drives a lime green Chevy Spark. I took some video of him. I can show you how drunk he is if you want."

"No, we'll check him out. How do we get up to the parking area?"

"I'll show you where the elevators are," Layla said.

"I'll go up," the older cop said. "Walt, maybe pull the cruiser down the street by the exit ramp. That way, if he happens to make it behind the wheel, you can pull him over when he comes out." The second cop nodded and headed back down the path and out the door. "You want to show me where the elevators are?" the cop said to Layla.

"Let me go with you. I can help you find him," I said, and we followed Layla through the 'Employees Only' door. Instead of heading down the hall toward the restrooms, we took a right and walked to a pair of elevators.

As we stepped onto the elevator, he said, "Ma'am, if you wouldn't mind waiting out in the Workshop area just in case he returns or a customer shows up."

Layla nodded and headed back to the Workshop. We rode the elevator up to the top floor and stepped out into a glass-enclosed area. The cop wrinkled his nose and said, "What the hell?"

"On the door," I said, pointing to the glass door leading out to the parking area. Someone, most likely Santa, had recently vomited. The stuff was dripping down the glass door and puddling on the floor.

"Charming," he said, taking a pair of latex gloves from his pocket and pulling them on. We walked toward the door. He pushed it open, avoiding the exit bar on the door, and said, "Watch your step."

There were only a half-dozen cars in the parking area. None of which were Soto's lime green Chevy Spark. Just to be safe, we quickly checked around and peeked in every vehicle, even though they were all locked. No sign of a drunken Santa. He radioed his partner, told him to be on the lookout, and then we walked down the spiral exit ramp. The entrances to the other levels were inaccessible from the exit ramp, and a gate at each level prevented access via the exit.

Eventually, we made our way out to the street, where the officer was waiting in the squad car. "No sign of him?" he said as we climbed into the squad car. It was only seven degrees above zero, and I was physically shaking. The squad car felt wonderfully warm, and for the first time in my entire life, I was happy to be in the backseat.

"Nothing. Maybe he was driving a different car?" I offered.

"No one came down the exit ramp since I've been here," the cop behind the wheel said. "How 'bout we give you a ride up to the front door, and we'll file a report. If he shows up, give us another call."

"Sorry to waste your time, guys."

"We'll put a BOLO out on him. The last thing we need is a drunk behind the wheel. You said his name was Arthur Soto?"

"Yeah, that's right."

"Any relation to the woman on the City Council?"

"She's his sister," I said. They looked at each other but didn't say anything.

Thirty-five

Layla half screamed, "Did they get him? Please, tell me they arrested that worthless piece of—"

"Sorry, Layla, but we couldn't find him."

"Couldn't find him? You mean he's still in the building somewhere?"

"No, I don't think so. His car wasn't up in the parking ramp. We walked down the exit ramp just to be sure but never saw his car. I'm thinking either he hurried up to his car and took off or he wasn't in the parking lot to begin with, and he got in his car, wherever it was, and took off."

"So they didn't arrest him?"

"Pretty hard to arrest the guy if we can't find him. Which reminds me. He left his gin in the men's room. I'm going to go get it. I think I can pull some strings and have the cops run it for fingerprints. I've got pictures of him drinking from it. This will be even better than the raisins. I'll be right back," I said and hurried into the men's room.

I pulled my cell phone from my pocket and took a couple of photographs of the paper towel dispenser. I opened the lid and took three more photos of the mason jar resting on top of the paper towels. I pulled two paper towels from the bottom of the dispenser, carefully picked up the jar by the lid, and set it on the counter next to the sink. I took two more pictures of the jar, now only about a quarter of the way full. I carried the jar into the Workshop and set it on the counter with the sign that read 'WELCOME TO SANTA'S WORKSHOP.'

"Do you have a plastic bag or something I can wrap this in? I don't want to mess up the fingerprints on the jar."

"He was drinking out of that?"

"Yeah, and I've got the pictures to prove it."

"I thought you said he was drinking out of the bottle."

"No, it was this mason jar. But the reason he was doing that was because he had this hidden in the paper towel dispenser, and a bottle wouldn't have fit in the dispenser."

"Oh," Layla said, nodding. "Clever, and that's why he was always going to the restroom. So he could get another drink."

"Yeah, and that's why he was so drunk because he was always running to the men's room."

"Oh, Dev, thank you for getting involved. If you hadn't done this, he would still be here ruining Christmas for families, frightening children, and being a major pain in the ass. For the first time ever, I feel like we are finally going to get rid of him."

"Do you have a plastic bag or something I can wrap this in?"

"Oh, yeah, sorry. How about this?" she said reaching below the counter and taking out a roll of white plastic trash bags.

"Perfect. Let me put the jar in there if you don't mind. I don't want to smear any of the prints," I said. Using the paper towels from the men's room, I picked up the mason jar by the lid and carefully set it inside the plastic trash bag.

"Okay, great. I'm going to run this down to the police station and try to cajole someone into checking it for fingerprints. I'm sure we won't have any results today, but maybe tomorrow or in a couple of days, we'll have something."

"Oh, God, I can't thank you enough. At least not here. Are you interested in coming over for a quick dinner and a late night tonight?"

"I would love that. Let me get this down to the police station, and since Santa is gone, are you closed for the rest of the day?"

"Obviously, but I'll have to file yet another report. I can only imagine what they'll tell me this time."

"Okay, I'll be over around 7:00 tonight. Let me send you those pictures right now. They'll help to add some credibility to your story and get them on record," I said. I took my phone out again and sent her six images plus the video of Santa staggering out of the Workshop the other day. Her phone began to ding a moment later.

Once all the images and the video were uploaded, she opened them up and viewed them. "Oh, this will be perfect. Thank you, Dev. Thank you so much," she said and gave me a kiss. "Now get that jar down to the police station and tell them it's okay with me if they lock him up until after Christmas. Honest to God!"

I phoned Aaron LaZelle once I was in my car. I got dumped into his voicemail after a couple of rings. "Hi, Aaron, it's Dev. On my way to your office to drop off a jar I need fingerprints on. Anything you can do to help would be appreciated. It's a jar partially filled with gin. Santa, at Santa's Workshop, is drinking on the job, and he ran off when I confronted him today. I've got photos of him drinking and a video of him staggering, and there are tons of complaints from staff and families. Unfortunately, he hasn't been fired, and we think that's because his sister is Melody Soto, on the City Council. Anything you could do to help the situation would be greatly appreciated. Thanks."

Three minutes later, I pulled into the parking lot across the street and hurried into the station.

"What can we do for you, sir?" the officer behind the front desk asked.

I explained my situation to him and finished up with, "Sir, if someone from Homicide could maybe come down, get this, and set it on Lieutenant LaZelle's desk, I'd appreciate it. He'll take care of it from there."

The officer gave me a look that suggested I was an idiot, but then he picked up the phone and made a call.

"Yes, I have a gentleman by the name of Dev Hassle down here with evidence Lieutenant LaZelle is expecting. Great, thank you," he said and hung up. "Okay, if you'll just take a seat, Sergeant Norris Manning will be down just as soon as he can."

"That was Manning you were speaking to?"

"It was. You know him?"

"I do," I said with a fake smile. I didn't see any point in explaining that Manning was not my biggest fan. I wandered over to the rows of black plastic chairs, wondering how many hours Manning would keep me waiting.

Imagine my surprise when Manning stepped out from the security door, spotted me, and hurried over. "Haskell, you have some evidence the LT is expecting?" Manning asked.

"Thanks for coming down, Sergeant. Just wanted to leave this for Lieutenant LaZelle," I said, lifting the white trash bag.

Manning took the bag and looked inside. "A mason jar? Is someone making moonshine?"

"Not exactly. A friend of mine plays the part of Santa's elf, at Santa's Workshop, and she's working with this guy who has to be the world's worst Santa Claus. In fact, I called 911 earlier today because he was intoxicated, making children cry and being obnoxious. All the families waiting in line walked out. He's just awful. The squad car showed up in just a couple of minutes, but we couldn't find the guy. He somehow got away."

"Back up for a moment. You said he's dressed as Santa Claus, and he's making children cry?"

"Yeah, he tells them they're not going to get what they ask for. I've heard him tell a couple of kids he won't be stopping at their house. My friend has to calm down irate parents while Santa hurries into the men's room where he has a bottle, or in this case, that mason jar of gin, hidden in the paper towel dispenser. He sneaks drinks during the day, which does nothing to improve his personality."

"This wouldn't happen to be at Santa's Workshop over on Cedar Street, would it?"

"Yeah, that's the place. You've been there?"

"No, but my wife and daughter have been there with the grandkids. The wife was ready to kill Santa. Told the little guy he didn't deserve the dinosaur truck he wanted and that Santa was going to bring a lump of coal. He told the granddaughter she was getting a Barbie doll instead of the American Girl Doll she wanted. It only took a full day to calm the two of them down. This is the guy you're trying to get fired?"

"Yes. In fact, there are tons of complaints on the guy from staff and customers alike, but nothing has ever been done about it. Turns out the guy's sister is on the City Council, which apparently makes him untouchable."

"Who's the council person?"

"Melody Soto," I said.

"Soto? She's my council person. Now, I have to say, she runs a pretty tight ship, and I like her style. Are you sure she's the council person?"

"Yes, sir, very sure."

Manning pursed his lips, nodded for a long moment, and said, "Would you mind if I made a suggestion?"

"Not at all, please do."

"Take this over to the BCA. You know where they are over on Maryland Avenue?"

"Yeah, I've been there before."

"Good, ask for Jim Dugan. I'll go upstairs and place a call to him. He had something like our situation happen to a couple of his kids last year. Now they don't want to go ever again."

"Jim Dugan," I said.

"Yeah, I'll make the call now," Manning said as he stood and held out his hand.

"Thank you, much appreciated," I said as we shook and I hurried out the door.

Thirty-six

The BCA is Minnesota's Bureau of Criminal Apprehension. It couldn't get any better than being sent there and Manning making a phone call. I repeated Dugan's name over and over on the five-minute drive to the BCA.

I pulled into the parking lot, paved, by the way, as opposed to gravel with potholes, and hurried into the lobby. I gave the guy behind the desk my name and asked to see Jim Dugan. Dugan was down in the lobby five minutes later.

"You're Haskell? The guy Manning from St. Paul called me about?"

"Yeah, thanks for taking the time to see me. Sorry to interrupt your day."

"Believe me, this is no interruption if you're going after that character at Santa's Workshop. Anything I can do to get that jerk off the street will be well worth it."

I gave him an update on Arthur Soto, his behavior, the raisins, the hidden mason jar, and the things he said to kids and parents, and then I handed him the trash bag with the mason jar.

"You got a business card? I'll get on this tonight. With any luck, it should be relatively easy."

"Oh, man, I can't thank you enough," I said and handed him the bag. We exchanged business cards, and I left so he could get started. I headed back to the office. Louie's car was parked just where it had been when I left. I parked in front of him and hurried up to the office. Louie wasn't there, but the empty coffee pot was still on the burner. I turned the burner off, set the pot on the file cabinet, and headed over to The Spot. At no surprise, Louie was seated on his stool.

"Get you a beer, Dev?" Mike asked.

"Afraid not, I'm just here for a minute. Pour another one for Louie, and I'll buy."

"I wasn't sure if you'd be in tonight," Louie joked and took a sip of his drink.

"Yeah, I can only stay for a minute or two, but I wanted to give you an update. I proceeded to tell him about Santa, the hidden jar, and everything else. I covered all of the afternoon's activity and ended up with my trip to the BCA and Dugan offering to stay late to get the fingerprints. We chatted for a bit more, and then I begged off and hurried home.

Morton met me at the back door when I walked in. All three kids were seated at the kitchen counter with Emmett, who was wearing a dark blue blazer to hide his shoulder holster. Everyone was dipping grilled cheese sandwiches in ketchup and devouring them along with potato chips. Christine was having a glass of wine, and Emmett was drinking a glass of water.

"How did your day go?" Christine asked.

"It went well. I think I got a problem cleaned up, and I've got some work to do tonight for a bit, so I'll be out late, but things went well. How about you guys?"

Christine gave Emmett a nod, and he said, "It went well. No problems. Had a car with two people stop in front of the house for a bit, but they went on their way after a few minutes."

"Nothing out of the ordinary?"

Emmett shook his head and glanced at the kids for half a second.

"What about you, Christine?"

"Well, we read stories, and Bryn dressed the doll. Kevin played with his dinosaurs, and Rowan built a really neat house with the Legos. Can I talk you into a grilled cheese sandwich?" she said.

"I don't know. What do you guys think? Were they good?"

"Real good," all three kids said at once.

"Well then, I guess I'd better have one, if you please."

"Coming right up."

Emmett picked up his plate and gave me a look. I gave a quick nod while Christine was busy slicing cheese. I picked up the kids' plates, stuffed what was left of Bryn's sandwich in my mouth, and once I swallowed it said, "Do you guys want to go play?"

They all nodded.

"Okay, go ahead."

As they hopped off their stools, Christine called after them and said, "We're going to be picking up toys in a bit. If you want to get started, that would be a good idea. Baths tonight before bed."

She set my grilled cheese in the pan, and it sizzled slightly. "Thanks again, Christine. You're doing a great job. You hear anything from Tommy?" I pulled a couple of potato chips from one of the kid's plates and started eating them.

"Only that they're very busy. Something is on the horizon. I can tell by the way he talks or doesn't talk, not that it has anything to do with us here. But I can pick it up. I've been there before."

"Do you need anything from me?"

"Oh, no, Dev. You've been wonderful. And thankfully, your place is large enough so that, if needed, and there are times when it is, the kids can get some space and some private time. Especially the boys. Rowan likes to read. Kevin has the dinosaurs chasing each other, and Bryn likes to give directions to her doll." She picked up the spatula and turned my grilled cheese.

"By the way, Christine, in case I haven't mentioned it, I love the fact you're doing all the cooking. It's really kind of you."

"Well, you're doing plenty, not the least of which is providing a safe place for all of us. Very much appreciated."

"My pleasure. I'm just glad everything is working out."

She turned the grilled cheese once more and then set it on a plate and placed it in front of me. "Would you like some ketchup?"

"Yes, please."

She squirted ketchup on the plate, piled the leftover potato chips next to my grilled cheese, and put the kids' plates in the sink.

"Leave those there. I'll rinse them off and load them in the dishwasher."

"Oh, thanks. It's pretty full, so you should probably run it once you've finished eating."

"You're the boss," I said.

"Let me go address the den," she said and headed out of the kitchen. A moment later, I heard her say, "Okay, time to pick up. Rowan, would you stack those four books back on the shelf, and Kevin…"

I finished my sandwich, ate the potato chips, placed my plate in the sink, and went out to the front room. Emmett was seated in a chair in the dark, staring out the window.

"You expecting trouble?" I asked.

"We saw the same car out front four different times, New Jersey plates. Haven't gotten the plate number yet."

"What were they doing?"

"Circling the block a couple of times. Driving past, looking for activity. I don't think they saw any, but you never know."

"You think they could be with Chillcot?"

"I'd say there's a pretty good chance, the Jersey plates here, in December. It's unusual any time of the year, let alone in winter."

"Is Chuck in the basement?"

"No, he's parked out on the street. Dressed for the cold, and he's got an FN SCAR 20S, perfect for long range up to a thousand yards, along with a sidearm, of course."

"And you?"

"HK 416, under your couch at the moment. A nine millimeter," he said, tapping his left shoulder, "and a Glock 22 strapped to my ankle."

"You want me to hang around tonight?"

"Actually, no. If they're watching and they see you go, that might just calm them down."

"You're sure? It's no problem to change—"

"No, Dev. I mean it. We get any sense we need help, the place will be crawling with cops in about thirty seconds, believe me."

"Okay, but if you think something's going to happen, call for backup first and then call me."

He looked up at me, smiled, and flashed a quick salute. "We already checked you out."

"Okay, well, I better get back in the kitchen and get that dishwasher running."

Thirty-seven

There was a security phone in the lobby of the Blair House. I phoned Layla and a moment later, the door buzzed. I took the elevator up to the fifth floor and walked down the hall to her place, number 505.

She opened the door while I was still knocking, grabbed me by my belt, and pulled me inside. As soon as the door closed, she pushed me up against it and gave me a kiss that lasted for a full minute.

She stepped back, revealing her short, black lace kimono. She smiled and said, "Oh, Dev, I can't thank you enough for the pictures, the video, and for getting fingerprints off that mason jar." She backed me against the door again and kissed me.

When we came up for air, I said, "Well, we haven't gotten the fingerprints back yet."

"But still, I mean, he was the only guy drinking out of that jar, wasn't he? You didn't drink from it, did you?"

"Yeah, Layla, that's right. I drank out of that jar because I knew we were going to kiss tonight, and now you've got Santa's germs."

She slapped me on the shoulder and said, "You really are nuts. Come on. I've got some nice brie and crackers in the living room. Oh, and you're in charge tonight."

It suddenly dawned on me that her unit was rather dark. Two dim lights attached beneath the upper kitchen cabinets were on in the kitchen that overlooked the living room. The gas fireplace was burning and two candles, one on either end of the fireplace, were lit. A blanket with two pillows was arranged on the floor in front of the fireplace, and an ice bucket with a champagne bottle and two champagne flutes next to it rested on the coffee table. The curtains were drawn back, and the large moon was glowing through the stained glass windows. We were two floors above the building across the street, and no one would be able to see in.

"How about some champagne?"

"I'd love it. The perfect celebration to creepy Arthur Soto leaving the Workshop never ever to return again."

I slowly loosened the cork on the champagne and filled the flutes. We clinked glasses, and I got another kiss. We each had two more glasses of champagne, got very personal, slept for a bit, and started all over again.

It was after midnight when I got dressed and kissed her goodbye. She promised to call me when she found out who the new Santa Claus was going to be. I took the elevator down to the ground floor then looked up and down the street before I stepped out of the building. The street was empty, and other than a city bus in the distance, there wasn't any traffic. I hurried to my car, climbed in behind the wheel, and locked the door.

I drove down the street and took a right turn, deciding I would drive past Chillcot's place. As I passed, there were two guys standing out in front. Both warming their hands over what looked like a space heater. I didn't count, but there were at least ten cars parked in front or on the side street. The third floor was illuminated, suggesting that the gambling area had been set up and was already in operation. I took an indirect route home, double-checking that I wasn't being followed. I pulled into my garage and entered the house through the back door.

The place was quiet. I was still in the kitchen when a text message came through on my phone. 'Welcome home. Everything quiet so far. Chuck.' I left the lights off and walked into the front room. Emmett was stretched out on the couch beneath a blanket. I looked out the front window at the car parked across the street, but I couldn't see anyone in it. I sent Chuck a thumbs-up emoji.

"Have a nice evening?" Emmett asked, causing me to half-jump.

"Oh, God, you almost gave me a heart attack," I said. "Yeah, it was a nice evening, caught up on a lot of things. Enjoyed one another's company. Everything okay here?"

"Everything's fine. We're just playing it very care-ful."

"I drove past Chillcot's place. Maybe ten cars were parked on the street, and it looked like all the lights were on up on the third floor."

"Yeah, we got word it's opening night over there. That's fine. With any luck, it will keep everyone busy."

"Well, get some sleep, Emmett. Sorry I woke you."

"Not to worry, sweet dreams," he said and rolled over with his back to me.

I gave a quick look out the window. Everything looked quiet. I could only hope it stayed that way. I climbed the stairs. Morton was on his feet as I stepped into the upstairs hallway. Once he saw it was me, he assumed the position for a head scratch, and when I finished, he stretched out again in front of the door to the kids' room. I went into my bedroom and was asleep about thirty seconds after my head hit the pillow.

Thirty-eight

Barely 6:00 and I was up the following morning. I'd forgotten to set my alarm, but apparently, that didn't matter. I showered, shaved, dressed, and quietly headed downstairs. Morton wasn't in front of the kids' room, and I wondered if one of them had gotten up in the middle of the night and let him in. It wasn't worth the risk of waking them just to check, so I quietly made my way downstairs.

I heard a voice coming from the den and peeked in. Bryn was sitting on the floor with her back to the door, pretending to feed a doll. "No, you have to have a clean plate before I can give you dessert. I made chocolate chip cookies just for you, so eat this mac and cheese. That's a good girl. You are much better than your brothers. Here, have some more," she said then bumped the spoon against the doll's cheek.

Morton was asleep on the couch. He opened an eye, saw it was me, snuggled down further on the couch, and went back to sleep.

I tiptoed into the kitchen, filled the coffee pot for ten cups, and turned it on. I stepped into the dining room.

From where I stood, I could see Emmett asleep on the couch in the front room. I looked out the window. The sun was just beginning to rise. The car was still parked across the street, and I wondered if Chuck had spent the entire night in there.

I went back into the kitchen and arranged things for breakfast. Bowls and boxes of cereal for the kids. I cracked a couple of eggs into a bowl and sprinkled in cinnamon for French toast then got out the syrup, butter, and silverware.

By the time the coffee was ready, I'd unloaded the dishwasher so I poured myself a mug. I got out three mugs for whenever the other adults appeared. I turned on my laptop and checked the news. Fortunately, there didn't appear to have been any shootings in town overnight. I heard the shower go on upstairs, and a half-hour later, Christine appeared dressed in jeans and a University of Minnesota sweatshirt. She poured herself a coffee, took a sip, and asked, "Anything in the news?"

"Looks to have been a fairly quiet night. No shootings and no snow."

"How long have you been up?"

"I was wide awake at 6:00 and thought I'd come down and get things ready. I'm in charge of breakfast this morning. Can I make you some French toast before the kids get down here?"

"Oh, that would be wonderful. I saw Bryn in the den, but she was feeding her doll, and I didn't want to interrupt."

"Yeah, she was doing the same thing when I peeked in. She was telling the doll she'd baked chocolate chip cookies but couldn't give her any until her plate was clean."

Christine laughed and said, "That must have been one of their parents' rules."

Christine and I were halfway through our French toast when Emmet stepped into the kitchen. He was wearing his blazer. "Good morning," he said and poured himself a coffee. I dipped three pieces of bread into the French toast batter and placed them in the frying pan.

The kids showed up in their pajamas. Bryn brought along her doll. They chose cereal over French toast, which was fine with me. After a quick breakfast, they adjourned to the front room and watched the same cartoon video they'd watched on previous mornings.

I cleared the empty dishes, loaded the dishwasher, then topped up all three coffee mugs. "Everyone slept well?" I asked.

Christine and Emmett nodded.

I didn't want to get into any information Emmett might have with Christine present. She had enough to worry about with the kids so I gave them an update on Santa's Workshop.

"Oh, my God, and they can't get rid of this character?"

"I think after the video, the photographs, and the fingerprints on the mason jar, that should be enough to force them into taking action. It's been an adventure," I said.

Emmett entertained us with a story of playing Santa Claus in college. It turned out to be how he ended up meeting his wife. It was safe to presume there were probably adult beverages involved.

Christine told us about meeting Tommy at a high school dance, how they'd both been at the dance with other dates who snuck off, leaving the two of them. Tommy gave her a ride home, and they'd been together ever since.

Once they'd finished with their stories, there was a very quiet period until Christine finally said, "Okay, Dev, your turn."

"Oh, God, the women I've dated. They were all very nice, well, most of them were, but they finally seemed to come to their senses and tell me not to ever call them again, ever. I've met them in bars and at dog shows. Two of them rear-ended me, you know, in their cars. I met one on an airplane. One was a dancer. She—"

"A dancer? You mean she was a stripper?" Christine asked.

"Well, yeah. I guess that's one way to describe her career." They both laughed at that. "The woman I'm seeing now is an elf at Santa's Workshop. Her goal in life is to get Santa Claus fired because he's so awful. I dated a couple of bartenders, some school teachers, a school principal, a lawyer, a doctor, two realtors, a—"

"Oh, for God's sake. Stop with the list. Is there anyone in town you haven't dated?"

"There are a few, but I've still got time."

"Well, I think you're nice," Christine said.

"Yeah, and you make great French toast. What's not to like?" Emmett said.

"Thank you both. If there's nothing else, I should probably head down to the office. Anything you need before I go?" They both shook their heads. I said goodbye to the kids in the front room. All three nodded but didn't take their eyes off the TV.

I took the roundabout way to the office, avoiding driving past Chillcot's place. I parked in front of Louie's car and headed into the building. He had stopped asking where Morton was a couple of days ago and instead said, "How did your evening go?"

I gave him the update on Arthur Soto and Jim Dugan from the BCA working late to run fingerprints off the mason jar.

"Oh, that's perfect. Someone Santa pissed off a year ago has a chance to get back at him. One can only hope he's successful." We chatted for a couple of minutes, and then Louie headed down to the courthouse.

I watched his car explode with a cloud of exhaust debris and drive off. Once he was out of sight, I called Tubby Gustafson. This time when I called, the creep answered the phone and said, "Are you calling to speak with Mr. Gustafson?"

"Yes, I am."

"One moment, and I'll connect you."

The phone rang twice before Tubby picked up, but instead of giving me a hard time, he sounded all business. "Yes, Haskell. What do you have for me?" I was actually stunned that he hadn't called me names or told me I'd never amount to anything. "Haskell? Are you there?"

"Oh, yes, sir. Sorry about that. I just wanted to report that I drove past the Chillcot residence early this morning, shortly after midnight."

"And?"

"Well, sir, there were a least ten cars parked out front. And the entire third floor was illuminated. My guess is they set up all the gambling equipment upstairs on the third floor and put the news out that they were open for business."

"Interesting," he said, not sounding the least bit surprised. "Did you see anyone keeping an eye on things outside?"

"Yes, as a matter of fact, I did. There were two men on the front stoop. It was cold out, and they were both warming their hands over what looked like a space heater."

"And they were at the front door?"

"Kind of. I think there are five, maybe six, stone steps that lead up to the front door. They were actually at the base of those steps."

"Did you see anyone at the side or rear entrance?"

Interesting Tubby knew there was a side and rear entrance. "No, sir, but then I wasn't looking, and I was driving, so I just had a second or two to glance."

"Did you recognize any of the parked cars?"

"No, but again, I was driving, and if you're asking, did I recognize who owned them? I have no idea. I will say they were all very nice, some SUVs, a couple of Mercedes, I think a BMW, and a Cadillac Escalade, you know, like yours, sir, only it was white."

"Interesting. Anything else?"

"No sir, just thought you should know he's apparently open for business."

"Well, with that sort of activity, it would seem the police might take more than just a passing interest. Time will tell. Thank you, Haskell. Enjoy your day," he said and hung up.

A pleasant phone conversation with Tubby Gustafson? Who knew? That was an absolute first for me.

Thirty-nine

Layla phoned in the middle of the afternoon.

"Hey, hot number. I was about to call you and thank you for a wonderfully lovely evening last night."

"All for nothing, I'm afraid."

"What?"

"Arthur, he's here. Nothing's happened."

"But, you showed them the pictures, didn't you? He was drinking from the mason jar. He was in the men's room, and the paper towel dispenser had that handwritten 'OUT OF ORDER' sign on it. The video showed him staggering around. You've got all the customer complaints, all the employee complaints, and—"

"And they're still telling me it's not good enough."

"What do they want? We called the police, for God's sake. The cops filed a report."

"But they never got hold of him. He somehow got away."

"Are you at the Workshop now?"

"Yes, and we're liable to be busy because there are just a few days left. Of course, that's only if anyone is stupid enough to have their kids sit on creepy Arthur's lap."

"Stay there, Layla. I'm on my way."

I quickly decided it would not be a good idea to bring a pistol. I'd want to use it on Arthur. I hurried out to the car and headed downtown. Word must have gotten out about Arthur because there were two empty parking places right on the street in front of the Workshop entrance. I hurried inside.

"That'll be five dollars," the same bored-looking kid I had to deal with my first time here said to me.

"Thanks, but I'm here to make a quick adjustment that should have been taken care of a long time ago," I said and stepped inside.

I hurried up the path, and there was Arthur, just now yelling at Layla. "I don't care what you think. I'm firing you, do you hear me? Now get your gorgeous ass out of here and—"

"Hey, Arthur, that's it. You're done. I want *you* out of here, now," I shouted.

Arthur took a step or two in my direction and attempted to focus. "Wait a minute, don't I know you from somewhere? Did you buy me a drink one time?"

"No one would buy you a drink, Arthur. You're a worthless jerk. I want you to take off the jacket and the beard. You are done ruining Christmas for everyone who comes in here."

"You, you can't talk to me like that. I'll have you know I've got connections with some very powerful people in this town, and—"

"And your sister is going to drop you like a hot potato when the word gets out that she's the reason you've overstayed your welcome."

"I don't know who—"

I grabbed hold of his beard and pulled it off his red face. He plodded forward a step or two and raised both hands. I pushed them to the side and grabbed his red, fur-trimmed coat by the collar with both my hands. I thought, if I pulled hard enough, the coat would unbutton.

"No, no, don't, don't," he groaned just as I pulled with all my weight.

Instead of unbuttoning, the velcro seam simply opened, and he stood there in a strappy white t-shirt with a red cushion belted around his midsection. I spun him around, pulled the coat off, and then kicked him in the rear. He staggered forward into a Christmas tree. Just as the tree was about to fall, he grabbed onto a branch, staggered back, then tripped and fell to the floor, landing on his back in a pile of Christmas-wrapped boxes.

The ten-foot tree rocked back and forth. Arthur grabbed onto a lower branch and attempted to sit up. Suddenly, the giant star on the very top of the tree wiggled back and forth and fell off. Arthur watched it with wide eyes as it tumbled toward him. The star landed dead center in the middle of his forehead, exploding into a thousand pieces. Arthur's eyes crossed, then rolled up into his forehead, and he collapsed backward, bouncing his head off the concrete floor twice.

"Oh my God. Dev, are you okay?" Layla cried.

"Yeah, I'm fine, but he's not doing so well. Better call 911 and tell them Santa is unconscious."

While Layla made the call, I pulled off Arthur's black, patent leather boots and then pulled his red velvet trousers off. He was lying on the floor in his underwear with an image of the Grinch over the fly on his boxers and white knee-high stockings when the EMTs arrived. They undid the cushion strapped around his stomach and were lowering the gurney when the same two police officers that had come the day before entered.

"Don't tell me that's Santa Claus," one of the cops said as the EMTs hoisted underwear-clad Arthur onto the gurney.

"Yeah, he ran out here in his underwear and was screaming things we couldn't understand," I said.

"Both families that were here ran back outside," Layla said and gave me a look.

"He was staggering around and started to fall. He grabbed onto a branch on that Christmas tree and the decoration on the very top—"

"It was a star, a great big silver star," Layla said.

"Yeah, that thing just fell and landed right on his forehead. Next thing we know, he was out cold."

"The guy reeks of gin," one of the EMTs said.

"Yeah, we've reported him countless times, and they still won't fire him. I've got complaints from parents and from other employees. We even have pictures of him drinking on the job and a video of him staggering around here, and they still let him come back to work. He's frightened at least half of our customers away. It's an absolute shame," Layla said.

"Well, he'll be in the hospital at least overnight," one of the EMTs said.

"We'll give him a breathalyzer as soon as he wakes up," the older cop said.

Layla grinned. "Oh, you are so sweet. Thanks, guys. We really appreciate your help."

The EMTs wheeled Arthur out of the Workshop. The cops took a brief statement from Layla and me and then hurried out to catch up with the EMTs.

"Oh, man, I can only hope this puts the final nail in Arthur's coffin," I said.

"Dev, I don't want him dead. I just want him out of here."

"Well, like they said, he'll be in the hospital overnight, so you have the entire day to work with someone—"

"Oh, this is the perfect opportunity for you to step in, Dev. We've got families coming in today, and the Santa costume is right there. Please. Please say yes. If I have to go through the idiots in HR, it will take all day."

"Me, play Santa? Arthur was bad enough. But parents wouldn't want me anywhere near their children. It would be a big—"

"Please, Dev. Please. You're already here, and it will just take you a couple of minutes to get ready. Come on. I'll show you where the locker room is," she said and took my hand.

"Layla, I've got some things I have to do and—"

"Please, Dev. I'll make it very worth your while," she said and gave me a kiss.

"Mmm-mmm. Yeah, okay. Let me just pick up this beard and the suit."

"Thank you. I'll get the boots," she said and gave me another kiss. "Oh, and here, you'll need these," she said and handed me a package of Mentos mint candy.

Forty

The line was long, then again it was the dinner hour. I'd lost count of the number of kids I'd had on my lap. Layla led a little girl over to me. Her hair was done in braids, and she was wearing a frilly pink dress. I lifted her up onto my lap and said, "Thank you for coming to see me. What's your name?"

"I'm Melisa," she said.

"Yes, I thought that was you, but you've grown so much since last Christmas." She smiled at that. "Have you been good this year?"

She nodded and then pulled out a sheet of paper. "I made a list because I didn't want to forget anything."

"I think that's a very good idea. Can you read it to me?"

"I can. My mom says I'm a very good reader."

"Okay, you read it to me," I said. She read off a list of about twenty different things. I didn't know what half of the items even were. Once she finished, I said, "Do you want to give me the list?"

She shook her head, "No, I'm going to give this to my dad. Don't worry if you can't bring everything on my list. When I give this to my Dad, he'll make sure I get everything I want."

"He sounds like a very nice father."

She nodded and said, "He is."

I had a little boy who, among other things, said he would like a train set.

"What kind of train?"

"A locomotive, box cars, and a caboose."

"Okay, but now you need to know that, if I bring you a train set, your father may want to play with it, too."

He seemed to think about that for a moment and then said, "Maybe you could bring two train sets, and then he would have his own and not have to share with me."

"I think that's a good idea."

The Workshop was supposed to close at 7:30, but it wasn't until forty minutes later that the last two children left. While Layla locked the door and dimmed the lights, I sat on the Santa throne with my head back and my eyes closed, thinking of all the kids and the things they said and asked.

"Well, you survived," Layla said, climbing onto my lap.

"Oh, man. What an experience. Some of the things they asked for I'd never even heard of, but I enjoyed it. Well, except there was that one little boy who needed his diaper changed."

"Comes with the territory," she said.

"An exhausting day and worth every single minute. I loved it. All the kids on their best behavior. It was great. You hear anything from the HR department?"

"No, which is surprising. I called twice and was told they were in a meeting. That's never happened before."

"Maybe they finally got the message with the police here two days in a row and Arthur getting carted off to the hospital. Hopefully, the cops were able to give him a breathalyzer test."

"I'm just waiting to hear because that ornament fell on his head that we have to let him back."

"Well, I'm willing to adjust my schedule and fill in if you need someone."

"Oh, Dev, that would be wonderful," she said, then pulled my beard down and kissed me.

"It's only two more days, isn't it?"

"Actually, it's three. We're open Christmas Eve until 4:00."

"I think I can deal with that."

"Oh, thank you," she said and kissed me again. This time on the forehead. I hung up the Santa outfit in the locker room and changed back into my clothes. I escorted Layla up to the parking ramp on the top floor. I noted the fact that the glass on the door and the floor around the door had been cleaned. I opened the driver's door for her and stole another kiss, then watched until her car disappeared down the exit ramp.

I drove over to The Spot and had a beer with Louie, telling him stories about Arthur being hauled away and all the kids.

"You hear anything from that guy at the BCA?" Louie asked.

"Oh, God, with everything going on, I completely forgot. He was going to work on it last night, and I should have gotten a call sometime this morning. Oh man, I hope he didn't run into some kind of problem. That would just be par for the course on this thing. I'll probably get arrested for impersonating Santa Claus."

Louie laughed at that. I headed home and pulled into the garage. Everything looked okay, and the lights were dimmed in the kitchen when I stepped in. There was a plate covered in tinfoil with a note that read, 'Dinner for Dev. Remove tinfoil and microwave.' I removed the tinfoil and glanced at the pork chop, red peppers, and mashed potatoes. I placed the plate in the microwave, set the timer for one minute, and pressed 'Start.' While the microwave performed, I wandered out to the front room. Emmett was stretched out on the couch, reading a book. He was wearing his shoulder holster, and the HK 416 was on the floor within easy reach. He lowered the book as I stepped into the room.

"How'd everything go today, Emmett?"

"Hi, Dev. Everything was wonderfully boring. No problems."

"Did you see that car from yesterday? The one that made four passes?"

"No sign of it. We're keeping our eyes peeled all the same."

"Is Chuck back in the car?"

"No, he's downstairs at the moment. He's doing a walk around every so often. We've got someone else in the car tonight. Everything all right with you?"

"Yeah, interesting day." I gave him the short version then headed back into the kitchen. I debated having another beer or a glass of wine and decided against it. I inhaled dinner in about five minutes, put my plate in the dishwasher, turned it on, and then set the cereal boxes, plates, bowls, and silverware on the counter. I got the coffee pot ready and set the timer so it would turn on in the morning. I checked the locks on the front and back door along with the chain locks and headed up to bed. Morton was stretched out in front of the kids' room. I was asleep in about ninety seconds, dreaming of the kids today and the things they said.

The digital clock read 3:51 a.m. Something woke me, not a noise, maybe more like a sense. I jumped out of bed, pulled on my jeans and black t-shirt, stepped into my slippers, and pulled my Glock from the drawer in the bedside table.

I left the light off, but as I stepped out into the hall, Morton was already on his feet, looking through the stair rail. I hurried downstairs. It was dark, and I couldn't see anything, but I didn't want to turn on a light. The front porch light was on, and things appeared quiet.

"Emmett?" I whispered. I heard what sounded like his thumb snapping twice and stared where I thought the noise had come from. I could just catch his figure standing against the wall next to the front window. As I hurried toward him, a small light beam suddenly flashed through the front window and scanned the room. Someone was on the front porch.

Forty-one

Emmett whispered and signaled with his fingers, "There are two." He was wearing a set of ear-buds. Actually, just one earbud, the other hung down on his chest. "Chuck is in the kitchen and—" The light on the front porch suddenly went off. He reached up and pressed a button on the earphones twice then leaned over toward me and said, "Stand over on this side of the front door. Things are about to get crazy."

I nodded and stepped next to the hinges on the front door. The door was locked, and the chain door lock was in place. I looked back at Emmett. The light beam from outside was scanning back and forth in the front room again, apparently checking for someone or something. Suddenly the light went off. Emmett looked over at me and gave a slight nod. A moment later, I heard a noise coming from the lock cylinder on the front door. I snapped my finger at Emmett, and when he looked over, I pointed to the lock cylinder. He nodded.

It didn't take more than ninety seconds before the door lock clicked open. A moment later, the door opened no more than an inch. The chain was pulled but not quite taut. Suddenly, the chrome steel head on a pair of bolt cutters appeared and snapped the brass chain in half. I had the Glock pointed at head height. A gloved hand appeared on the edge of the door and began to open the door slowly. No doubt waiting to see if a security alarm sounded.

The door opened another two inches. I took a step back and kicked the door as hard as I could. A voice on the porch gave off a high-pitched scream as the gloved hand slammed between the door and the door frame. I shouldered the door as hard as I could, crashing it into the fingers of the gloved hand again. I tore the door open and grabbed the guy by his jacket, swinging my Glock as hard as I could across his forehead three times. He stumbled forward and landed face down on the floor, unconscious, with a puddle of blood spreading around his head.

Emmett brushed past me, stepped onto the front porch, and a second later, I heard a gunshot, followed by another heavier round being fired. Almost immediately, there were flashing red lights out on the icy street as three squad cars slid to a stop. I looked out the open door, and Emmett had his pistol pointed at a body twitching on the sidewalk leading up to the front porch.

I placed a knee on the back of the unconscious body on the floor and quickly searched for a weapon. Rolling him over on his back, I pulled a pistol from the front of his belt. I shoved his pistol into my belt and studied his forehead. I could actually see what I thought was his skull bone, although there was so much blood I couldn't be sure. I took hold of his ankles and dragged him out the front door and onto the porch. His head thumped, going over and off the oak threshold. I glanced back into the house, and there was a long bloody streak leading from the puddle on my polished oak floor and out the door.

"You okay" Emmet called.

"Yeah. You?"

"Fine, just fine."

"Did he shoot at you? I heard two shots."

"No, he picked up on the red laser sight dot and fired across the street. No real choice for our guy except to fire back," he said and chuckled.

Two EMT vehicles arrived. Both men were pulled onto gurneys, and the EMTs began to wheel them away. Before they left, Chuck joined us out front, and he and Emmett did a more thorough search of both individuals. The guy I'd dragged out of the house was now conscious, or maybe semi-conscious would be a better term. From what I could hear, he was still pretty incoherent. Going back inside, I grabbed a sponge and a bucket. A couple of cops asked me questions as I attempted to sponge up the blood in the entry as best I could. Then I walked into the kitchen, turned on the coffee pot, and got a bunch of mugs out.

Tommy Bishop arrived thirty minutes later. When I took him upstairs, Morton gave a growl toward Bishop, and I let Morton into the kids' room. Christine was in the room holding a gun. She rushed toward Tommy and began to sob quietly as he wrapped his arms around her and kissed her.

Aaron LaZelle arrived and took charge. Emmett, Chuck, and I gave brief recorded interviews. Each one lasted around fifteen minutes. Aaron gathered up the billfolds, the bolt cutters, and the weapons we'd taken from the two guys. Everything was placed in evidence bags. Two BCA officers were parked out front photographing the front porch, the front door, and the blood stains in my entryway.

We were close to the end of the second pot of coffee when Tommy and Christine came into the kitchen. Christine was dressed, but her eyes were still red and puffy from crying. I thought maybe Tommy had climbed into bed with her, but it turned out she'd made him stand guard outside the door until she was sure the kids were back asleep.

Gradually, people left. Two uniformed officers remained, and a squad car was parked on the street. A couple of news people showed up, but an officer out front read them a formal statement and made it pretty clear there would be nothing to see.

At 9:00, I drove down to the station for a more formal interview. I got a handshake from the two officers at the front desk and was led up to the third floor by one of them. He led me down the hallway past Homicide and into Interview Room Two. Detective Manning and Aaron were seated at a table along with Denny Jackson, a detective in Special Investigations I'd met a few times. He'd been in the interview room up in Special Investigations when Bishop asked if I'd be willing to take the Hogan kids.

"Thanks for coming down, Dev," Aaron said. "Because of our conversation earlier this morning, Detective Jackson will be in charge of your interview. Merely a formality, but we want to have all the t's crossed and the i's dotted. Grab a seat. This shouldn't take long."

Jackson started with the normal format. I was there of my own choice. I understood the ramifications of the interview, and on and on. I gave my version of the night's events. How I woke up and checked things out. Morton was up and growling. I left the lights off and went downstairs. Emmett was standing in the dark, and someone was shining a flashlight through the front window.

"Did you call the police?" Jackson asked.

"There really wasn't time, and I was afraid if I called, whoever was outside might be able to hear me, and they would shoot into the house. Besides, I had two officers in the house with me."

"Were you aware other officers were in the vicinity?"

"Other than Emmett and Chuck in the house, I had no idea, but I was awfully glad to see them. There is no doubt in my mind those two guys were on a mission to kill the Hogan kids and anyone else in the house, including Christine Bishop and me. They weren't going to leave if I turned on the lights or told them to leave. There was no time for a warning. I couldn't have been out of bed more than three or four minutes, and the guy who picked the lock was opening the front door."

He asked three or four other routine questions and then thanked me for my time and brought the interview to a close. Once the recording equipment was off, I asked, "What can you tell me about these two guys?"

Aaron leaned forward and said, "Both have long records from out east. They've done substantial time, been involved in a series of incidents, and they're connected to the New Jersey mob. You're all very lucky to be alive. Once they're out of the hospital, they'll be held, tried, and convicted."

"Are they part of Chillcot's gang?"

Aaron glanced around the table for a brief moment and then said, "No way to prove it at this point, but I would say that's a pretty safe bet."

"You're aware that he's running an illegal operation on the third floor of his home, aren't you?"

"We are, and this incident at your home has sped up the investigation of that particular operation."

"But you're still investigating?"

"We have to follow the law, Dev. You know as well as we do that we can't just go in there without a warrant and actual proof that they're operating illegally."

I bit my tongue for a moment and simply nodded, then said, "Just curious, but what were the names of those two guys last night?"

"The gentleman who picked the lock is Michael Morelli. You'll be interested to know he is, or at least was as of 8:00 this morning, comatose, and three of the four fingers on his right hand are damaged to the point of needing amputation. The individual who was shot, Dexter Zeller, is currently on life support."

"Hopefully, they'll decide to pull the plug," I said. "Anything else you need?"

Aaron glanced around the table and then said, "No, Dev. Thank you for coming down."

"And thanks for being there last night," Jackson said. "Christine and Tommy Bishop have had the door open for all of us. We've always been welcome in their home, and we won't forget what you did to save her and those kids."

"Well, don't forget Emmett and Chuck. God bless those two."

The three of them walked me out of the room, and after handshakes, Manning escorted me down to the main floor. We were alone on the elevator, and once the doors closed, he turned and said, "Two new officers will be replacing Emmett Casey and Chuck Steiner."

"They're not in any trouble, are they? If it wasn't for them, I'd be in the morgue right now."

"Just policy, they're getting a break and on desk duty. Believe me, we're proud of both of them and you, too." The doors opened, and he escorted me out to the lobby. We shook hands, and Manning said, "Glad you're okay, Haskell. Hell of a fine job. Well done."

Forty-two

I drove back home and parked in the driveway. A squad car was parked out front with an officer in it. Two uniformed officers were sitting at the kitchen counter, talking with Christine and drinking coffee. Bryn was sitting on one of the guy's lap. I recognized both of them, but I was drawing a blank on their names.

"Hi guys, I'm Dev Haskell. No, no, stay seated, relax. Hey, I know we've met before, but in my old age, I've forgotten your names."

"Carey Rustad," the blonde guy said and held out his hand.

"Ed McCormick, nice to meet you again. Glad things went your way last night. If you don't mind me saying."

"Not a problem, and thanks for being here today."

"You kidding? Coffee, breakfast, a pretty girl like Bryn talking to me. What could be better?"

Bryn smiled and snuggled in a little closer.

"Well, if you'll excuse me, I'm going to change and head down to the office. You guys are going to stay here?"

They both nodded. "They've got a new team from Special Investigations coming in sometime later today. We heard everyone in Homicide and Special Investigations volunteered," Rustad said.

"That's because of Christine's cooking," McCormick added.

"Yeah, well, I knew it wouldn't be because of me. I'm going upstairs to change. If you need anything, Christine is in charge. Are the boys around?"

Christine nodded, "They're in the den with Morton."

"I'll pop my head in." I walked out of the kitchen and looked in the den. Rowan and Kevin had beach towels tied around their necks, and they appeared to be pretending they were flying. Morton had a beach towel around his neck, but he was on the couch, standing on his towel and bobbing his head back and forth. I said, "Hi guys," and both kids waved but kept running in a circle.

I stepped out of the den and headed toward the stairs. A throw rug was covering most of the bloodstain on the entryway floor. That was probably Christine's idea to cover it up, which was great since the thought had never occurred to me. Up in my bedroom, I took off my button-down shirt and pulled on a sweatshirt. I changed my shoes to a more comfortable pair and headed back downstairs. I chatted in the kitchen for a couple of minutes, and then Christine said, "Go on, get down to your office. We're fine here."

Louie's car was nowhere to be seen, so I parked in my usual spot and hurried up to the office. At no surprise, the coffee was still on, and the pot held about a sixteenth of an inch. I turned the burner off and set the pot in the sink. I settled in at my desk, pulled out my cell phone, and called Tubby Gustafson.

The phone rang only once before the creep answered, "Are you calling to speak with Mister Gustafson?"

I was tempted to say I wanted a large sausage pizza with extra cheese, but instead, I just said, "Yes."

"One moment, and I'll connect you."

It was three rings before Tubby picked up. "Are you okay, Haskell?"

"Yeah, I'm fine, just fine."

"I heard you had an interesting early morning."

To my knowledge, there hadn't been a news report. Even if there was, my name and address wouldn't have been mentioned. It probably meant that someone in the police department had given Tubby the information, and it wasn't even noon.

"Well, fortunately, things went our way. I wanted to let you know that the two individuals who attempted to break in have extensive records back east. Their names are Michael Morelli and Dexter Zeller."

"And they're hospitalized, right?"

"Yeah, Zeller's on life support. He was shot. Morelli was still semi-comatose as of 8:00 this morning. He's the one who picked the lock on my front door. I was able to stop him. I damaged three of the fingers on his right hand to the point where they'll probably have to be amputated."

Tubby chuckled and said, "Sounds like you ended his career."

"I wish I'd ended his life. The cops have no definitive proof that either piece of shit is associated with Chillcot, but they're pretty sure that's the case."

Tubby muttered something just under his breath and said, "I'm positive that's the case. Well, I'm glad you're okay and that everyone is safe and sound. The children are all right?"

I was about to answer and then remembered I'd never told Tubby about the Hogan kids. In fact, I hadn't told anyone. "I don't have any children. I've never married, sir."

Tubby chuckled and said, "Yeah, okay, Haskell. Hope you have a good night's sleep tonight. Don't let the bed bugs bite."

"You, too, sir," I said, and Tubby hung up.

I spent the next half-hour looking online for anything and everything about Michael Morelli and Dexter Zeller. Morelli was forty-three, originally from Fairfield, New Jersey. There were a half-dozen images of him, and they more or less matched what I remembered he looked like, although his face had been covered in blood when I rolled him over and dragged him out of the house. If I'd been thinking, I would have pulled off his jacket in the hope that he'd die of exposure. He'd been in and out of jail from the time he was sixteen when he was tried as an adult for assault.

Dexter Zeller was forty-six and had a similar background. He was from Paterson, New Jersey. No mention of family. He'd been a ward of the state up until he turned eighteen. He received a dishonorable discharge from the Army a year later, and from there, he'd been in and out of jail for the next twenty-five years. There were three photos of Zeller. None of them suggested he would be the sort of person you'd want to strike up a conversation with. His pictures showed a serious scar on the left side of his face from roughly the middle of his ear down to almost the tip of his chin.

Louie was back in the office just as I was headed out the door to Santa's Workshop. He asked how things were going. I just said, "Fine," and didn't add anything else. I was concerned for two reasons. First, I didn't want to mention the Hogan kids. Second, I wanted to keep Louie safe, and I figured the best way was to keep any and all information to myself.

Forty-three

Santa's Workshop was busy all afternoon, and once again, at the 7:30 closing time, there was still a line of parents and kids. It took another half-hour, but everyone got to tell me what they wanted for Christmas. Layla was pleasant but a little standoffish. We chatted for a couple of minutes and then went our separate ways. I couldn't tell if it was her or me that had cooled things down, but after the early morning break-in and eight hours of playing Santa, I wasn't just tired, I was exhausted, and I headed home.

There was still a squad car parked in front of the house, and I waved at the officer as I entered the driveway and parked in the garage. I stepped into the kitchen. Christine was seated at the counter eating dinner, a pork chop and some roasted red and yellow peppers. There was a guy standing next to her, sipping from a coffee mug.

As I stepped in, she looked over and said, "Oh, Dev, I was beginning to wonder. Pork chop and peppers on the stove for you. They should still be warm."

The guy set his mug down and extended his hand. "Hi, Mr. Haskell. My name is Jim Walters. My partner, Pat Leary, and I are with Special Investigations, and we'll be taking over for Emmett Casey and Chuck Steiner. Pat's in another room reading. It's a pleasure to meet you, and we both want to thank you for your involvement earlier this morning."

"Nice to meet you. Thank you for being here."

"You kidding? We won the lottery. I'm not fooling. Everyone in our section wanted to be here, well, plus we all know about Christine's cooking."

"Oh, stop," Christine said.

"No, I get it. You're absolutely right, Jim. No offense, but I hope you guys are bored out of your mind while you're here."

"That would be just fine with me. Pat's reading a book to the kids. When he found out we got this assignment, he went out and bought a kid's book series, The Misadventures of Michael McMichaels. He wants to read them a story every night. He'll be on duty during the day shift, and I've got the nights."

"How long is that squad car going to be out front?"

"Is that a problem? After those idiots attempting to break in this morning ended up in the hospital, a squad car out front would probably go a long way in giving anyone else second thoughts."

"Oh, God no, it's not a problem. In fact, let me just run out now and see if he'd like some coffee. Is there any left?"

"Pot's half full," Walters said.

Christine nodded toward the refrigerator. "We've got another pork chop I could cook up for him if he wants it."

"I'll ask him," I said as I filled a coffee mug and headed toward the front door. The kids were in the den sitting on the floor with Detective Leary. Bryn was on his lap, and they were all focused on the book Leary was reading. Morton appeared to be asleep on the floor next to them. I didn't want to interrupt and headed for the front door.

I glanced out the front window and checked the street. There was some light traffic, but it was cold, and I couldn't see anyone walking. I stepped onto the front porch, closed and locked the door behind me, and walked down the steps. It was dark, and I looked left and right over my shoulder a few times as I approached the squad car.

The officer saw me coming and lowered the window on the passenger side. Once again, he looked familiar, but I couldn't recall his name. He leaned toward me and smiled.

"Hey, just wanted to thank you for being out here tonight. Can I talk you into some coffee?" I said and extended my hand with the steaming mug.

"I'd love it," he said and took the cup from my hand.

"We've got a pork chop we can cook up for you if you'd like."

"Oh, thanks, but I'm dining on health food," he said then laughed and nodded toward the McDonalds bag and wrappers on the passenger seat.

"Okay, just give a yell if you want anything or need to use the bathroom."

"Much appreciated, and thanks for the coffee," he said.

I hurried back up onto the porch. The porch light was still off, and I reached up into the light fixture. I felt the lightbulb and turned it to the right, tightening it. The light suddenly flashed on, and the officer in the squad car tooted the horn a couple of times. I waved and stepped inside the house. I hung my jacket in the kitchen and started to get things ready for the morning.

"Stop. You are not doing that tonight. I'll get things ready," Christine said. "Why don't you quietly head on up to your room and lie down? You look tired, Dev."

Suddenly, a wave of exhaustion seemed to wash over me. It was as if Christine had given me the okay to feel exhausted. "You sure? I can—"

"No, you can't, Dev. Now, I'm going to sound like I'm talking to one of the kids, and just maybe I am. You need to go upstairs and lie down. Anything happens, we'll let you know."

"I think—"

"No, don't think. You need to rest while you can, Dev. Good night."

"Thanks, Christine. Okay, good night and sweet dreams," I said and headed up to bed. I settled down on the bed and closed my eyes, thinking a quick nap would work.

The loud noise seemed to echo as it woke me from my sleep. At first, I wondered if it had been a dream, but the mirror above my dresser had vibrated. I distinctly heard it. It was 3:27 on my digital alarm clock. I was still dressed, and after standing and straining my ears, I grabbed the Glock from the bedside table and stepped out of the bedroom in my stocking feet. The hall light was on. Morton was on his feet in the hallway. He gave me a look just as I heard the door down the hall open. I turned as Christine stepped out of the bedroom, tying the belt on her white terrycloth robe.

"You heard that, too? I thought maybe I had dreamed it," she said.

From downstairs, I heard the voices of Walters and Leary. "No, it wasn't here. It was some distance away. Squad, this is security. Over."

Whatever the response on the radio was, it was garbled, and I couldn't make it out.

"Stay up here, Christine, and I'll go downstairs." I walked over to the light switch and turned off the hall light. "I don't know what that noise was, but I don't think it was in the house."

"It sounded, I don't know, distant, maybe."

Walters and Leary were in the front room, staring out the window. Walters was dressed, and Leary was wearing boxers, a blue t-shirt with St. Paul Police in white letters across his chest, and a shoulder holster.

"You guys heard it too?" I asked. "What the hell was that?"

"Not sure," Leary said. "All we know is it wasn't here."

Walters was wearing a set of earbuds. "Explosion over on Summit Avenue. Hell of an explosion," he said.

"Maybe a gas leak?" Leary asked.

Walters just shrugged. I could hear the sound of a distant siren. The squad car was still parked in front of the house, but the computer screen illuminated the front seat, and I could make out the officer behind the wheel tapping on his keyboard.

"Explosion at 441 Summit Avenue," Walters said and pressed both earbuds a little deeper into his ears.

"441? That's Chillcot's address."

"Are you sure?" Leary said.

"Yeah, positive. I saw guys there the other night unloading a craps table and a roulette wheel. They got it out of the gambling site above Sweeny's Auto Repair down on Jackson Street. The guy who was running the joint, Leroy Ross, was shot outside the building."

They both nodded, and Walters said, "Sounds like they're calling every fire station on this end of town."

"Well, look at that," Leary said and nodded at the window. The two-story building across the street was closed, but above the roof of the building was an orange glow, and even though it was the middle of the night and four blocks away, we could make out plumes of smoke and sparks rising up to the sky. Sirens, and there were a number of them, were loud. Two fire trucks raced past, heading east. They slowed and took a right at the corner.

"I'm going to check it out," I said.

Leary looked at me and then said, "Okay, just be careful and phone me when you get there. Things are going to be jammed. You'll probably get there faster if you walk."

"Thanks," I said and hurried upstairs.

"What's going on?" Christine asked. She was standing at the top of the stairs with Morton at her side.

"Are the kids okay?"

"Sound asleep. What happened?"

"An explosion at Chillcot's house over on Summit Avenue. Fire trucks from all over town are on the way. You can see the smoke and sparks from the fire rising in the sky. I'm going to go over there and check it out."

"Do you think that's a good idea?"

"The place will be flooded with police. Walters and Leary are staying here. The squad car is still parked in front, so you and the kids will be okay."

She nodded and said, "Promise me you'll be careful."

"I promise. Scouts honor," I said and held up my hand.

I stepped into my room and put on a pair of hiking boots. I slipped the Glock into my shoulder holster and went back downstairs. I grabbed a pair of leather gloves and a black stocking cap from the first-floor closet, slipped on my jacket, and stepped out the front door. I told the officer in the squad car where I was going and then hurried across the street in the direction of Chillcot's place.

Forty-four

Before I was close enough to see it I could hear and smell the fire. The street I was on, Arundel, was blocked off by a squad car, and I had to walk east for another block and then head south two more blocks before I reached Summit Avenue. The street was blocked at the corner of Western Avenue, but Overlook Park was just across Summit, and right now, it was filled with people watching the fire. I could see three fire trucks, and I was pretty sure there were more. What remained of the roof on Chillcot's place was engulfed in flames. Fire crews were on ladders attached to trucks as well as on the ground. They were all aiming hoses into the mansion where the roof used to be. From what I could tell, their efforts were having little, if any, effect on subduing the fire.

I checked the crowd for Layla but didn't see her. I recognized a few people, and over the course of the next half-hour, I asked if they knew what had caused the blaze. Three people mentioned the explosion I'd heard, but no one had any thoughts as to the cause of the explosion. The people I spoke to seemed to be unaware of the gambling operation.

After nearly an hour, the fire was still roaring. Flames could now be seen in the windows of rooms on the first floor, and fire crews were spraying water through the smashed bulletproof glass windows with the wrought iron burglar bars.

I had the sense that the firefighters had gone from attempting to extinguish it to simply maintaining a perimeter control of the blaze. People were leaving the crowd, and I joined them, walking home along Western Avenue with a number of other folks.

I talked to the officer in the squad car in front of the house. When we'd finished, he handed me the empty coffee mug Leary had brought out to him. Leary, Walters, and Christine were in the kitchen eating pancakes. Leary was now dressed in a gray sweatshirt and sweatpants. Christine placed three pancakes on a plate and set it in front of me while I told them what little I knew.

"When I left, I could see flames burning on the first floor. The roof over the entire house was gone, and the rear portion of the third floor had collapsed. I think at this point, the fire crew is just controlling the fire from spreading to surrounding structures, but the place is going to be a total loss."

"Based on the damage you're describing, this doesn't sound like a gas leak," Leary said.

"What else could it be? We all heard the explosion. In fact, we felt it," I said.

"A bomb?" Leary wondered.

"Sounds like that's entirely possible," Walters answered. "Be interesting to see if they find anything in the rubble. I would guess we had someone recording license plate numbers of people there earlier tonight. What time did that explosion occur, 3:30?"

"My digital said 3:27."

"I think they'd close the gambling down around 3:00, 4:00 at the latest. I'm guessing they weren't all that eager to attract neighborhood attention. So much for that thought after waking everyone up in the middle of the night," Walters laughed.

I suddenly recalled Tubby's earlier line about having a good night's sleep and don't let the bed bugs bite. "Well, they've got the entire city's attention now. It was interesting talking to the couple of folks I knew watching the fire. None of them had any idea of a gambling operation going on there."

"Par for the course," Leary said. "Say what you will about this Chillcot, but he knew what he was doing with regard to setting up the gambling operation."

"If you gentlemen will excuse me, I'm going to send a text message to my husband telling him we're all okay, and then I'm going back to bed. I've got a busy day ahead of me," Christine said.

"Yeah, I'm going to try to grab some sleep, too," I told them and followed Christine upstairs. Morton was stretched out in front of the kids' room. He opened one eye as we stepped into the hallway, recognized us, and went back to sleep.

I stepped into my room and suddenly felt exhausted again. I placed the Glock back in the top drawer of the bedside table. Pulled my shoulder holster off, set it on the dresser, and decided not to set the alarm on my clock. I tossed my jeans and shirt on the end of the bed and crawled under the covers.

It was after 9:00 when I finally woke up. I grabbed a quick shower, pulled on the same clothes I'd worn yesterday, and headed downstairs. The kids were involved in some cartoon on the TV in the den. I called, "Good morning," and got a couple of nods in return.

The coffee was on in the kitchen, and Christine was on the phone placing an order for something. I poured a cup of coffee and walked into the front room. Leary was seated on the couch watching a local news channel.

"Anything on last night's fire?" I asked and took a large sip of coffee.

"Nothing we didn't already know. You were right. The place is listed as a total loss. No word as to the cause of the fire, although they did mention an explosion. Investigators are on the scene now, but God only knows what, if anything, they'll be able to find."

My cell phone suddenly rang. I set my coffee mug on the fireplace mantel and pulled the phone out. Jim Dugan with the BCA. "Hi, Jim, sorry I haven't called. I completely forgot about getting in touch with you." I went on to tell him about Arthur Soto. I cleaned up the story quite a bit and eliminated me telling Arthur to get out of the Workshop. I did tell him about drunken Soto falling down and the star ornament falling from the top of the tree and knocking him out. I mentioned that I was filling in as Santa Claus and taking his place.

"Well, then it's probably a good thing Christmas Eve is tomorrow. Your man Soto has been arrested and—"

"Arrested? You mean they finally got the message that he was drinking on the job and ruining Christmas for all sorts of kids?"

"Not exactly. It turns out to be a little more serious than that. There was a liquor store robbery back in 2018. The owner of the store, a man named Sonny Rosinni, was murdered. He'd been struck on the back of the head with a liquor bottle, the cash register was emptied, and a case of gin was stolen. We got the fingerprints from the bottle but never found a match until you brought in that mason jar. Suddenly, we had a perfect match on a thumb and three fingers. Your friend Mr. Soto will be charged the day after Christmas with that murder."

"Really? Oh, that's wonderful. Oh, Jim, you made my day, and it's not even 10:00. I have to ask, how come there wasn't a record on Soto? No fingerprints?"

"Basically, because he's never done anything. He wasn't in the service. Never really traveled or did any-thing other than drink and be a pain in the ass for his entire life. But his prints on that mason jar matched the prints on the gin bottle that was used to kill Rosinni."

"You know, in a way, it's not surprising. He's never done anything, well, except ruin Christmas for lots of kids. Thanks for the good news, Jim."

"Thanks for the mason jar, Dev."

"Sounded like some good news, " Leary said.

"Yeah, surprisingly good news," I agreed and went on to tell him the story. I said goodbye to the kids, still deeply involved in the cartoon, and headed down to the office. I was going to drive past Chillcot's place, but the street was still blocked off. Louie was already in the office, so I told him about the fire and Arthur Soto being arrested for murder.

"I don't know, Dev. Two big wins like that, and it's not even noon. Maybe this is the day you should buy a lottery ticket."

"Yeah, I'm trying to think of a faster way to ruin my good luck."

"You doing the Santa gig again today?"

"Yeah. Just today and only a half-day tomorrow, on Christmas Eve, and then I'll be finished."

"You spending Christmas with Layla?"

"She hasn't mentioned it, and I don't want to push her."

Forty-five

I was in the locker room and had just strapped the red cushion around my midsection. I was pulling up Santa's red velvet trousers when Layla said, "Oh, you're here. I didn't know if you'd be coming in."

I didn't ask what she was doing in the men's locker room. I was just glad to see her. "I'm bound and determined to finish this up tomorrow and tell as many kids as possible that they're going to get whatever they want for Christmas. You know, Layla, this has been hard work. I'm really beat when I go home at night, but it has been so worth it. All these little kids, real believers, I don't want to let them down."

"Well, I'm just glad you took matters into your own hands and got rid of Arthur."

"Oh, speaking of which. I got a call from a friend at the BCA this morning."

"The BCA?" she gave me quizzical a look.

"The state's Bureau of Criminal Apprehension. At the suggestion of a detective friend, I took Arthur's mason jar to the BCA, and they got his fingerprints."

"Oh, good. So now, if, or rather when, the HR department questions us, we can tell them Arthur's fingerprints are all over that jar, and he was drinking just like we told them a dozen times before."

"Well, yeah, but I don't think they're going to be questioning us."

"Dev, with everything we've given them so far, and they've always managed to find a way around it, believe me, they'll question us."

"Well, here's the other part. Apparently, Arthur had never been fingerprinted. He was never in the military. He'd never held a job where they did a background investigation. Actually, I'm not sure he ever really held any job, but, they did find a match to his fingerprints."

"What? How?"

"A liquor store robbery a few years ago, in 2018. The owner of the store was murdered, and whoever did it took the money from the cash register and stole a case of gin. Turns out the fingerprints on the mason jar were an exact match to the fingerprints on the bottle that the owner was hit with, and surprise, surprise, they were Arthur's."

"He actually killed someone, and he was here playing Santa Claus?"

"Compliments of the HR department and Arthur's sister on the City Council."

"Oh. My. God," Layla said. She stepped forward, tugged on the red cushion strapped around me, and said, "Promise me you'll never get this fat, for real."

"I promise," I said.

The line of kids never stopped. We had kids all afternoon long and then for another forty minutes after the official closing time. When we were finally finished, and it was just the two of us, I was still seated on the Santa throne with the large candy canes on either side. Layla climbed onto my lap and said, "Are you going to ask me what I want for Christmas?"

"Oh, yeah, of course. I've just been waiting for the right moment. Umm, what would you like for Christmas, Layla?"

Her eyes welled up with tears, and she said, "I want you to tell me the truth about the woman you have staying at your house. If there's someone else, I can accept that. I just need to know." Her eyes watered, and she looked about to cry.

"What?"

"Don't lie to me, Dev. I know she's there. I drove past the other night on the way home, and I saw the two of you at your front window."

I closed my eyes, exhaled, and thought for a moment. "Okay, I'll tell you, but you can't tell anyone about this. All right?"

She leaned back, studied me for a moment, and then said, "What? Is she your wife?"

I laughed and said, "No, she's not my wife. Here's the deal, you remember a while back when the FBI agent and his wife were murdered downtown?"

"Yes, I remember. It was awful. She was pregnant, and they'd just been to the obstetrician's office."

"Yeah, their last name was Hogan. It hasn't been proven yet, but it's suspected they were murdered on orders from a gangster named Alex Chillcot. Anyway, the Hogan's had three children, two boys and a little girl. The children have been hiding at my house with Christine Bishop, who is the wife of a St. Paul cop named Tommy Bishop. The Hogan's were friends of theirs, and there is a real fear that Chillcot and his gang will try to kill the children. As a matter of fact, two men attempted to break into my house a couple of nights ago."

"What happened? Did you chase them away?"

"Something like that. I'm pretty sure they won't be back. But the kids are still hiding at my place. Now, you are the only person, aside from some police officers, who know they're there. You can't tell anyone. You can't mention it. And I shouldn't have told you to begin with."

"This, this is so crazy. So you're telling me that you're protecting these children? You, Dev Haskell. A person who has never had children. A person who spends his nights in a bar called The Spot. Out of all the people in town, somehow, they chose you. Really?"

"Well, me and a number of people. Not the least of whom is this woman who is watching over them and all sorts of police officers."

"But how long is this supposed to last?"

"Until we know they'll be safe. Now things may have changed recently for this bad guy, Alex Chillcot.

So maybe things will get better sooner rather than later. We'll just have to see."

"Oh, and then this woman will move out of your place, and what? Go back to her husband? Gee, thank you for telling me. I never would have guessed," she said and climbed off my lap. She stared at me for a long moment and then walked toward the 'Employees Only' door.

"Hey, Layla, wait a minute. I think you've got this all wrong. I'm just helping look after the kids, and I—"

"Actually, Dev. I think I get it," she said, then pushed the 'Employees Only' door open and disappeared.

I thought about going after her, but then what? Tell her the same thing again? Take her to my place so she could see the kids? No, if she wasn't going to believe me, there wasn't much I could do. Maybe she'd calm down overnight.

I stopped at the grocery store on the way home and picked up two packages of cinnamon rolls and a bottle of nonalcoholic champagne. I made it home just in time to get one of Christine's delicious cheeseburgers made with Swiss cheese and caramelized onions. I think I devoured half the bowl of her homemade barbecue potato chips. For dessert, Walters had a patrol car drop off a half-gallon of peppermint ice cream. We had to share with the kids, but it was still delicious.

I was tired and went to bed just before 10:00. Once again, Morton was stretched out in front of the kids' room. Christine had been on the phone for most of the evening, and once the kids were in bed, she went to her room.

Forty-six

My alarm hadn't gone off yet when I climbed out of bed. I showered and dressed, all the while trying to be as quiet as possible. I tiptoed downstairs. Morton opened his eyes and watched as I passed him but didn't make an effort to follow. It was Christmas Eve morning. I put the coffee on, prepared eggs for cheese omelets for the adults, and put the cinnamon rolls in the oven. While they baked, I mixed up a bowl of sugar frosting.

I had just taken the rolls out of the oven when Christine came into the kitchen in her bathrobe and fuzzy slippers. "Dev? What are you doing up this early?"

"Getting things ready for breakfast. You're not cooking this morning. It's Christmas Eve, and you get to be off for at least the breakfast hour. You can even go back up to bed if you want."

"Oh, thanks. That's so nice of you, but I've got a very busy day."

"Yeah. I'm sorry, but with everything going on, those two idiots the other night, then that house burning down, and all the Santa Claus stuff. All of a sudden,

Christmas is here, and I haven't gotten a tree, and I need to run out and get presents for the kids, and I—"

"Dev, relax. The kids are taken care of. They're going to have a wonderful Christmas."

"But I haven't done anything. I've still got a bowl of Halloween candy on the counter, for God's sake."

"Will you relax? Trust me. We have a very special Christmas planned, and you're going to play a big part in it."

"Well, can I at least get you a glass of champagne? It's nonalcoholic, unfortunately."

"That would be perfect, thank you."

I made an omelet for her, dished it up, and placed a cinnamon roll on the plate. While she sipped the champagne, I set the plate in front of her and said, "How's the champagne?"

"Nonalcoholic," she answered, and we both laughed. I filled a coffee mug and set it next to her plate. I made omelets and cinnamon rolls for Walters and Leary. They both took a pass on the champagne.

When the kids came in, I set plates in front of them with cinnamon rolls. I gave each one a table knife and let them frost their own rolls. I think the frosting was a half-inch thick on each roll, and they licked their table knives clean. I insisted on cleaning the kitchen. Christine went off to take care of whatever her latest task was. The kids settled in front of the TV. Walters went to bed, and Leary went into the front room.

I arrived in the office after 10:00. Louie was already at his picnic table, and there was a six-pack of Summit beer with a big red bow sitting on my desk.

"Louie, God bless you, but you didn't have to do this. I'm sorry, but I wasn't even thinking of Christmas gifts. I've had so many things going on and—"

"Dev, relax. I understand. Whatever you're involved in must be very important. You don't need to tell me. I just want to know that you're okay and somewhat sane."

"Well, I'm okay. But I'm not sure about the sane part."

"That'll do," Louie said. We gossiped for a couple of hours, and then it was time for me to head to the Workshop. For once, there weren't any parking places in front of the building, so I parked on the top level of the parking ramp. I got suited up in the men's locker room, half-hoping Layla would come in, but that never happened. When I stepped into the Workshop, there was a woman dressed in an elf costume, but it wasn't Layla.

"Oh, so you're the replacement Santa I've heard so much about. Thank God! My name is Denise, by the way. It's wonderful to meet you," she said and held out her hand.

"Nice to meet you, Denise. Thanks for the kind words. Is Layla around?"

"No, she called in. I guess she's got a flu bug. Wouldn't you know, and on Christmas Eve, too. Honest to God. I only got the call from HR less than an hour ago.

Thank goodness I had my elf costume back from the cleaners. Say, there's already a line waiting outside. What do you say we get started?"

"Oh, yeah, sure. I think that's a good idea," I said and assumed my position on the Santa throne while Denise hurried over to unlock the door.

There was a non-stop line for the next two hours. Things started to thin out after that. I guessed families were getting ready for Christmas Eve. All of a sudden, Tommy Bishop was hurrying up the path past the Christmas trees and the cardboard fireplace.

"Tommy, is everything okay? The kids? Christine? Is there a problem?"

"Everything's fine, Dev. I'm just going to need your help with something."

"Yeah, sure. What is it?"

He told me then stepped back, looked at me, and said, "Dev, are you okay?"

"Oh, I'm…I'm yeah, believe me. I'm fine. Happy to help. Thank you."

"Back in a bit," he said and hurried down the path.

It was almost closing time. We hadn't had any visitors for the past fifteen minutes. Denise was checking her watch every three or four minutes. I was wondering about Tommy Bishop when he and Christine suddenly appeared with the three children all dressed up and holding hands. They made their way up the path. Once Bryn saw me dressed as Santa, she began to hold back, but her brothers picked up speed and then stopped in front of Denise.

"Well, hello, and Merry Christmas. Are you here to see Santa?" All three children nodded but didn't speak. Denise took Bryn by the hand and said, "Well, let's go see Santa. He's waiting just for you. Come on."

She led them toward me, and as they approached, I said, "Ho, ho, ho. I was hoping I'd see you. Now let me see Rowan, Kevin, and Bryn. Is that right?"

All three nodded and stood there wide-eyed and staring.

"Well, come on. Don't be afraid. Tell me what you'd like for Christmas. Come on," I said and patted my thigh. Bryn suddenly hurried over and jumped up onto my leg. Kevin jumped up on my other leg. Rowan remained standing but snuggled in next to his sister. They each gave me a laundry list of gift items. Dolls, and a dollhouse for Bryn. Kevin wanted a dinosaur truck and a dinosaur helmet. Rowan wanted a battery-operated race car. And then, when they were finally finished, Rowan looked at me with a tear in his eye and said, "Santa, can you help us? We really want a mom and dad."

I looked at each one of them. I suddenly felt a lump in my throat and cleared it once or twice. "Well, now. It's funny you should ask because I have a present for all of you. A very special gift for you. Are you ready?"

They nodded, and now all four of us looked about ready to cry. "My special gift is you're going to be a family, with a mom and dad. Here is your new mom and dad," I said as Tommy and Christine hurried forward. Christine reached down and grabbed Bryn and Tommy hugged Rowan and Kevin. Now there were six of us with tears running down our cheeks, make that seven as Denise's mascara dripped down her face.

Once we calmed down, Tommy said, "We'd like to have you over for Christmas Eve dinner at our place. The kids will be sleeping there from now on and—"

"Tommy, this is wonderful, but will they be safe? Will you and Christine?"

"We've got it on good authority that Mr. Chillcot won't be a problem."

"You sure about that? I mean he—"

"Yes, he apparently left before the fire and won't be coming back. I guess he found the city was not to his liking."

It was possibly the best Christmas Eve ever. The Bishops' house was decorated with a tree and lights. The boys had their own bedroom with brand new bunk beds, and Bryn had a pink room with a pink bed right next to Christine and Tommy's bedroom.

As it turned out, the children were officially placed in foster care with the Bishops. Tommy and Christine had begun adoption proceedings and were on the fast track to getting that completed.

I got home around 10:00 that night. The house was spotless. All the books and toys had been transferred to the Bishops' house. My bed, the beds in the guest room, and what had been Christine's room had clean sheets.

The cots were out of the basement. Morton was focused on his pillow in the kitchen with a new chew toy. A bottle of wine, a plate of Christmas cookies, and a note from Christine were on the kitchen counter. I opened the note. There were just two words, 'THANK YOU,' and below that, a lipstick kiss.

Epilogue

Jim Dugan had been right. Arthur Soto was charged with the murder of Sonny Rosinni the day after Christmas and remanded in custody. That evening, Arthur's sister, Melody, issued a statement saying she had not seen or spoken to Arthur since 2017, even though he lived in the unit in her backyard.

Two days after Christmas, a photo of Alex Chillcot appeared in the obituaries announcing his passing and stating,' No information available at this time.'

What remained of the Chillcot mansion was leveled and cleared away during the week between Christmas and New Year. The lot was placed on the market for the princely sum of one million dollars.

I was just finishing up in the office around 4:00 on New Year's Eve when my phone rang. I didn't recognize the number but answered anyway.

"Haskell Investigations."

"Mr. Gustafson would like to see you. Now! You've got sixty seconds to get your ass out here, or we're coming up to get you."

I glanced out the window, and sure enough, there was Tubby's black Cadillac Escalade parked behind my car. There was no point in arguing. "I'll be right there," I said. I tossed Morton a biscuit, grabbed my jacket, and hurried out the door.

As I opened the rear door, Fat Freddy handed the cell phone to the driver. Freddy was seated in the passenger seat, eating what looked like a soft-shell taco. There appeared to be a bag of tacos on his lap, and I hoped he might be in a sharing mood.

"Great to see you, Freddy. Happy New Year to you," I said, trying to sound positive.

He looked at me, shook his head, and took another bite of the taco. We drove the rest of the way in silence. The only sound was from Fat Freddy eating two more tacos.

We climbed out of the Escalade at the front door to the mansion. When Fat Freddy searched me, I had the distinct feeling he was wiping taco debris off his hands in the process. I noticed that the number of people armed and standing around the front door was about a third of what it had been over the previous week.

I was searched again when we stepped inside, but today, there was only one guy reading a comic book at the front door. I followed Freddy down the hallway to Tubby's office. No one was sitting in a chair outside the office door.

Freddy opened the door as he knocked, and said, "Haskell, as you requested, sir."

We stepped into Tubby's office. There was a large Christmas tree in the corner with the lights on. Two women, a brunette and a redhead in lace negligees, were sipping flutes of champagne in front of the tree. Four Christmas stockings hung from the mantel, and above the fireplace, the landscape painting that had been there for years had been replaced. I stared at the new painting for a long moment. It had a gilt frame, and the painting was of two guys playing cards at a table. One of them was smoking a pipe. It had to be the same painting I'd seen taken to Chillcot's mansion in the middle of the night with the roulette wheel and the craps table.

"Happy New Year, Haskell. Wanda, maybe pour some champagne for Haskell. He looks like he could use it," Tubby said and laughed. Fat Freddy laughed then stopped a half-second after Tubby.

The redhead filled a champagne flute and strutted over toward me. She handed the glass to me and raised her eyebrows in a suggestive manner.

I took the flute, said, "Thank you," and tried not to stare.

"Here's to a profitable year," Tubby said and raised his glass. Everyone did the same, including me, and we all took a sip. "Haskell, I just wanted to thank you for keeping me informed on Chillcot. Not that we wouldn't have eventually obtained the information, but your timing made a difference."

"Thank you, sir. I just wanted to pass on whatever information I had. By the way, I like the new addition to your art collection," I said and raised my glass toward the painting above the fireplace.

"Oh, yeah. A generous, umm, gift from your friend, Chillcot. It's a Paul Cézanne, entitled 'The Card Players'."

"A Cézanne, the French painter?"

"Yes. Chillcot decided he really didn't have a need for it, and I, well, let's just say, I happened to be there at the right place, right time."

Fat Freddy chuckled.

"I haven't heard anything about Chillcot since the fire. Is he still in town?" I asked.

"Not that I know of. If I remember correctly, he mentioned a dislike with our winter and said something about taking up residence near a beach."

Fat Freddy laughed at that.

I nodded and said, "Probably best for all involved."

"Absolutely," Tubby said and raised his glass once more.

I was back in the Cadillac Escalade five minutes later. Fat Freddy dropped me off at my office. I took Morton for a walk. We ended up celebrating New Year's Eve with Louie at The Spot. We were home around 9:00, and I went online to look up 'The Card Players' by Paul Cézanne. It turns out the painting was one in a series of five paintings. One of the paintings sold for two hundred and fifty million dollars to the Royal family of Qatar back in 2011. Lucky Tubby Gustafson. I was in bed just after 10:00, which made for a much nicer New Year's day.

On February fourteenth, Valentine's Day, the adoption of the Hogan children by Christine and Tommy Bishop became official. Good things were still happening in the world.

There was a stretch of unseasonably warm weather the last week of February. The ice melted on a number of lakes in town, and a black 2022 Mercedes-Benz S 500 was discovered in about eight feet of water not more than a dozen feet from the shore of Lake Johanna. When the Mercedes was pulled from the lake, Alex Chillcot was found handcuffed to the steering wheel. Apparently, he'd finally found his residence near a beach.

The End

Thanks for taking the time to read <u>Suspect Santa</u>. If you enjoyed the read please consider leaving a review, it really helps.

Better check out the sample of the next book in the Dev Haskell series, <u>P.I. Apprentice</u>.

Sneak Peek

P.I. Apprentice

Second Edition

MIKE FARICY

Prologue

For the past fifteen minutes I'd been in my office watching through my binoculars as the two women in the third-floor apartment across the street sipped coffee and applied makeup. They were standing next to one another with makeup mirrors on the island counter and mugs of coffee next to the mirrors. The topless blonde had a white towel wrapped around her head. The redhead's hair was pulled back, and she was wearing a black bra.

They got me thinking it might be a good idea to phone my close personal friend Crystal and set up a play date. She answered on the second ring. "Well, Dev Haskell, I was beginning to wonder. What have you been up to?"

"Oh, nothing much. I wanted to see if you might be interested in getting together tonight." I had the binoculars up. The blonde said something, and the redhead nodded excitedly.

"I'd love it, say dinner around 7:00, and it might be a good idea to bring an overnight bag. I've got a new toy you can help me try out."

"More than willing to help, Crystal. I'll see you tonight."

"Rest up," she said and disconnected.

A car had just parked across the street behind my car, and a young woman climbed out. She draped a large tote bag over her shoulder. The bag looked like it was made from a southwestern Indian rug, and I figured she was probably heading into the hairdressers across the hall from my office. As long as it wasn't my office mate, Louie Laufen, I could keep watching the ladies across the street.

The staircase creaked ever so slightly as the young woman made her way up to the second floor. Now, both ladies in the apartment were laughing as the redhead brushed some sort of powder onto the blonde woman's cleavage and blew her a kiss. Just as I adjusted the binoculars for a closer view, the office door opened.

"Oh, excuse me. I'm looking for Mr. Haskell. Is this his office?" the young woman asked and then looked at the door for my name. There was nothing on the door identifying either Louie or me, except for the unit number 200.

"What? Err, umm, good morning," I said and spun around in my office chair. The binoculars hung around my neck by a black leather strap as I pushed the chair closer to the desk. "What can I do for you?" I asked as I studied the woman, her age couldn't have been more than mid-twenties. She may have looked familiar, but I couldn't place her. Morton, my Golden Retriever, was off his pillow and in the process of attempting to place his nose up her skirt.

"Are you Mr. Haskell?" she asked as she twice brushed Morton away.

"Yes, I am. No one else would want to be me," I laughed. She responded with a confused look. "What can I do for you?"

"My dad told me that if anything ever happened to him, I should talk to you."

"Who's your dad?"

"John Carter."

"John? I know or knew a Jack Carter. He passed away a while back."

"Yeah, that was my dad. Both my parents were killed in a car accident."

"Oh, wait, are you Melissa? No, you can't be. You should be in high school and—"

"Yeah, that's me. I graduated from high school eight years ago. Now, I work in the city attorney's office.

"Melissa, oh, please, please come in and sit down. Your parents were such wonderful people. Umm…belated condolences. I've been out to the cemetery to pay my respects. I know, because of Covid, there wasn't a funeral. It must have been very difficult, losing both parents in a car accident. It was labeled a hit and run, wasn't it?"

She nodded and said, "Yes, that's what I wanted to see you about."

"Okay, here, umm…take a seat and let me get you a cup of coffee. Do you take it black?"

She nodded. "Black would be fine."

I pulled out one of the client chairs in front of my desk, and she sat down. She took a manila envelope out of her tote bag. I grabbed Louie's coffee mug off his picnic table desk. I poured what was left down the sink, rinsed it out and refilled it with the remnants in the pot. The coffee had been on since yesterday morning, and I had meant to turn it off and make a fresh pot when I came in, but then the women across the street had served as a bit of a distraction. I quickly set my binoculars on the file cabinet and grabbed the mug.

"Here you go, Melissa," I said and set Louie's mug down in front of her. "Sorry, but we're fresh out of pastries," I joked.

"That's okay. Thanks." She ignored my attempt at humor and took a sip from the mug. She seemed to shiver for a second or two and then placed the mug as far away as possible.

I settled into my desk chair. "So, how can I help you?"

She looked at me for a long moment, took a deep swallow, then handed me a manila envelope. She was visibly shaking. "I'm pretty sure my parents were murdered."

One

It took a long moment for that last statement to sink in. Finally, I came back to reality. "Murdered? Melissa, that's a pretty strong statement. Obviously it's upsetting. In fact, I can't imagine the pain you must be going through, but—"

"I didn't make an offhanded comment. Look, my folks are gone. They're dead. Okay. As much as it pains me to say it, I accept the fact. I don't like it, but I accept it. They're not going to answer my phone calls. They're not going to open the door when the doorbell rings. That said, I've been checking some things out, and it's all in that file. You don't have to read it now, but I'm hoping you'll take a look at it sometime and tell me what you think. I know you did some work for my dad, and if you feel up to it, I'd really like you to check things out. I need someone like you to confirm the information I've assembled."

"You said you're in the city attorney's office?"

She nodded, "Let me stop you right there. No, I didn't run that file past anyone in the office if that's what you're thinking. People there are too connected. As a matter of fact, other than me, you're the only person who will have seen the file."

"What do you mean? Too connected? I'm not following."

"I can't afford to have someone go off the deep end based on the information I've put together. Please, just take a look and tell me what you think. If you go through it and you decide you don't want to be involved, that's not a problem. I won't like it, but I get it. Oh, and I'll probably never talk to you again. Just kidding," she said and smiled.

"All right. Don't say anything else. Let me take a look and I promise you this. I'll go through it and do the best I can. Fair enough?"

She nodded, and her eyes suddenly looked watery. I passed her the Kleenex box I keep on my desk for just such an emergency. Five minutes later, I watched out the window as she climbed into her car and headed down to her office in the St. Paul courthouse.

I took a long look at the manila envelope, eventually took a deep breath, and took out the multi-page file. It was more than just a few pages, probably about twenty. I pulled out my phone and placed it in airplane mode. I'd met Jack Carter years ago when I'd dropped out of college after my first semester. He was a real estate developer, and he offered me a job instead of enlisting in the army, but of course, being nineteen, I knew better. When I got out and came back home, he steered me toward a couple of job opportunities that I immediately screwed up. He was always supportive of me, shook his head when I got my Private Investigators license, and sent me the occasional case. I usually checked out an insurance claim or the work history of someone he wanted to hire. Over the years, his office grew from four people to, maybe fifty or sixty, and he made millions.

Me? Well, I share an office with Louie Laufen, who handles DUI cases, and our local crime lord Tubby Gustafson drives me crazy on any given day.

It was close to four in the afternoon when Louie finally made it into the office. He'd had three court appearances, the last one at 3:00. "Oh, man, what a day," he said as he tossed his briefcase onto his picnic table and settled into his desk chair. As he turned on his computer, he asked, "Everything okay on your end?"

"Mmm," I said and turned to the next page in Melissa's file.

It was close to 5:00 when Louie shut down his computer and asked, "You thinking about going over to The Spot for one? Dev? Hey, earth to Dev."

"Oh, sorry, checking out some stuff here. What did you say?"

"Asked if you were interested in going over to The Spot for a little relaxation?"

"Yeah, let me just finish up here. I'll take Morton on a quick walk, and we'll join you in fifteen or twenty minutes."

"See you over there." He rose from his chair, grabbed his briefcase, and gave a quick wave as he hurried out the door. I watched out the window as he crossed the street and headed into The Spot.

I glanced at the clock on the wall. Louie had left over an hour ago. I was on my third read of Melissa's file. I placed it back in the manila envelope and grabbed Morton's leash. As soon as I grabbed the leash, he was off his pillow and standing at the door. I clicked the leash onto his collar, and we went outside. We crossed the street, I tossed the envelope on the front seat of my car, and we walked for three blocks. Morton investigated every other fence gate and registered his visit on both fire hydrants.

Once we entered The Spot, Morton nearly pulled my arm out of its shoulder socket as he strained on the leash. We headed toward Louie on his stool at the corner of the bar. As we rounded the corner, Louie reached down with a handful of pork rinds and said, "Well, Morton, you had me worried, afraid Dev had fallen asleep or was scanning the apartment building across the street again."

"Sorry about that, Louie. I got involved in a file, and the next thing I knew, an hour had gone by."

Louie checked his watch. "Actually, it's been an hour and a half, but who's counting? Oh wait, I'm counting because it's your turn to buy."

"How 'bout a beer, Dev?" Mike, the bartender, asked.

"I'll take a Summit and better give Louie a refill before he starts to throw a hissy fit."

"He's been complaining ever since he came in." Mike laughed and headed down the bar.

"You seemed really into whatever you were reading. Everything okay?" Louie asked.

"What? Oh, yeah. Just a file someone dropped off that I'm going through."

"Oh, so then you're not being sued. Or are you?"

"Me, no, the file has nothing to do with me, well, other than the woman wants me to check some things out."

"You going to do that?"

"Yeah. I owe it to the family. Her father gave me a lot of good advice, not that I ever followed any of it, but he was a friend, a mentor of mine as a young guy. So yeah, I'm going to check some things out. How'd the day go for you? You had three appearances in court today, didn't you?"

Louie gave a nod and went on to tell me about his day over the course of two beers and another handful of pork rinds for Morton. It was after eight when we headed home. I tossed Morton a biscuit in the kitchen, warmed up some pasta that had been in the refrigerator for a few days, and we settled in front of the TV. We headed up to bed around 11:00. I was wide awake at 2:00, and after lying there for fifteen minutes, I went downstairs, grabbed Melissa's file, and started reading it for the fourth or fifth time.

TWO

My alarm woke me at 6:30. I turned it off, and Morton woke me an hour later. I went downstairs to the kitchen, let him out the backdoor, then grabbed a shower and put on a reasonably clean t-shirt and jeans.

We were down in the office just after 9:30. Louie was on his computer, and amazingly, a fresh pot of coffee was going. I poured a mug and topped off Louie's.

He gave me a friendly nod. "Thanks, Dev. Long night? You look tired."

"Oh couldn't sleep and ended up reviewing that same file for a couple of hours."

"Oh, you're kidding. Here I was thinking you had some incredible erotic night lined up with a beauty queen."

"No, not by a long shot. I was—oh shit, wait a minute," I said and looked at my phone. It was still set on airplane mode. "Oh, no. I was supposed to meet up with someone last night, and I got so involved reading that damn file I completely forgot. I adjusted my phone, so I wouldn't be interrupted. Oh, God." I checked my recent phone calls, four of them twenty minutes apart, all from Crystal. I wasn't sure I wanted to hear the messages she left. There were six text messages: 'Are you okay? Are you coming over? Did you forget? Please let me know you're okay. Call me when you see this. I don't care what time it is.' And then the last one, 'Dev, please let me know you're okay. Please.'

Her audible messages, there were four, with the last one coming through about midnight, were more of the same. She sounded worried and concerned rather than mad. I had to play this carefully. I thought for a minute and then made the call.

The phone barely rang, and she answered, "Oh, God, Dev, are you okay?"

"Yes, Crystal, I'm okay. It was just a harrowing night."

"Oh, my God, I knew it. I just knew it. What happened?"

"Oh…ah…two toddlers were missing. Three and four years old. The babysitter fell asleep, and when the parents came home from work, the little ones were gone. Somehow they got out of the house. I was so focused on finding them I completely forgot. The police were involved. Must have been fifty or sixty people looking for the little children. It was getting dark. Even the police were starting to think that maybe they had been kidnapped. It was close to midnight when I found them. They had climbed a ladder up to a treehouse in the backyard two doors away. When I found them, they were sound asleep. I carried them back to the parents' house, then had to show the treehouse to the police and a bunch of newspaper reporters. I didn't get home until sometime after 2:00 and just collapsed in bed. I would have called sooner, but I didn't want to wake you after the long night you had. I'm really sorry, Crystal. I was afraid—"

"Oh, Dev. Not another word. You saved them? Those two little ones? Oh my God, it's a miracle they didn't fall out of that treehouse. How old did you say they were?"

"Three and five, I think. I really can't remember, and I'm still so tired." I glanced over at Louie. He was sipping his coffee and shaking his head.

"Oh, Dev. God, I'm so proud of you. I can't wait to read about this in the paper. Which papers were the reporters from?"

"Oh, I'm not sure. They told me, but I was too focused on the little kids. I told them not to take pictures of me carrying the kids. I was afraid the camera flash might wake them."

"The camera flash?" she said.

"I just wanted to get them back to their parents, who, obviously, were very worried."

"And the babysitter. Was it a woman?"

"Oh, no, it was a neighbor girl. I think she was ten or eleven. You know, kids just being kids."

"Any chance you're free tonight? We might be able to catch it on the news before we get down to business."

I nodded at Louie. "Why yes. I'd love to come over. What can I bring?"

"Just bring yourself, and you had better rest up. We're going to be very busy. 6:00 sound okay?"

"Yes, I'll see you tonight."

"Oh, Dev, you're my hero. You're going to see all of me tonight, up close and very personal. We're going to celebrate like you won't believe, honey" Crystal said and disconnected.

I breathed a sigh of relief.

Louie shook his head. "You gotta be kidding me. She actually bought that fabrication?"

"Not bad for coming up with something right off the cuff. Yeah, I should have put it on speaker for you. I'm her hero, and she wants to thank me in an up close and very personal way, and those are her exact words. Oh, and she told me to rest up."

"Unbelievable. And just what are you going to tell her when there's nothing on the news, the internet, or in the newspaper?"

"Yeah, I'm going to have to think about that. Hopefully, something big will happen today, and I can just say it was bigger news and took over the media."

"Just be careful, Dev. These things have a way of getting out of control, and suddenly, you're living the lie. She's going to ask you names, where this happened, and all kinds of stuff. And you're going to have to get your story straight and keep it that way."

"Thanks for the advice, Louie. Not to worry, I'll think of something."

Three

I headed out to one of the main locations in Melissa's file just before noon. A massive multi-unit apartment complex called The White House. I'd heard of it but had never actually been in it. It was just to the east of St. Paul in the suburb of Woodbury. The complex was three years old and made up of five, five-story buildings arranged in a pentagon. Each building housed one hundred units, which rounded out to twenty units per floor, or five hundred units in the entire five building complex. I had passed the place countless times on the freeway but never really paid much attention to it other than they were new and took up a large amount of space along the freeway corridor. I took the exit and drove along the frontage road toward the five-story buildings in the distance.

There was a visitor's parking lot in front of each building. I turned into one of the parking lots and headed toward the door in the center of the building. The door had a box-gable roof over it, extending out about six feet from the building. The sign on the front of the roof read

'Leasing Office' in blue letters. I stepped into the building. The leasing office was just off to the right. Straight ahead was a security door with a phone next to it to contact residents. I headed into the leasing office.

There was a brown leather couch against the wall just to the right of the door. A framed poster of the the White House Apartments hung on the wall above the couch. Straight ahead was a marble-topped counter. The woman behind the counter was on the phone. She signaled me with her hand and nodded, suggesting it would just be a moment.

"But if you'll check your lease, our policy is that you have agreed to pay rent for a twelve-month period, which means you are liable for that rent payment of two thousand one hundred dollars until next November, which is five months from now. Yes, I understand that, and I will be happy to place your unit on the available list once you have vacated and we have restored the unit for the next occupant. No, ma'am, that will be up to our maintenance department to determine. Yes, very well, thank you." As she hung up, she muttered something under her breath that I presumed wasn't all that polite.

She turned to face me, flashed a quick smile, and said, "Good morning. How may I help you?"

"I'm interested in renting a unit."

She looked surprised for a brief moment before she said, "I'd be happy to help you." She reached over to the credenza behind her, grabbed a clipboard off a stack, and handed it to me. "If you would just fill this form out, we can get you started."

I took the clipboard and sat down on the brown leather couch. The form on the clipboard asked for basic information. My name, address, that sort of thing. Among other things, it listed that the building was pet friendly and that smoking was prohibited. There was a second page that displayed two floorplans, a single-bedroom and a two-bedroom unit. It also mentioned a social room on the fourth floor available for rent and a workout room, also on the fourth floor. Underground parking was available for an additional one hundred and twenty dollars a month.

As I was filling out the form, the phone rang, and the woman went through a similar conversation to the one I'd heard minutes ago, explaining what was required in order to move out of the apartment.

She flashed another fake smile when I handed her the clipboard, gave it a ten-second glance, and said, "Are you interested in a one or two-bedroom unit?"

"Oh, definitely a two-bedroom unit. I work from home, so the second bedroom will serve as my office."

"I see," she said and nodded. "And what exactly do you do, Mr. Haskell?"

"I have a marketing firm. I sell items all over the world on the internet. You do have internet access, don't you?"

"But of course. Would you have a moment to tour a two-bedroom unit?"

"Yes, I was hoping to see one."

"Wonderful. My name is Jennifer, by the way. Please follow me," she said as she stepped out from behind her desk. We walked out of the office. She locked the office door and then unlocked the door leading out of the small lobby and into the actual residential area. The carpet in the hallway was worn, and for being a no-smoking building, it smelled an awful lot like cigarettes. The two-bedroom unit was the second door on the right. I figured the first door was probably the one-bedroom unit.

She unlocked the door, and we stepped into the unit. It seemed to be a fairly standard layout. There was a small entry area and a bathroom off to the left. Off to the right was a small dining area with a table and four chairs. Just beyond that was the kitchen with a four-burner stove, dishwasher, refrigerator, and veneer wood cabinets. On the left was a living room area with a couch, a matching wingback chair, and a coffee table. A window looked out onto a large concrete courtyard with permanent tables and benches bolted to the concrete. Four more five-story buildings surrounded all sides of the courtyard. There were probably twenty people outside, but the area was large enough that it didn't appear crowded. A few kids were using the swings, and two boys, ten or eleven years old, were shooting baskets.

"Let me show you the bedrooms," Jennifer said and stepped over to a closed door. She opened the door and stepped inside. The room had a double bed and a chest of drawers. It would have been too small for a king-sized bed and maybe even a queen size. There was a closet with two sliding doors, one of which was opened, displaying not all that much room.

"Very nice," I lied.

"Let me show you the other bedroom," she said and stepped out of the room. The other bedroom was roughly the same, only smaller. A set of bunk beds were against the far wall. There was a double chest of drawers, three drawers high and presumably for two children. The closet had two sliding doors, one of which was open, revealing a similar closet to the other one, only smaller.

From there, we toured the bathroom, which was barely large enough for both of us. A small sink and cabinet with a mirror were attached to the wall. The tub had a shower head and no shower curtain. Two towel bars were opposite each other. One next to the tub and the other above the toilet.

"Any questions?" Jennifer asked.

"No, it's very nice. Very comfortable. Oh, one question, what is the availability?"

"So not a problem. Units are available on every floor."

"Do you have a lot of people leaving?"

"No more than usual. We're in the midst of the moving season. Things come pretty much to a halt from November to April. No one wants to move in the Minnesota winter."

"Yeah, of course."

I followed her out to the lobby, where she turned and faced me. "Now, we can get you started on a lease. It's fifty dollars to complete our credit report. As I mentioned, we have units available on every floor, so once your credit is approved, which takes just three or four days, you can start moving in."

"Let's do it," I said, and we went back into her office.

She gave me another clipboard, this time with a credit form. I filled out the form in about five minutes. I listed my annual income at a quarter of a million dollars. The only accurate information I put on the form was my name, a credit card number, and my phone number. I had to pay fifty bucks so they could check my credit. I handed the clipboard back to her and said, "Thanks so much. I appreciate you taking the time, Jennifer."

"I'll let you know just as soon as we receive credit approval," she said, and I headed for the lobby and out into the sunshine.

Four

As luck would have it, there was a car with a trailer two parking places away from my vehicle. Just now, two guys were lifting a couch onto the trailer. Six dining room chairs were lined up on the sidewalk next to the trailer. The guys looked to be around thirty. I walked over to my car and waited until they were finished with the couch. "You guys moving out?" I asked.

They looked at me like I was nuts after watching them move the couch onto the trailer. "Yeah, I am, this is our third load, and we've got four or five more after this," a guy with the goatee said.

"How long have you lived here?"

"Just a year, one of the worst years of my life."

"I just had a tour of the two-bedroom unit. I was thinking of moving in. I guess they've got openings on every floor."

The goatee nodded. "That would make sense. The internet is out a couple of times a week. We've had power outages every month that last for hours. No garbage disposals, the sinks back up, and sometimes the toilets. The place is a dive. Whoever built it cut costs everywhere they could. The garage door for the underground parking wouldn't work over Christmas, so no one could leave. That didn't make people very happy."

"I guess not. The place is only a few years old, and you've got power outages?"

"Oh yeah, every month, even in nice weather, all of a sudden, everything goes off, including the elevators. They've got all sorts of lowlifes living here. Did she have you fill out one of those credit forms?" he asked.

"Yeah, I just finished filling it out."

"Well, don't worry. They'll wait a bit and call you, tell you things are filling up, and you'd better act fast. It's all bullshit. When you pay the fifty bucks for the credit report, they keep the money and never actually send the report to be verified. They'll call you later today and tell you that you've been approved. God, my car has been broken into three separate times in the so-called secure underground parking. The last time whoever did it broke the driver's window. You'd think they'd have security cameras down there, but they don't. The alarm went off for hours in my car, and no one did anything. There are some decent folks that live here, but there are some real jerks, too. Save yourself the hassle and go somewhere else."

"Are you moving to one of the other buildings?"

He shook his head. "They're all the same. Lousy internet, the plumbing is half-ass, and the phone lines are out from time to time too. I had three different friends in the other buildings, I'm the last one here, and I can't wait to get out. You'd be better served if you could qualify for low-income housing."

I chuckled at that.

"I'm not kidding, man. Oh, did I mention they apparently don't pay the trash hauler on a regular basis? Twice in the last six months, it wasn't picked up for a couple of weeks. God, we could smell it up on the fourth floor. My wife threatened to leave me if we didn't move. She's been living at her parent's house for the last month. Won't come back here."

"We need to keep moving, Donny," the other guy said.

"Yeah, why don't you watch this stuff, so no one takes it? I'll get that other cart down here." He turned toward me. "Sorry to be such a downer, dude, but take my word. You don't want to be here." With that, he grabbed the cart and began to push it back toward the building.

I climbed into my car and headed back to the office, stopping at McDonald's on the way to grab a couple of cheeseburgers that I ate while driving. Back at the office, Louie's car was nowhere around. I tossed the McDonald's bag in the trash bin in front of the building and headed up the stairs. I wrote a note reminding me of my dinner date with Crystal, telling me to leave by 4:00 and take Morton for a long walk before getting cleaned up for my wild night. I checked out the White House Apartments online and read the reviews, largely complaints echoing what the guy with the goatee had told me. Louie was still out of the office when it was time to leave.

To Be Continued . . .

Thanks for checking out the first couple chapters in P.I. Apprentice. Better grab a copy and see what happens. Crime Lord Tubby Gustafson might be about to insert himself . . .

Books by Mike Faricy

Crime Fiction Firsts

A boxset of the first four books in four crime fiction series:

Russian Roulette; Dev Haskell series
Welcome; Jack Dillon Dublin Tales series
Corridor Man; Corridor Man series
Reduced Ransom! Hot Shot series

The following titles comprise the Dev Haskell series:

Russian Roulette: Case 1
Mr. Swirlee: Case 2
Bite Me: Case 3
Bombshell: Case 4
Tutti Frutti: Case 5
Last Shot: Case 6
Ting-A-Ling: Case 7
Crickett: Case 8
Bulldog: Case 9
Double Trouble: Case 10
Yellow Ribbon: Case 11
Dog Gone: Case 12
Scam Man: Case 13
Foiled: Case 14
What Happens in Vegas… Case 15
Art Hound: Case 16

The Office: Case 17
Star Struck: Case 18
International Incident: Case 19
Guest From Hell: Case 20
Art Attack: Case 21
Mystery Man: Case 22
Bow-Wow Rescue: Case 23
Cold Case: Case 24
Cash Up Front: Case 25
Dream House: Case 26
Alley Katz: Case 27
The Big Gamble: Case 28
Bad to the Bone: Case 29
Silencio!: Case 30
Surprise, Surprise: Case 31
Hit & Run: Case 32
Suspect Santa: Case 33
P.I. Apprentice: Case 34
Rebel Without a Clue: Case 35
Puppy Love: Case 36

The following titles are Dev Haskell novellas:
Dollhouse
The Dance
Pixie
Fore!
Twinkle Toes
(*a Dev Haskell short story*)

The following are Dev Haskell Boxsets:
Dev Haskell Boxset 1-3
Dev Haskell Boxset 4-6
Dev Haskell Boxset 7-9
Dev Haskell Boxset 10-12
Dev Haskell Boxset 13-15
Dev Haskell Boxset 16-18
Dev Haskell Boxset 19-21
Dev Haskell Boxset 22-24
Dev Haskell Boxset 25-27
Dev Haskell Boxset 28-30
Dev Haskell Boxset 1-7
Dev Haskell Boxset 8-14
Dev Haskell Boxset 15-19
Dev Haskell Boxset 20-24
Dev Haskell Boxset 25-29

The following titles comprise the Jack Dillon Dublin Tales series:
Welcome
Jack Dillon Dublin Tale 1
Sweet Dreams
Jack Dillon Dublin Tale 2
Mirror Mirror
Jack Dillon Dublin Tale 3
Silver Bullet
Jack Dillon Dublin Tale 4

Fair City Blues
Jack Dillon Dublin Tale 5
Spade Work
Jack Dillon Dublin Tale 6
Madeline Missing
Jack Dillon Dublin Tale 7
Mistaken Identity
Jack Dillon Dublin Tale 8
Picture Perfect
Jack Dillon Dublin Tale 9
Dublin Moon
Jack Dillon Dublin Tale 10
Mystery Woman
Jack Dillon Dublin Tale 11
Second Chance
Jack Dillon Dublin Tale 12
Payback Brother
Jack Dillon Dublin Tale 13
The Heist
Jack Dillon Dublin Tale 14
Jewels To Kill For
Jack Dillon Dublin Tale 15
Retirement Scheme
Jack Dillon Dublin Tale 16
The Collector
Jack Dillon Dublin Tale 17

Jack Dillon Dublin Tales Boxsets:
Jack Dillon Dublin Tales 1-3

Jack Dillon Dublin Tales 4-6
Jack Dillon Dublin Tales 1-5
Jack Dillon Dublin Tales 1-7
Jack Dillon Dublin Tales 6-10

The following titles comprise the Hotshot series;
Reduced Ransom! Second Edition
Finders Keepers! Second Edition
Bankers Hours Second Edition
Chow Down Second Edition
Moonlight Dance Academy Second Edition
Irish Dukes (Fight Card Series)
written under the pseudonym Jack Tunney

The following titles comprise the Corridor Man series:
Corridor Man
Corridor Man 2: Opportunity knocks
Corridor Man 3: The Dungeon
Corridor Man 4: Dead End
Corridor Man 5: Finger
Corridor Man 6: Exit Strategy
Corridor Man 7: Trunk Music
Corridor Man 8: Birthday Boy
Corridor Man 9: Boss Man
Corridor Man 10: Bye Bye Bobby

Corridor Man novellas:
Corridor Man: Valentine

Corridor Man: Auditor
Corridor Man: Howling
Corridor Man: Spa Day

The following are Corridor Man Boxsets:
Corridor Man Boxset 1-3
Corridor Man Boxset 1-5
Corridor Man Boxset 6-9

All books are available on Amazon.com

Thank you!

Contact the author:
- Email: mikefaricyauthor@gmail.com
- Twitter: @Mikefaricybooks
- Facebook: Mike Faricy Author
- Website: http://www.mikefaricybooks.com

Published by

MJF Publishing

9 781962 080552